BORN UGLY

Also By Beth Goobie

Novels for Young People
Hello Groin
Fixed
Flux
Sticks and Stones
The Lottery
Before Wings
The Dreams Where the Losers Go
The Colours of Carol Molev
The Good, the Bad, and the Suicidal
I'm Not Convinced
Kicked Out
Who Owns Kelly Paddick
Hit and Run
Mission Impossible
Group Homes from Outer Space

Poetry
Scars Of Light
The Girls Who Dream Me

Novels
The Only-Good Heart
Could I Have My Body Back Now, Please?

BORN UGLY

Beth Goobie

Red Deer PRESS

The author gratefully acknowledges the Canada Council for the Arts grant that funded the writing of this novel.

Published by Red Deer Press, A Fitzhenry & Whiteside Company 195 Allstate Parkway, Markham, ON, L3R 4T8 www.reddeerpress.com

Edited for the Press by Peter Carver
Cover and text design by: Daniel Choi
Cover Image Courtesy of: Getty Images
Printed and bound in Canada by Webcom

5 4 3 2 1

We acknowledge with thanks the Canada Council for the Arts, and the Ontario Arts Council for their support of our publishing program. We acknowledge the financial support of the Government of Canada through the Book Publishing Industry Development Program (BPIDP) for our publishing activities.

ONTARIO ARTS COUNCIL
CONSEIL DES ARTS DE L'ONTARIO

Canada Council   Conseil des Arts
for the Arts   du Canada

Quote by Masaru Emoto used with permission from Beyond Words Publishing © 2001 by Masaru Emoto. English translation © 2004 by Beyond Words Publishing. From the book *The Hidden Messages in Water*. Reprinted with permission from Beyond Words Publishing, Hillsboro OR.

Library and Archives Canada Cataloguing in Publication
Goobie, Beth, 1959-
Born ugly / Beth Goobie.
ISBN 978-0-88995-457-1
I. Title.
PS8563.O8326B67 2011   jC813'.54   C2011-901435-1

Publisher Cataloging-in-Publication Data (U.S)
Goobie, Beth
Born ugly / Goobie, Beth.
[272] p. : 13.3 x 18.4 cm.
Summary: A young girl struggles with her negative self-image and feelings of being a victim, as she learns to assert herself for the first time in her life.
ISBN: 978-0-88995-457-1 (pbk.)
1. Bullying -- Juvenile fiction. 2. Self-perception in adolescence – Juvenile fiction.
I. Title.
[Fic] dc22   PZ7.G663Bo 2011

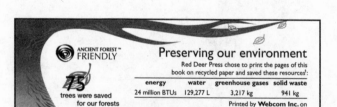

ANCIENT FOREST™
FRIENDLY

75
trees were saved
for our forests

Preserving our environment
Red Deer Press chose to print the pages of this book on recycled paper and saved these resources[1]:

	energy	water	greenhouse gases	solid waste
	24 million BTUs	129,277 L	3,217 kg	941 kg

Printed by **Webcom Inc.** on
Legacy Hi-Bulk Natural 100% post-consumer waste.

FSC
www.fsc.org

MIX
Paper from
responsible sources
FSC® C004071

[1]Estimates were made using the Environmental Defense Paper Calculator.

The earth is searching. It wants to be beautiful.

– *The Hidden Messages in Water* by Masaru Emoto.

One

The house party rocked with sound. Standing in the back entranceway, a beer in one hand, Shir let her body fill with the vibrations coming from the living room stereo. Beneath her feet, the floor was pulsing; she could feel the bass traveling like a live thing through her soles, then up her legs and spine, to where it became one with the supersonic throb of her brain.

Metallica, she thought. *An old CD, but a good one. Yeah, this was good. This was really good.* Grinning sloppily, she lifted her can of beer and let the dregs pour into her mouth. It was her third since her arrival an hour ago, but she was managing fine. She had always been good at holding her booze. "Drunk as a stone," her mother often said, whether Shir had been drinking or not. But then, she had already been saying that way back when Shir was four years old and too young for anything except apple juice.

Well, anyway, thought Shir, the night was yet young and she had brought a twelve-pack, which made it three down and nine to go. And based on the rate the rest of the kids at this party were downing their favorite fluids, it was either suck back those nine soon or kiss them goodbye. So, putting a hand to the wall, she began feeling her way tentatively along the back hallway toward the kitchen. Things were admittedly wobbly, the floor doing a slow waltz under her feet.

Because it's dark, Shir giggled uneasily to herself. *That's what you get when you stick a ten-watt bulb into the ceiling. Bunch of cheapskates running this place.* Stumbling on a loose shoe, she straightened to find the kitchen doorway to her left, its sudden brightness gouging deep into her brain. *God!* she thought weakly, holding onto the doorframe as she stared blurrily at the overhead light. With the difference between the hall and kitchen lighting, it felt as if she had gone from ten to a thousand watts in half a teeny-tiny second. What was it with the interior decorating in this place?

At that moment, several guys and a girl entered the kitchen from another entrance. Immediately, Shir shrank back into the hallway's comparative darkness, watching in silence as the group opened the fridge and pawed through the booze stacked inside. The girl was familiar, having shared a math class with Shir last year, and the guys also attended her high school. Still, Shir waited without speaking until they had pulled their beers out of a Budweiser six-pack and left the room. Then, her eyes blinking in overdrive, she entered the kitchen and stood, letting her vision adjust to the light. This was the kind of situation, she thought fuzzily, staring around herself, that was murder to a brain on multiple beers—in addition to putting a thousand-watt bulb into the overhead socket, some no-brainer had painted the walls virgin white. The place was absolutely nuclear with light.

"Headache," she muttered, opening the fridge door and

peering at its contents. Well, another beer would fix that soon enough. Coors—she had brought a twelve-pack of Coors Light, but she couldn't see the label anywhere among the six- and twelve-packs crammed onto the bottom shelf. Some jerk must have filched the rest of her pack. Oh well, that gave her the right to filch someone else's. She had brought twelve, she had the right to drink twelve. Molsons would do fine.

Carefully, Shir slid a can out of the nearest pack and closed the fridge door. Then she leaned against the counter, steadying herself as she popped the tab. *Molson Canadian*, she thought, surveying the can with hazy satisfaction. *Yeah, Molsons.*

But as she raised it to her mouth, readying herself for the first sluice of cold fluid, several guys entered the kitchen. As she caught sight of them, Shir instinctively lowered her drink and covered the label with both hands. *Damn!* she thought frantically. What if this particular can of beer belonged to one of these guys? Sure, there was lots of Molsons in the fridge, but sometimes kids marked their beer to make sure no one else drank it. Why hadn't she thought to check first? Easing the can behind her back, Shir began a cautious sideways shuffle toward the back entrance.

"Hey, wait a minute," said one of the guys, a tall, blond grade-twelve student Shir knew from afar as Wade Sullivan. Part of the drama crowd, he was also in the school band and played on the soccer team. "Shirley Rutz, right?" he said with a grin, coming toward her. "Don't run away on me now. I've got a proposition for you."

Still holding the Molsons behind her back, Shir regarded him suspiciously. A proposition? she thought warily. What kind of proposition would Mr. Big-Shot Drama Star want to make her? This was her third year at Collier High, and try as she might, she couldn't recall a single time previous to this moment when Wade had spoken to her, even glanced in her direction. So why the sudden interest? He didn't look drunk. At least, not *that* drunk.

"Oh, yeah," she said cautiously.

Reaching into his pocket, Wade pulled out a toonie. "Two bucks," he said, holding it in front of her face.

"Two bucks for what?" asked Shir. Glancing at the guys behind him, she felt a sinking sensation. Something was up, obviously. These guys weren't subtle—it was written all over their sneering, leering faces.

"Two bucks if you let me kiss you," grinned Wade. "I've never kissed a girl as ugly as you, and I figure the experience would be worth that much."

Loud guffaws broke out behind him and a flush hit Shir hard as a cruise missile, blowing her brain to bits. "Fuck off," she squeaked, her voice going high and crawling into the back of her throat. Ditching the can of Molsons, she lunged toward the back hallway.

"Uh uh," said Wade, cutting her off. "I really want to, Shirley. I figure maybe a kiss with you will change my life. Y'know, love is blind and all that. Maybe we'll kiss and I'll fall head-over-heels in love, and we'll get married and have a couple of dog-faced, shit-ugly kids who'll look just like you. And I'll love them as much as I love you, because I'm so blind with love, I'm living my whole life by Braille." Pursing his lips, he leaned toward her. "What d'you say, babe? This could be the moment we've both been waiting for."

He was so close, Shir could feel his beer-soaked breath on her face. Grunting low in her throat, she shoved him. Wade shoved back.

"Shirley, Shirley," he said, still grinning, but his eyes had narrowed. "You wouldn't say no to *blind* love, would you?"

Her mind a complete blank, Shir stared at him. Why hadn't she seen this coming? she thought bleakly. There was *always* something coming. "Fuck off," she hissed again, her flush deepening. "Just fuck off and leave me alone."

"Oooo, she's hot for you, Wade," said one of the guys behind him. "Look at that heat." Reaching around Wade, he grabbed Shir's right arm.

"No!" she cried, trying to jerk away, but he tightened his grip. At the same time, Wade leaned closer, pushing her against the counter with his hip. He was hard down there, Shir thought, panicking—she could feel it. Fear oozed stickily up her throat.

"Okay, leave it alone," said a voice from across the room. "That's enough."

Without backing off, Wade turned to look over his shoulder. "What for, Brett?" he demanded. "We're just talking kissing, here."

"No making her," said Brett, his eyes flicking uneasily across Shir's face. Also in the school band / soccer team set, he was another of Collier High's senior male students who had never before given her a second glance. "If she says no," he continued, flushing slightly under the concentrated stares of the other guys, "that's it, okay?"

"C'mon, Brett," grumbled Wade, but he took a step back. "That's why I got Dana to invite her to this party. Why else would I walk into a house with a face like that in it?"

"Tough luck," shrugged Brett, turning back to the living room. "You asked and she said no. I guess love isn't blind when it's looking at you, Wade."

Another guffaw rocked the group, and they drifted carelessly out of the kitchen after Brett. No one paused to give Shir a backward glance, but she was already gone, squinting in the back hall's ten-watt light as she fumbled through a pile of unfamiliar shoes. *Shit!* she thought desperately. Where had she left her runners? She was sure she had dropped them here by the back door when she came in, but now she couldn't see them anywhere. Oh, well, these two shoes fit okay. A sandal and a Nike runner—who cared if they matched?

Too bad about the nine missing beer, though.

Shoving open the back door, Shir took off and ran like a scream.

She woke to the sound of a different stereo, its muffled throb coming from across the hall. *Celine Dion*, she thought dismally, recognizing the familiar voice. That meant sister Stella was up and at 'em, raring to go, even on a Sunday morning. Probably had a five-star, next-year-it's-the-Olympics sports meet or something. With a long-suffering groan, Shir stuck her head under her pillow. Faintly, from further down the hall, she could hear the living room TV, which meant her mother was up, too. Hadn't anyone explained the purpose of weekends to these people—sleeping in, crashing out, digging your own grave, and crawling into a comatose stupor until Monday forced a return to consciousness?

Lifting the edge of her pillow, Shir peered at her clock radio, then rolled carefully onto her side and sat up. *Not bad for 11:10*, she thought, assessing her body's response. The usual headache was there, but at least it wasn't slamming her like a tidal wave. Blearily, she tried to recall something from the previous evening. What had it been—a full six-pack night? *No, not quite*, she realized as memory started to kick in. After ditching that dickhead party at Dana Lowe's, she had headed over to the alley behind the liquor store on 23rd Street, where there was always someone on a Saturday night, reselling beer to minors. At a fairly stiff hike-up of course, but she'd had enough on her to buy two cans, and this time she wasn't stupid enough to leave them sitting around where they could get ripped off. No, the beer had all gone sluicing down her throat the way it was supposed to, and then she had spent the next hour weaving up and down back alleys, belting out fifty-proof opera as she took the long way home.

"Somewhere Over the Rainbow"—it was the song she always sang when she got plastered. Over and over, the same dorky song and the same dorky tune. Her dad had been like that, too, except the song he had sung when he got ripped was "Rule Britannia." It was the only thing Shir could remember about him now, even when she got out the sole picture she had of him and studied every detail—a bent, aging photograph that showed him in undershirt and jeans, holding her on his knee and grinning like a wild man. One glance was all it took to prove beyond the slightest doubt that they were father and daughter. The evidence was unavoidable, from the skimpy red hair and huge honker of a nose, to the thick wide lips and narrow face that looked as if it had been placed on a rack and stretched five or so extra centimeters. Their close resemblance hadn't seemed to bother her dad—he was beaming at the camera like any proud father— but it hadn't been enough to keep him around for more than a few months at a time, either. "Here today, gone tomorrow," Mom used to say about him, and Shir's fifth birthday had been the last time she had heard from him—a birthday card displaying an elephant with a balloon in its trunk, and the words *Miss you Shirley* written inside. She still had it, stuck into her photo album next to the photograph.

"Probably dead," was all Mom would say about him now. "Beer fight or driving drunk. That man never could hold his beer."

Well, Shir could hold hers, that was for sure. *Five and a half beers*, she thought groggily, *and only a low-grade hangover to show for it.* Cautiously, she got to her feet, then sat down again as the floor gave a mild warning wobble. Okay, she thought, reassessing the situation. Maybe today's hangover was closer to medium—

somewhere between several extra-strength Tylenol and slamming your head against a wall to give yourself something else to think about. But after an hour or two and a bowl of Cheerios, last night's side effects would fade into history where they belonged. If only last night, and everything she was starting to remember about it, would fade into nothingness, too.

Standing up again, Shir grabbed a sweatshirt from a nearby chair and pulled it on over her pajamas. Then she eased open her bedroom door, bracing herself as Stella's stereo hit full force, Celine Dion's voice attacking from every possible angle— cat squall after cat squall, scratching its way deep into Shir's raw, throbbing brain. Briefly, she considered ramming her way through the locked door opposite and tossing her younger sister's stereo out the window, but ditched the thought. It would be too much effort, *way* too much. Besides, Stella was taking a self-defense course at the Y. No, all things considered, thought Shir, the best course of action would be to skulk into the bathroom and give her mouth a thorough going-over with Crest before Mom got a whiff of her breath. *If* she wanted a future, that is.

Morosely, she shuffled into the bathroom, where she flicked on the light, heard the fan kick in, and flicked the light off again. After the Cheerios, she thought, wincing, maybe she would be able to handle the fan—*and* the bathroom mirror, come to think of it. At that moment, without warning, a voice came into her mind, cutting off her thoughts. *Two bucks if you let me kiss you*, it said, clear as anything, and Shir's mouth dropped soundlessly open as memory hit full force, bringing back the kitchen scene at

Dana Lowe's and the sensation of Wade Sullivan's hip pressing her against the counter. *Shirley, Shirley,* she heard him jeer a second time. *You wouldn't say no to blind love, would you?*

Shir's throat tightened and she pulsed with dull, slow shame. No, she thought heavily. This morning she was definitely keeping the bathroom light off and leaving the mirror until later—later this afternoon, later this week, maybe later this year. Fumbling in the dark, she used the toilet, then pulled a toothbrush out of the medicine cabinet, loaded it with Crest, and started brushing. The toothbrush probably wasn't hers—it tasted different than usual and the handle felt wider—but it wasn't as if anyone had to worry about catching an STD from her. Not now, not ever.

Brushing furiously, Shir cleared last night's ugly aftertaste from her mouth and spat it into the sink. Then she splashed her face with water and headed for the kitchen. As expected, she passed her mother en route, sitting on the living room couch and watching a TV church show. Every Sunday morning like clockwork, Janice Rutz tuned into TV preachers for what she called her "God fix." Apparently, it made up for everything she said and did the other 167 hours of the week.

"Dragged yourself out of your drunken stupor, eh?" she called as she caught sight of Shir coming down the hall. "How many did you slosh last night, Shir—six? Or did you manage to work your way through an entire twelve-pack?"

"I'm all right," mumbled Shir, realizing her mother's tone wasn't angry—just needling, digging in with her voice. Ducking her head, she edged past the end of the couch. "I wasn't drinking, just hanging around. Why d'you always think I'm out drinking?"

"Because you *are* always out drinking," snapped her mother. "Just like your father—drunk as a stone. The first time I saw your face, a minute after you were born, I knew you'd grow up to be just like him."

A savage pounding started up in Shir's head. *Pot calling the kettle black*, she thought, but all she said was, "I told you, I'm all right." Receiving no reply, she chanced a glance at the couch and saw her mother staring at the TV, her eyes glazed the way they got when she ditched whatever was going on around her and went off someplace in her head. Janice Rutz spent a lot of time in her head, which at the moment was just fine with Shir. Relieved, she continued into the kitchen and got out the Cheerios and the milk, then set herself up at the table, squirreled in behind it, her back to the wall. With no one there to watch, she could go to town on the special effects. Maple syrup, corn syrup, chocolate syrup, and a big dollop of honey—the more the merrier. Squeezing happily, Shir watched the various liquids flow out of their containers into her cereal bowl, then added several tablespoons of brown sugar for good measure.

"If Mom catches you at that, your head's going straight into the TV," said a voice, and Shir looked up to see her sister walk into the kitchen. Hair curled, her makeup impeccable, even Stella's jeans were ironed. Quickly, Shir refocused on her cereal bowl.

"So?" she mumbled. "I could probably preach a better sermon than that guy she's watching."

Leaned against the counter, Stella gave a hissing laugh. "About what?" she demanded. "How to drink the entire liquor store and still come home standing?"

Shir shrugged. "I always come home standing," she said.

"Barely," said Stella, sliding some bread into the toaster. "You were banging into the walls coming down the hall last night. Lucky Mom was asleep."

Again Shir shrugged. "My lucky night," she muttered.

A long silence followed. Ignoring it, Shir concentrated on the gooey mess in front of her. It was one of her better concoctions, the accumulated mass of syrup outweighing the Cheerios and milk combined. Besides, if she looked up now, she knew what she would see—Stella's dark doe-like eyes, boring into her skull with utter disbelief. One year younger, Stella spent a lot of time staring at Shir whenever they were alone in a room together. It was as if she still couldn't believe, even after fifteen years, that they were genetically linked.

Not such a surprise, really, thought Shir, watching a thick gob of syrup slide off her spoon. Stella's dad had been one of a long list of guys who had floated into Janice Rutz's life during one of the many periods Shir's dad had floated out of it. With long dark hair, chestnut brown eyes, what could be considered a fairly normal nose, and a wide smiling mouth, Stella's face verged on pretty. At least, a lot of guys seemed to think so.

After Stella had been born, Janice Rutz had gotten a hysterectomy. As far as Shir was concerned, it had been one of her mother's better ideas.

"Would you mind not staring so hard?" she asked, keeping her gaze fixed on her cereal. "Your eyes are, like, doing major brain surgery on my head."

"No prob," Stella said casually. Pulling her bread out of the toaster, she smeared it with cinnamon spread. The sound of brisk munching followed. Out in the living room, a loud warbling erupted as a church choir took over the TV screen with "Amazing Grace." Shir rolled her eyes. The song never seemed to wear out—for anyone, that is, but her.

"So, did he kiss you?" asked Stella.

The question, coming out of the blue like that, caused an immediate choke-up of Cheerios in Shir's throat. "Kiss me?" she gulped. Guardedly, she shot a glance at her sister. "Did who kiss me?" she asked in a half-whisper.

"Wade Sullivan," said Stella, flashing a quick, bright smile— quick and bright as the edge of a razor blade. "That's where you were last night, wasn't it—at his party?"

A heaviness settled over Shir, and she stared at the bloated Cheerios floating in her cereal bowl. "I wasn't at *his* party," she said finally. "And anyway, how did you know I was at a party?"

"Just did," said Stella, the smile in her voice speaking louder than her words. Shir didn't have to look up to feel the smugness written all over her sister's goddam pretty face.

"Just did *how*?" she asked hoarsely.

"I don't think you really want to know," Stella singsonged softly. "But I'll tell you anyway. Everyone knew. Well, maybe not *exactly* everyone. Maybe only *half* the school. You know, the ... Well, *you* know."

Shoulders slumped, Shir sat turning her spoon over and over, watching the curves catch and throw light. Stella didn't have to come out and say it in so many words, it was obvious who she meant—the popular kids, the ones that mattered. Altogether, they comprised maybe ten percent of Collier High's student population, and Stella was definitely on their outer fringes. She was exaggerating, clearly; still, if she had known about Wade's plan in advance, others had, too—probably quite a few.

"So, if you knew," mumbled Shir, the realization pouring through her, "why didn't you warn me? So I didn't waste my time going to that fucking party."

Another brisk chewing episode ensued, followed by a little Stella-type giggle. Little Stella-type giggles made Shir want to grind eggshells with her teeth.

"Thought you might enjoy the experience," her sister said finally. "It was your first kiss, right?"

Shir's hands were shaking. In her mind's eye, she kept seeing it—a skyscraper-sized fist zooming across the kitchen and pulverizing Stella into a tiny, giggling pile of dust. Setting down her spoon, Shir placed both hands carefully in her lap.

"Do you have swimming practice at one?" she asked, fighting the wobble in her voice.

"Um ... *yeah*," said Stella, as if this was the dumbest question she had ever been asked.

"Well," said Shir, keeping her eyes fixed on the table. "I would suggest you get your ass out of this kitchen and go put on your swimsuit or *something*. Because if you stand there for, like, five seconds more, I am going to do massive physical damage to you."

"Oh, really?" said Stella, her voice rising.

Lifting her eyes, Shir looked directly at her sister. "Yeah, *really*," she said quietly, her voice even, but her meaning crystal. *Fuck Mom sitting in the next room*, she thought grimly, *and fuck the YWCA self-defense course*. With the way Shir was feeling right now, Stella was five seconds away from termination. And one warning was all she was going to get.

Stella got the drift. Dark, doe-like eyes widening, she pushed herself away from the counter. "Well," she muttered vaguely, glancing around herself as if consulting with the air. "I guess it *is* getting late."

Without another word, she left the kitchen. Seconds later, Shir heard the careful click of the lock sliding into place on her sister's bedroom door. Alone in the kitchen, she stared glumly at the mush in her cereal bowl. Truth be told, the stuff looked like a before and an after shot that had been merged together. Just looking at it, you couldn't tell if this was food that was still supposed to be eaten, or glop that had already been digested and then regurgitated.

Sort of like my life, Shir thought dully. Most days, it felt as if she was living something that someone else had swallowed, then chucked back up in disgust.

Out in the living room, the TV preacher was calling for the offering and reminding the congregation that God had commanded them to tithe a full ten percent. Anything over that was extra, something that would get them bonus points with the divine. Getting up from the table, Shir carried her bowl to the sink and dumped the contents. Then she turned on the tap and stood watching the clean water sluice the murky guck down the drain. It was all gone now—her conversation with Stella, last night's party, and Wade Sullivan's ugly comments.

The question was, did that leave anything worth living for? A sudden stinging blurred Shir's eyes. Turning from the sink, she left the kitchen and headed to her room.

Two

Ugly, she was ugly, thought Shir. No question about it. Glumly, she stared at her reflection in the bathroom mirror. Born ugly in a way that was never going to change. No Cinderella slipper here, no Sleeping Beauty to wake with a kiss, even for a toonie. No, hers was the kind of face that fairy tales reserved for dwarfs and goblins, a face without a single redeeming feature. Even the eyes were ugly—small, squinty, and of a queer, pale blue that never seemed to hold any expression. It was almost as if they were made of glass.

Maybe the eyebrows were okay, she thought, running a fingertip over the right one. Not too bushy and not too thin, they covered the area they were supposed to in your basic parallel arches. And her body was normal, neither fat nor rail-thin. But after that, it was all downhill. The worst aspect of her appearance was obviously her nose. It wasn't just that it was so enormous the rest of her had no choice but to skulk along in its shadow, there was also the size of her nostrils to consider. They were huge, cavernous. In grade five, it had been the favorite lunch-hour pastime to stick various objects inside them. Sometimes Shir had been the one to stick in something; sometimes a group of boys had held her down and done it. Stones, shoelaces, dill pickles—the inspiration had been endless. One boy had even brought his pet guppies to school and inserted them live.

They had died in her nose. Occasionally Shir still woke in the middle of the night, sweat pouring off her as she relived the sensation of those desperately wriggling guppies. It had been her choice; she had agreed in advance to having them stuck in there, but not to being held down or having her nose plugged after the guppies had been shoved in. Even now, years later, she could feel the exact moment the guppies' little fishy souls had left their bodies—two brilliant bursts of energy that had swum straight up her nose and into her brain. They were still there, those guppy souls, swimming the inside of her head. Telling her things: *Don't believe anything you hear. There's an enemy lurking behind every smile. Never let yourself get so small, they can do to you what they did to us.*

The thing about those guppies was that they had been pretty, Shir thought bleakly. Silvery fins, quick twisting bodies. Lines of light flashing in their fishbowl water. And still, hands had reached for them and squished out their tiny guppy breaths.

Quickly, she turned from the mirror. Shakes, she was getting the shakes. Well, it served her right—getting herself worked up over a couple of dumb guppies that had died five years ago. God, was she dumb, thought Shir. Drunk as a stone, like Mom said. Gently, she thunked her drunk stone forehead against the bathroom wall. Knock some sense into herself, yeah—*bang, bang, bang.* There, that was better. Now the shakes were gone and she could no longer remember what she had been thinking about. Which was fine with her, because as far as she could tell, it hadn't been too pleasant.

A long sigh shuddered through her. Glancing at her watch, Shir saw it was 1:54. The day was yet young; the floor had stopped its bleary wobble; and her headache was on the mend. What should she do? she wondered. Homework? Nah, homework was a disease. Reaching for the window-latch, she opened it, stuck out her head, and breathed deeply. *That's better*, she thought, fingering a nearby poplar branch. Already the first buds were beginning to show, the last of the snow long gone.

"Shirley," called a voice from down the hall, sharp and with a bit of an edge.

Mom, thought Shir, stiffening slightly. "Yeah?" she called back, keeping her voice neutral, in the nothing zone.

"The phone's for you," continued her mother, her tone still edgy, as if put out about it. "It's Mr. Anderson. He wants you to come in and do some deliveries."

Instantly, Shir straightened. Slamming the window shut, she erupted out of the bathroom and took the entire length of the hall in one expert slide. "Hello, Mr. Anderson!" she sang into the phone, as she grabbed it from her mother's outstretched hand. Mr. Anderson ran Bill's Grocer, a neighborhood corner store over on 12th Street. Six months ago, he had hired Shir part-time to stock shelves and do deliveries. Sunday-afternoon deliveries came about once a month, and they usually meant good tips.

"Hi, Shirley," said Mr. Anderson, his voice booming into her ear, slightly nasal because of the phone. "Can you make it here by three? I've got four deliveries for you."

"Sure thing, sir," Shir said immediately. "I'll be there in ten minutes."

"No need to rush," said Mr. Anderson, but she could hear the smile in his voice. "Three o'clock is fine."

"Great, sir," said Shir. "I'll be there *right away*, sir." Hanging up the phone, she headed for the door.

"Shirley Rutz, you put on a clean sweatshirt before going out," called her mother from the couch. "And brush your goddam hair, for Chrissake!"

Briefly, Shir considered ignoring the order, then remembered she hadn't brushed her hair since yesterday afternoon. "Gotcha!" she called, snapping a military salute as she passed the couch, then taking off in another long slide down the hall. A few swipes with her hairbrush, a clean Toronto Maple Leafs sweatshirt, and two Tylenol capsules to take care of the tail end of her headache, and she was once again making tracks for the door.

"Take your jacket!" hollered Mom, her butt still glued to the couch and her eyes fixed on the TV. "And remember to be *respectful*. None of that filthy mouth you show around here."

With a quick slam of the door, Shir cut off her mother mid-sentence. No sense in listening to *that* any longer than necessary, she told herself. Pulling on her jacket, she ran down the apartment block's back stairwell two steps at a time, then took the bottom five in one fell swoop. A few seconds to allow her legs to absorb the shock upon landing and she was out the door, unlocking the communal storage shed behind the building and dragging out her bike. "The Black Stallion" was what she called it, just a cheap Dunlop, and blue to boot, but who cared—nobody knew its soul name but her. Swinging a leg over the seat, she took off down the alley, and then it was just her and the Black, riding out the long sheer gusts of an early April wind.

Twelfth Street was three blocks south, and Bill's Grocer five blocks east. Zooming along a series of back alleys, Shir called out to every barking dog, taunting as the animals leapt furiously against fences, their teeth snapping her tailwind. Too quick coming out onto 14th Street, she had to swerve to miss a car, then took off again, ignoring the driver's shouts. Good thing Mr. Anderson couldn't see her now, she thought with a grin, or he would think twice about letting her drive the delivery van. Before hiring her, he had taken her for a test drive, watching as she had maneuvered corners and changed lanes. She had been sweating but she had done okay, at least, well enough to be hired. Fortunately, her mother had insisted Shir get her license as soon as she turned sixteen, mostly so she could send Shir out for groceries on weekends when she was too plastered to do anything but lie splayed on the couch and grunt.

The thing Shir hadn't been able to figure out yet was why Mr. Anderson had even *thought* of hiring her. After all, he had plenty of nephews, and there were always lots of neighborhood kids hanging around the store. But one day last September, when she had come in for a pop, he had looked at her, as if seeing her for the first time, and asked how old she was. Then he had asked if she wanted a job. "You bet!" she had said right off, then quickly added, "sir." Every week since, she had come into work expecting the situation to have somehow backfired and Mr. Anderson to sorrowfully tell her the whole thing had been a mistake; he had never intended to actually hire her, and she now had to pay back all the wages she had earned. But instead, here she was, six months later, still showing up three days a week, after school and on weekends, and walking out at the end of a shift with money in her pocket. Today's four deliveries could take as long as two hours if Mr. Anderson had her pack the boxes first. With tips, she should make enough to keep herself in beer for most of the week.

A swing out of the alley brought her onto 12th Street, with a view of Bill's Grocer at the next corner. As she caught sight of it, Shir slowed her pace, bringing the Black down to a gentle canter. No matter what her mother said, Shir thought proudly, she knew how to handle herself at work. She was a *professional*, always speaking respectfully to customers and never giving any back talk. Coasting into the curb, she dismounted and locked the Black to a stop sign, then headed into the store. As she entered, she was hit with the usual combination of aromas— lemons and apples, celery and Spic'n Span. To her left, a few customers were lined up at a till; Cathy, Mr. Anderson's niece, gave her a quick wave from the cash register. Ducking her head, Shir waved back. Bill's Grocer was a good place to work, she thought fiercely. Yeah, it was a friendly place—there must be hundreds of kids in this city who would like to work here—but Mr. Anderson had picked *her*; out of them all, he had chosen dog-faced, shit-ugly Shirley Jane Rutz.

With a sigh, Shir stooped to pick up an orange that had fallen off a nearby stack, and set it on top of the pile. Then she walked to the back of the store, pushed open the door marked *Employees Only,* and entered the main storage area. Shelves packed with boxes lined the walls, and three meters to her right was Mr. Anderson, standing with his back to her while he spoke into his cell phone. Coming to a halt, Shir waited quietly. Her boss was talking in a low voice, pacing back and forth, and it was a minute before he saw her. When he did, he seemed to start, then lifted a hand, waved, and walked out of the store's back entrance into the alley.

Instant alarm shot through Shir—had she done something wrong; should she have made more noise coming in; was she about to be fired? Then common sense took over, and she stood, letting her breathing slow. The boss was just having a private conversation, that was all, she told herself shakily. Maybe he had a mistress and was running a hot secret affair. Whatever, it wasn't her concern.

On a nearby counter, she noted four boxes packed to go, their delivery addresses written in black marker across the top. Crossing the room, Shir scanned them intently. Joe's Pizza, Mrs. Duran, and the Pleasant View Seniors' Home—she had made deliveries to each of these places before and they tipped okay. The last address, however, was new—the Sunnyville Rec Center on 9th Avenue. *Oh yeah,* she thought with a flash of recognition. She knew the place, having attended a day camp at the center the summer she turned eight. But that was twenty blocks west, she thought, a frown crossing her face. Why in the world would a rec center twenty blocks west phone in a Sunday afternoon delivery to, of all places, Bill's Grocer?

Briefly she pondered the question, then ditched it with a shrug. *Whatever*, she thought. A customer's reasons were his own private business. She just made the delivery. Picking up the nearest box, she hefted it experimentally. *Heavy enough*, she thought, grunting softly. From the sound of it, the box was full of cans. For this one she would put on an extra-sweaty, worn-out look when she carried it to the door. That should bring in an extra buck on the tip.

"Early and raring to go as usual, I see," said a voice behind her.

Startled, Shir turned to see Mr. Anderson coming through the back entrance. As usual, he was smiling, his upper lip hidden under a dark, bushy mustache, his plump face wreathed in congenial lines. *Just looking at that smile*, Shir thought, smiling back instinctively, *you don't notice what a porker he is. Or how bald.*

"Yes, sir," she said. "Lucky I did most of my homework last night so I was free today."

A flicker passed through Mr. Anderson's eyes the way it always did when she lied about schoolwork. As if he didn't quite believe her, thought Shir. But why wouldn't he? she wondered, giving him an uneasy glance. What would Mr. Anderson know, one way or another, about what she did when she was off work?

"Great," he said heartily, coming toward her. "Just what we

need—a scholar on staff. Now, like I told you on the phone, I've got four deliveries for you. You've done three of them before, but one is new. It's a rec center—"

"Yes, sir," Shir said immediately. "I know it."

"You do?" asked Mr. Anderson. Inexplicably, his eyes narrowed, and he shot her a sharp glance. Panic hit Shir, jagged heartbeats there and gone.

"Just went to summer camp there, sir," she blurted, cursing herself angrily in her head. Damn it all, what was the matter with her? She should know better than to interrupt the boss. So what if she already knew the way to the rec center? If Mr. Anderson wanted to explain every millimeter of the route, she could just goddam stand there and listen.

"Great, just great!" Mr. Anderson exclaimed heartily, the brief sharpness gone from his face. Reaching out a hand, he touched Shir lightly on the shoulder, and she was released from the frightened, angry yelling in her head. "You're sure you know the way there?" he asked gently.

"Yes, sir," said Shir. Flooded with relief at the change in her boss's tone, she stared fixedly at the floor. So, she wasn't going to be fired, she thought wearily. At least, not yet. *Not yet, not yet ...*

"Great, just great," repeated Mr. Anderson, and handed her the keys to the delivery van. "When you get to the rec center, ask for a Mr. Dubya. The order is to go directly to him and no one else."

"Yes, sir," Shir assured him.

"And keep to the speed limit," he added with a wink. "Don't

do anything I wouldn't do."

"No, sir," Shir grinned back. "I definitely won't, sir."

Grabbing the box that contained the rec center's order, she headed out to the van, a nondescript gray vehicle parked in the alley behind the store. Since the rec center was her furthest delivery, she placed the box on the back passenger seat, then returned to the storage room for another one. Mrs. Duran's was the closest address, only a few blocks away, and then there was the seniors' home. If she drove slowly, she should be able to stretch the four deliveries into an hour, maybe an hour and a half.

With a satisfied grin, she unlocked the van's front door and settled in behind the wheel. As usual, the raised front seat, with the van's mass of horsepower revving under her feet, made her feel as if she was sitting on a mobile throne. After a careful shoulder check, she backed out of the parking space and headed down the alley. At 12th Street, she scanned for traffic, but the thoroughfare was empty. A small sigh escaped her. Nothing ahead but sunshine and the faint lacy green of newly budding trees; the world was her oyster.

Giving it some gas, Shir started off slowly. Over the past six months, she had come to realize that two things were of the utmost importance when making deliveries—driving carefully, and using up as much time as possible so she could bump up her earnings and spend the rest of the week swimming in beer. At the first four-way stop, she turned on the radio to find it tuned to a couple of talking heads, the usual CBC stuff Mr. Anderson listened to. With a snort, she adjusted it to CJSR, and the world was rocking. Both hands firmly on the wheel and a wide grin plastered across her face, Shir continued rolling down the street.

At 34th Avenue, she turned right and parked. Mrs. Duran's house was the second from the corner—a small yellow bungalow with a garden to one side. This early in the year, there was nothing but a few green shoots poking out of the ground, but still she could see the tiny elderly woman pottering around, working the earth loose with a large gardening fork.

"There you are, Shirley!" she exclaimed as Shir opened the van door. Getting laboriously to her feet, Mrs. Duran started across the lawn in her ancient wobbly way. Hastily, Shir snatched a clipboard that lay on the passenger seat, and booted it to the back of the van. If she didn't watch it, the old lady would try to grab the box that contained her order and lug it into the house herself. Didn't come up to Shir's shoulder, but still thought she was Wonder Woman or something.

"Where would you like this, Mrs. Duran?" asked Shir, hefting the box securely into her own arms and giving the elderly woman her best smile.

"This way, dear," Mrs. Duran beamed back. "Follow me."

Slowly, she started off along the side of the house, creaky step by creaky step. Not bothering to hide her grin, Shir followed. She got a real kick out of this old lady, the way she was always doing something—painting her porch, raking the lawn, or gardening. One time, she had actually caught Mrs. Duran halfway up a stepladder, trying to knock a dead squirrel out of the eavestrough. Shir had helped her down off the ladder, then done the job for her. It had gotten her an extra toonie, but she had turned it down. A tip for deliveries was one thing, but helping little old ladies knock dead rodents out of eavestroughs—well, you couldn't take money for that.

As she turned the back corner and mounted the porch steps, Shir could smell cinnamon and nutmeg. *Baking again*, she smiled to herself. Mrs. Duran had about a million grandchildren, and was always mixing up another batch of cookies.

"Just set it over there, Shirley," said the elderly woman as they entered the back hallway. "On that chair there. Now, let me see if I can't find you a lovely loonie for helping out an old geezer like me." Fishing around in a jewelry box of loose change she kept by the phone, she placed a toonie firmly in Shir's hand. "Now, don't you think you need a cookie and a glass of iced tea after all that hard work?" she asked, peering up at her.

"I sure do, Mrs. Duran," grinned Shir, knowing this was the way Mr. Anderson would want her to respond—polite and friendly, treating the customers like real human beings. Hefting the delivery box higher in her arms, she carried it into the kitchen and set it on the table where it would be easier for Mrs. Duran to unpack it. Then she sat down and munched her way through several cookies while the elderly woman sat opposite, warbling on about her zillion children, grandchildren, and great-grandchildren, and what it had been like during the war years. And that wasn't the Iraq war, or Afghanistan, or even Vietnam, thought Shir, studying the wrinkled face opposite. It was World

War II, which put Mrs. Duran well into her eighties. And she wasn't *anywhere* near dying yet. Just sitting there, Shir could practically hear the little old lady's heartbeat, steady and sure, filling the walls of this pretty yellow house.

A feeling of softness crept over Shir and she let herself sink back into her chair, breathing in the room's quiet, nutmeg-scented air. It was nice here, her favorite place to make a delivery, and with Mrs. Duran's quavery storytelling, they managed to knock off twenty minutes before the elderly woman signed the clipboard, acknowledging delivery, and Shir was back in the van, waving goodbye and heading down the street.

The seniors' center was more businesslike. Shir didn't know anyone personally, and the old people didn't seem to do much more than sit around, staring out the windows. Still, the kitchen staff were friendly, and Shir left with a loonie tip in her pocket and a smile on her face. Next was Joe's Pizza, which was packed with customers, waitresses hollering back and forth, and kitchen staff madly shredding cheese and slapping on anchovies. So it was just a quick stop—in and out, with a wave to Lucille, Joe's wife, and another toonie in her pocket.

Back in the van, she mentally rehearsed her route to the Sunnyville Rec Center and started off. It would take at least fifteen minutes to get there—the place was halfway across town. You would think, thought Shir, there would be a grocer in the Riverdale area that did deliveries, but maybe not on Sundays. Tapping her fingers against the steering wheel in time to an old AC/DC song, Shir made good time down Madden Road, a four-lane route, then slowed as she entered the city's west end. Sunnyville was on 9th Avenue, just past St. John's high school. *Yup*, she thought, as she caught sight of the familiar building. *There it is.* Carefully, she swung into the parking lot and parked the van.

Glancing out the side window, Shir saw that the grounds were empty except for a single guy, who was leaning against the rec center's closest wall and smoking a cigarette. Beside him, the door to the gym stood open, releasing the sounds of shouts, squeaking runners, and a bouncing basketball. Obviously, a game was in process. Getting out of the van, Shir opened the back door and slid out the last box. Then she hefted it into her arms and walked toward the guy.

He was in his twenties, tattooed, and wearing a muscle shirt despite the coolish weather. As Shir approached, his eyes flicked casually across her face and she ducked her head, wanting to avoid the inevitable expression of shock that hit strangers the first time they saw her. "Delivery for the Sunnyville Rec Center," she said, studying the tear in the tip of her left runner. She was back to wearing her old pair again—her new ones were probably still lying somewhere in Dana Lowe's rear hallway. "Do you know where I can find a Mr. Dubya?"

"In there," said the guy, jerking his chin at the open doorway. "He's reffing the game."

"Thanks," said Shir. Hefting the box, she stepped through the doorway and stood, letting her eyes adjust to the indoor light. As she had thought, a basketball game was in progress, two teams of teenage boys sprinting around the court. A few meters to her left stood the only adult in the room, a man in his fifties, wearing a whistle around his neck.

"Mr. Dubya?" asked Shir, approaching him.

"From Bill's Grocer?" responded the man, and she nodded. "Okay, put it over there," he said, pointing to a bench along the wall.

Setting down the box, Shir held out her clipboard. "Could you sign here, sir?" she asked, the way she always had to with a new customer. "Just to say you received your order?"

Mr. Dubya's eyes flicked across her face, then came back to linger with casual curiosity. Sucking her lower lip, Shir fought the urge to look away. She could just imagine the thoughts running through his head: *How'd you get to be so ugly, kid? Someone drop you when you were a baby? Onto a freeway? A busy one?*

But instead of signing, the man simply said, "Just tell Anderson that Dubya got the goods. He'll be okay with that." Then he turned back to the game.

"But I'm supposed to get a signature," protested Shir, riding a small wave of panic. "To prove that you got it, I mean."

Mr. Dubya glanced at her, his eyes suddenly so cold, she felt a shiver run up her spine. "You tell him Dubya got the goods," he repeated tonelessly, as if reciting something, then turned once again to watch the game.

Bewildered, Shir blinked at him but Mr. Dubya ignored her, his eyes fixed on the rapidly shifting players. Abruptly, he grabbed the whistle around his neck, blew it and shouted,

"Foul!" A collective groan rose from the boys on the court and he strode toward them. Mouth open, Shir stood staring after him, then jammed the clipboard under her arm and headed for the door. No point in hanging around—she had obviously been dismissed.

Back in the parking lot, she stood beside the van, breathing in the sun and the late afternoon air. *That was odd*, she thought guardedly. Kind of creepy, actually, as if weird little ghosties were hanging around, sending out bad vibes. And no tip. With a sigh, she climbed into the van and wrote *Mr. Dubya wouldn't sign* onto the clipboard. Then, turning on the ignition, she backed cautiously out of her parking space. Over by the gym door, the wall was now empty, the guy in the muscle shirt no longer leaning against it. For a moment, Shir idled the van at the curb and stared thoughtfully at the place he had been standing. Why had a guy like that been hanging around here? she wondered. He was too old to be part of the game going on inside, and too tough to listen to anyone's goddam whistle.

Frowning, she sat a moment longer, trying to work it out. But no answer came to her, so she made her usual careful shoulder check and started off down 9th Avenue. A quick glance at her watch showed that it was 4:25. If she drove at a reasonable pace, she would make it back to the store around 4:45, which Mr. Anderson would be sure to bump up to 5:00. That meant she would be paid for a full two hours' work. With the five bucks she had made in tips, that was more than enough for an eight-pack, which would keep her going until Tuesday, her next shift. *Yeah!*

Shir thought, exhilarated. She was doing fine; she was *laughing*.

With a broad grin, she turned up the volume on the radio and settled in for the drive back to Bill's Grocer.

Three

The school halls were the usual, packed with students yakking at their lockers and coming and going from homerooms. Braced against the inevitable onslaught of noise, Shir let the south-entrance door swing closed behind her, then ducked her head and pushed her way into the melee. This year her locker was on the school's west side, in the languages department, which put it across the building from the east-entrance bike racks. Last year it had been outside the gym, and the year before that beside the music room. Maybe next year, her grad year, the cross-eyed schizoid in the front office who was responsible for assigning lockers would give her one within radar detection range of homeroom 32, a science classroom located in the basement under the principal's office. *Which put it*, Shir thought grumpily, as she climbed the stairs leading to the second-floor languages wing, *directly under Mr. O'Donnell's butt.* You would think, as compensation, they could at least cut back on the daily locker safari ... and the social joys that went with it.

With a sigh, she dropped her gym bag in front of her locker and mentally rehearsed her lock combination. Several times this year, as she had reached for her lock, she had gone into a complete blank—hadn't been able to remember the correct combination for the life of her. She must have looked a real dork, standing there stockstill and staring at the lock in her hand. It had been a weird kind of mind warp, there and gone, the combination surfacing seconds later in her thoughts. Alzheimer's for the adolescent—maybe if she ate more broccoli, her brain would improve.

Today, it seemed to be functional—at least, the lock opened on her first try, with its customary satisfying click. Carelessly, Shir stuffed her gym bag into the bottom of her locker. The only thing it contained was her lunch—what with her shift at Bill's Grocer on Saturday, the party that evening, and then the Sunday-afternoon deliveries, there hadn't been time for homework. Anyway, she thought derisively, homework was a disease. Who needed history or English to stock shelves and drive a delivery van? School was for eggheads who wanted to become prime minister. And prime ministers were also a disease.

Grabbing her binder and textbooks, Shir slammed her locker door and started off down the hall. From all sides came the usual banter and jokes; head down, she caught a few phrases as she passed.

"Pottberg really tied one on Friday night—smashed in the front end of his dad's car."

"No way, you got that hickey from Larry Adawee?"

Overhead, the occasional security camera whirred, taking in whatever it was security cameras took in; at floor level, Shir continued to weave through the jabbering crowd, then down a flight of stairs to the first floor. Next, it was a short hall and another set of stairs to the basement. Here she turned left, and continued her daily locker-to-homeroom odyssey along another crowded hall before making the final turn to the right, and heading toward the open doorway of homeroom 32.

"Hey, what d'you know—it's Wade Sullivan's blind love!" called a voice behind her.

A jolt of something ran up Shir's back, a sensation somewhere between fear and electric shock. Ducking her head lower, she put on a burst of speed.

"Wade Sullivan's in love?" another voice asked dubiously.

"Blind love," said the first voice. "We're talking eyes-gouged-out-of-the-head blind. Take a look at it."

Behind Shir, someone seemed to be pointing her out. Without glancing back, she could feel the sudden intensity of eyes focused on her back.

"What? *That?*" demanded a voice, disbelieving.

Shir didn't wait to hear the rest of it. Practically launching herself through her homeroom doorway, she veered to the right and scurried down the wall aisle. Back corner desk—it was the seat she always headed for, and this year she had been lucky enough to snag it in homeroom. She was supposed to have a partner—all the desks in this room were two-seaters—but on the first day of classes, the other desks had filled up quickly, leaving her sitting alone. That was all right, she had eventually decided. She wasn't the only one, and besides, it saved her having to make conversation. Conversations, especially in the morning, *especially* in homeroom, were a disease.

Sliding onto the stool at her desk, Shir opened her binder to the first empty page and sat staring at it. Years ago, she had discovered that empty pages were a good way to blank the mind and get rid of all the things she didn't want to think about. Eyes narrowed, she concentrated on the page's white areas, blurring out the blue and pink lines, and trying to turn her brain into nothing. But this morning, her gray cells refused to cooperate. Instead, a crowd of voices started up inside her head—mean, ugly, school-hall, power-trip kinds of voices.

Eyes-gouged-out-of-the-head blind. Take a look at it.

What, that?

It was happening the way she had figured it would—the blind-love joke was too good to let die after only one kick at the can. No, it was worth at least a week of cheap shots, and then there was the "love by Braille" line. That one had enough going to last another few weeks. With luck, they could keep tossing it around until mid-May.

A snicker sounded, and Shir heard the slide of jeans on varnished wood as the girls seated ahead of her turned around on their stools. "So, how was Dana's party?" a voice asked casually.

Shir's eyes narrowed. Jenny Shamayyim and Bev Mulholland were grade ten nobodies—heavy on the makeup, tight on the jeans, two *very* basic metalheads from the curbside smoking crowd. They certainly hadn't been at Dana's party Saturday night, and whatever they had heard, it was scraps.

"It was fine," she said, forcing herself to meet their gaze. People's faces did weird things when she looked them dead-on. It was the complete blankness in her eyes, she was sure of it—that pale, boundaryless blue that gave back nothing, *nothing*. Focusing on the sensation of pure nothingness in her eyes, Shir stared the two girls down. Whatever happened here, she reminded herself sternly, she had to make sure her nostrils didn't flare.

The girls' gaze flickered and their sneers wavered slightly. "Just *fine*?" giggled Jenny and rolled her eyes at Bev.

"Seen better," Shir said coolly, zeroing in on Jenny's left pupil. It was a trick she often used that allowed her to blur out the rest of a person's face. Then it was like talking to a black smudge, or perhaps the period at the end of a sentence. Period, as in *over*, time's up, see ya later, loser.

"So, did you see Wade?" asked Bev, leaning forward eagerly.

"Yeah," Shir said tersely. Now it was her gaze that was wavering. Angrily, she forced it back to Bev's face. "I saw him," she added grimly.

The girls grinned at each other. "Oh, yeah," said Jenny, "Well, did he—"

"Well, *nothing*," snapped Shir, the blood beginning to pound in her cheeks. Goddam it, she could feel it—any second now, her nostrils were going to flare. If that happened, they would expand at least a centimeter. They would be titanic, gargantuan, a monstrosity. Screaming at her nostrils in her mind, *willing* them to remain calm, relaxed, and of reasonable human diameter, Shir refocused on a beauty spot Jenny had drawn above her upper lip.

"Just nothing," she repeated, trying to keep her voice steady. "Nothing happened, all right? *Nothing.*"

For a long, stretched moment she stared at the girls and they stared back, the air between them taut as the skin over the pulse in a throat. "Okay," Jenny said finally, glancing at Bev. "No need to freak about it. You look like a dork when you stare at people like that, you know."

"I know," Shir said evenly, keeping her gaze fixed on the beauty spot. Years of experience had taught her that a minimal response was safest. After all, it was difficult to maintain an all-out, no-holds-barred, aim-for-the-jugular assault on a void. And if anyone was an expert at transforming herself into an absolute void at whim, it was Shirley Jane Rutz. For several seconds longer, the two girls continued to stare at her. Then, with a sniff, Bev turned to face the front of the room, followed by Jenny. As soon as their backs were turned, Shir went into meltdown—her stomach, her spine, even her brain dissolving into a series of nauseating puddles. Letting her eyes drop, she focused on the blank page in front of her and just got rid of it.

With a quick breath, Shir stepped up onto the ramshackle stoop, knocked rapidly, and jumped back to the grass. Then, retreating several steps, she waited. As expected, it took Gareth almost a minute to come to the door, and when he finally arrived, the first thing he did was lift a slat in the window's ancient venetian blind and peer out balefully. After ensuring that she wasn't a cop or social worker, he opened the door, poked out his miserable seventy-proof head, and sniffed blearily at the air.

Shir rolled her eyes. They went through this routine every time. "Beer," she said tersely. "How many d'you got?"

"It'll cost you $3.50 a can," said Gareth, scratching his unshaven jaw.

Shir's mouth dropped. "Three-fifty!" she almost shouted. "Last week it was three bucks."

"Price of oil's gone up," said Gareth, studying her through heavy-lidded eyes. "When oil goes up, everything goes up. Cost of transportation, you know."

Speechless, Shir glared. The cost of oil had goddam nothing to do with it. Gareth had what she wanted, and on a Monday afternoon he was her only option. He knew it and she knew it.

"Three-fifty for the first and three even for the second," she bargained, swallowing hard.

"Three-fifty for both," he replied coolly. "That's seven dollars for two. *If* you want them, that is."

Sucking in her breath, Shir fought to keep calm. She had nine dollars on her, enough—at last week's price—to buy three cans. Whenever she came knocking on Gareth's door, she brought exact change. Hand him extra and you could count on it being a sure loss.

"Okay," she said grudgingly. "I'll take two."

A smug smile came and went on Gareth's whiskery face. It was a smile she had seen often, and had learned to be wary of. A terminal welfare case, Gareth Fenske was a forty-something, dead-end loner always looking to make a buck. She had met him about a year ago, collecting bottles outside the liquor store, and had offered him a toonie to go inside and buy her a six-pack. He had bargained for the toonie and two beers. It hadn't taken them long to come to a thorough understanding of each other.

"Want to come in?" he asked, his voice carefully casual.

"I'll wait here," Shir replied gruffly. It was the response she gave every time he asked. And he asked every time she showed up at his door, even though she would have had to be certifiably crazy to take him up on the offer. Gareth's apartment was at the back of a dilapidated house that had been subdivided into low-rent units. His was the only apartment that could be entered from the building's rear, and the yard was surrounded by a high wood fence. From the alley, no one could see who went into this door, or if they ever came back out. Gareth might not be blind, but he didn't look picky, either, especially about issues like consent.

"Suit yourself," he shrugged and disappeared from the doorway. A moment later, he returned and set two cans of Budweiser on the stoop.

"Here," Shir said grimly, and placed a five and a toonie in his outstretched hand. Then, bending down quickly, she grabbed both cans. Just that brief second of vulnerability, with the back of her neck exposed, was so excruciating, she almost went into vertigo. Flushed, her heart pounding, Shir managed a strangled, "Thanks," then turned and booted it toward the gate. Once in the alley, she leaned against the fence and simply breathed, her ears peeled for the quiet click that would tell her Gareth had closed his door and gone inside. As usual, he had stood on the stoop and watched her walk all the way out of the yard. The guy was *weird*, she thought heavily. There were sicko little ghosties fluttering all around him.

Well, at least she had two beers. With a sigh, she placed the cans carefully into her gym bag. Then, slinging the bag over her shoulder, she unlocked the Black from a nearby fence and took off down the alley. It was 4:10, the afternoon yet young, and there was more than enough time to guzzle two beers before heading home for supper and family time. At the end of the alley, she turned left and booted it down the street. A steady stream of children was flowing along the sidewalk, little kids from a nearby elementary school. Little kids' schools, Shir thought as her eyes skimmed the laughing faces, shouldn't be allowed near houses that had people like Gareth living in them. There should be signs posted all over this block, especially up and down the alley, warning kids to stay clear.

When she reached the corner, she turned right and headed toward the river. Since she had left Gareth's place, the sun had come out, giving the air a dusky golden glow. Earlier in the day it had rained, but now the sidewalk ahead of her was clear and dry. Which meant that the arches running along the underside of the nearby walking bridge would also be dry, and she would be able to park her butt on one of them in utmost comfort while she partook of life's greatest pleasure. Whooping loudly, Shir veered off the road, across the sidewalk, and onto the muddy, faintly green lawn of an old Anglican church. Here she dismounted, walked her bike down a short slope to the parking lot behind the church, and locked it to a *Parking—Church Patrons Only* sign. Then she headed over to the footbridge.

She had visited this bridge at all times of day, but late afternoon was her favorite, when the sun slanted down in heavier angles and colored the concrete a warm amber. In the fall, it was prettiest, the trees scattering their vivid yellows up and down the river. Now, in early April, was probably the ugliest of times, with the last of the snow melted and all the winter grunge showing. Still, it was pleasant, a quiet restful scene—somewhere she could come like a lost thought looking for a home.

Myplace was what she called it, and the bridge seemed to know its name, seemed to agree that it belonged to her. Hiking her gym bag more securely over her shoulder, Shir lodged a foot between the base of the bridge's outer pillar and the beginning of the first western support arch, and started her climb. There were four support arches under the bridge, two on each side, and she usually climbed to the peak of the first western one to catch the warmth of the afternoon sun. The trick was working her way around the outside of the vertical pillars that kept the arches in place, especially in winter when the concrete was icy, but so far she had made it without a problem. Once, she had even traveled both western arches, ending up on the opposite bank and the bottom of someone's backyard. Their German shepherd had convinced her never to try that again.

Between the first and second pillars, the incline was steepest, and still layered with grit left behind by the melted snow. Holding onto the arch with both hands, Shir climbed slowly. This wasn't difficult, the surface of the arch about a meter wide, and just before the second pillar, she momentarily straightened and stood midair with the breeze, watching the river flow past. Back on the bank, or even walking across the top of the bridge, a person didn't get a sense of what it was like here, with the breeze coming low and full-out across the water, and the sun so golden glowing, unobstructed by buildings or trees. Eyes tranced, Shir leaned her cheek against the pillar's warm concrete and stood, riding the breeze with her mind. Then, swinging her left foot around the second pillar's outer edge, she stepped onto the next section of the arch. The incline leading to the third pillar was easier, just a simple crawl, and finally she was easing around that pillar onto the peak of the arch, seven meters above the water, where the breeze ran freest and the sun laid itself heated and dense across her skin.

Paradise, thought Shir, sliding her back down the pillar until she was sitting comfortably. With a sigh, she took the first can of Budweiser out of her gym bag. *Three-fifty,* she thought disgustedly, popping the tab. *The price of oil.* Hissing softly, she raised the can and saluted the late-afternoon sun. Then, putting the can to her lips, she drank steadily. Almost immediately, a burn started up in her gut, and she pounded her stomach gently with a balled-up fist.

"Shut up, tummy," she scolded. "Don't you know what's good for you? This is medicine, stupid. Happy medicine for when things get down."

Raising the can again, she drank until she was sucking the dregs. There, that was better, she thought. One beer down the hatch, and the world felt quiet and steady again. She reached into her gym bag, pulled out a sandwich bag, dropped the empty can into it, and sealed the bag. Then she dropped the bagged can into her gym bag. One thing she had learned over the years was that her mother had a nose for beer fumes. Sandwich bags sealed in the odor until she could dump her empties into a back-alley garbage bin. What her mother didn't smell wouldn't hurt her.

Task completed, Shir reached for the second can, popped the tab, and lifted it to her mouth. From 9 AM on, today had been nothing but ugly. A sizable number of Collier High guys seemed to have fallen in love with her—blind love, of course—and they had all had propositions to make. With the number of toonies she had been offered, she could have been swimming in beer by now. Yeah, Shir thought bleakly, she could have *built* a swimming pool, filled it with beer, and then gone swimming in it. And after swimming in the damn thing, she would have drunk the entire pool dry. After a day like today, she needed it.

Instead, all she had were two lousy beers and the memory of all those jeers, taunts, and one starkly pornographic limerick:

My love is uglier than sin
Who knows where the hell she's been
But since I'm so blind
It's just a bump and a grind
Then I leave her for the next dog to find.

The guy who had written the limerick had read it to her in front of a tittering cafeteria audience, then apologized for the incorrect rhyme scheme. *Poetic license*, he had called it. As he was reading it, she had seen Brett at a nearby table—the guy who had put the brakes on Wade Sullivan Saturday night. Face in neutral, he had listened without comment, then abruptly gotten up and walked away. He hadn't tittered like the others, hadn't, in fact, shown the slightest sign of amusement, but neither had he demonstrated any inclination to intervene. She wasn't about to be raped in a crowded cafeteria; nothing illegal was going on; as far as he was concerned, this wasn't his problem. And that, Shir reflected bleakly, was as good as things got in her life.

A brief choking sensation came and went in her throat, and the sun blurred into a stinging mess along the top of the tree line. The second can jammed tight against her lips, she began to drink, sucking in the cold familiar taste, pulling it over her tongue, then forcing the fluid to the back of her throat and swallowing, swallowing hard, *harder*.

Yeah, this was good, she told herself grimly. Beer on a bridge, with the sun going down into the trees, and alone with the wind—this was what she wanted, this was *good*.

The dregs trickled over the back of her tongue and left her sucking air. With a grunt, Shir bagged the can and tossed it into her gym bag. Then she simply sat, eyes half closed, watching the sun work its way slowly into the trees. A noticeable chill had come into the air and she pulled her jacket tighter, waiting for the beer to warm her up. Yeah, there it was, she could feel it now—a gently heated blur oozing out of her gut and working its way up toward her brain. Yeah, this was good, she thought again. This was too good; she was *laughing*.

Pulling her jacket tighter, Shir watched the sun lose itself in the trees.

Four

Supper was Sloppy Joes and a bowl of carrot sticks, a bit on the dry side because Stella had cut them up yesterday and hadn't thought to store them in water. The Sloppy Joes, however, were one of her better concoctions—at least Mom seemed to think so. "Delicious, Stella!" she had exclaimed after the first approving spoonful. "You've done something different this time. What's your secret ingredient?"

Beaming, Stella had refused to tell. She liked to keep cooking secrets; they were important to her. Cooking secrets were not important to Shir. Neither were scrubbing-the-tub secrets or scouring-the-sink secrets, although if there were any, she had yet to discover them. Slouched in her chair, she stared blearily at the mass of steaming hamburger on her plate. Midway through her Budweiser high, she didn't have the slightest interest in nibbling carrot sticks or chewing her way delicately through well-mannered spoonfuls like Stella, who at the moment was seated kitty-corner and talking eagerly to Mom. No, what Shir wanted to do was break into a full-out roar of the chorus to Queen's "We Will Rock You" and whack her fist *splat!* into the middle of Stella's carefully sculpted plateful of Sloppy Joes. Years ago, Stella had developed the annoying habit of sculpting her food into castles, cats, or what-have-you; just looking at the circle of peaks on her current masterpiece, Shir could guess what this one was supposed to be—Prince Charming's palace. Either that, she mused, or the carriage he had sent to fetch Cinderella. Stella would never have admitted it, but Shir knew how her sister's mind worked. Sloppy-Joes palace, that was what it was. Fifteen years old, and Stella was still waiting for Prince Charming and happy-ever-after. What she needed was a good *splat!* to get rid of that nonsense.

Suppressing a hiccupy giggle, Shir tightened a fist, then relaxed it. On second thought, she decided, reconsidering, Sloppy Joes all over the wall was not a good idea. And Mom at full blast, screaming into her face was another definite negative. Too bad, because the moment of the actual *splat!* and the resulting astonishment on Stella's face was a memory Shir would have liked to relive time and time again while sipping a contemplative Myplace beer.

"Would you mind not breathing your alcohol-laden breath all over my food?" demanded Stella, breaking off her description of a no-doubt riveting, after-school home basketball game to glare at Shir.

"My breath is not alcohol-laden," Shir snapped back, then ducked her head to direct any possible beer fumes at her plate. *Godammit*, she thought grimly. She had been late getting back, and had only managed to squish some toothpaste onto her tongue before coming to the table. That obviously hadn't been enough.

"You smell like a beer factory," Stella said angrily, waving her fork. "I don't see why we should have to eat at the same table as you if you're going to come to it absolutely *reeking*."

Blood began to beat in Shir's cheeks. "I am *not* reeking," she snapped again, shooting her sister a malevolent glance. There, within arm's reach, sat Stella in all her glory—hair in its usual neat ponytail, makeup subtly accentuating her doe-like eyes, and looking a lot like Mom had probably looked twenty years ago.

"You are, too," hissed Stella. "You stink. You're *putrid*."

Fury erupted in Shir like a live thing. She surged to her feet, only dimly aware as her hip caught the table edge. Glasses of milk wobbled, slopping their contents, and Mom and Stella grabbed for sliding cutlery with cries of alarm.

"I am not *putrid!*" roared Shir, the breath raw in her throat as she leaned over her obviously frightened sister—one of Collier High's finest, *most* kiss-ass students. "I smell beautiful, gorgeous! I am a goddam *fucking* rose—"

Without warning, Mom was on her feet and coming around the table, her hands reaching for Shir and shoving her back down into her chair. "Oomph!" grunted Shir as her head slammed into the wall. For a long moment, everything dissolved into a loud ringing darkness. Then the darkness faded and she was back in the middle of family time—Mom yelling, Stella crying, glasses of milk tipped onto their sides and milk running everywhere.

"Now look what you've done!" wailed Stella. "I've got my defense class at seven, and I'm going to have to change all my clothes."

Slumped in her chair, the back of her head in a massive throb, Shir sat with her eyes closed and listened to the furious breathing going on centimeters to her left. *Mom*, she thought carefully. Years of experience had taught her that the best way to assess her mother was to listen to her breathing. It wasn't watching the woman that told you when she was going to blow, it was listening. When Mom was angry—*really* angry—her breath wheezed in and out like a rabid accordion.

"You are a disgrace to the human race," Mom hissed slowly, her breath pumping in and out, in and out. "Can't have a conversation with you, can't sit at the same table without a catastrophe. All day long, I'm on my feet slaving away, cleaning people's houses, and then I come home to this. No respect, no gratitude. A dog would treat me better."

Dog, thought Shir, and the memory of that afternoon's hallway limerick returned, snapping her eyes wide open. Wordless, she stared directly into her mother's slitted gaze.

"You disgust me," said Mom, the words slow and final, like the tolling of a bell. "Drunk as a stone, just like your dad. Take your goddam supper and go eat in your room."

"I'm sorry, Mom," blurted Shir, a flush searing her face. "Honest. I didn't mean—"

"Get out," said Mom, pointing in the direction of Shir's bedroom.

For a moment longer, Shir sat rigid, staring at the face that hovered in front of her. Contorted, twisted, it glared back with a look of ... hatred. *Mom hates me*, Shir realized with a sickening lurch in her gut. *She hates me.*

Taking hold of her plate, she got to her feet and shuffled out of the kitchen without a backward glance.

It was 7:23 PM. Alone in her room, her Budweiser high long gone, Shir was sitting on her bed, jabbing a capped pen methodically into her leg as she listened for whatever she could pick up from beyond the closed bedroom door. For the last forty minutes, things had been pretty quiet. Stella had left at twenty to seven for her self-defense course at the Y, and Mom had turned off the TV fifteen minutes ago. Which was weird, thought Shir as she jabbed the pen harder into her thigh, because Mom usually had the thing going day and night. Janice Rutz lived for the TV, keeping careful track of her favorite characters' fashion styles and often quoting lines of dialogue from recent shows. The only time she shut off the TV was when she headed to bed, so why would it be off now, when one of her favorite shows was on and the rerun season barely started?

Jab jab jab went the pen, digging deep into the flesh of Shir's outer leg. On her lap sat her empty dinner plate—empty except for her right hand, which was covered with tomato sauce. When she had left the table, she had forgotten to take her fork and had been forced to eat her Sloppy Joes by hand. With Mom in her current mood, she reflected grimly, it would have been risking life and limb to return to the kitchen for cutlery. All things considered, she had gotten off easy tonight—just a bump on the head. Bumps on the head went away; the memory of the expression on her mother's face would not. Ever. Better to avoid Mom until her mood changed, and her expression along with it.

Jab jab jab went the pen. Shir was aiming for sore spots now, places she had already bruised, wanting to drive the pain so deep it would hit overload and fade into oblivion. And it was working—the pain was beginning to disappear. If only, she thought miserably, the pressure from her massively overloaded bladder would disappear along with it. She had to go to the can *bad*. Two Budweisers in quick succession had a way of doing that to a person, but for now, she was going to have to hold it. No way was she moving from this bed until she heard something—anything—that told her Mom had calmed down completely and it was once again safe to venture from her room.

Abruptly, from the hall, came the sound of footsteps, each a clear half-step followed by a shuffle, the way Mom walked in her slippers. Stiffening, Shir listened to see if the footsteps turned into the bathroom, but, continuing along the hall, they came to a stop outside Shir's closed door. A sickening swallow locked in Shir's throat, and her heart began to thud. Eyes riveted to her closed bedroom door, she listened.

"Shir?" said Mom, her voice muffled as if she had her face pressed to the door.

Not angry, Shir thought slowly, assessing her mother's tone. Well, not *exactly* angry. More ... just dull, as if things were going pretty much as expected.

"Yeah?" she asked cautiously.

Her bedroom door remained closed. "You get out here,"

Mom said in a monotone. "We've got to talk. I'll be in the living room."

Without waiting for a response, she walked back down the hall. As the sound of her footsteps retreated, Shir sat bug-eyed and frozen, staring at the closed door. *Talk?* she thought wildly. *About what?* She and her mother never talked, they just yelled back and forth about chores and whose turn it was to go grocery shopping. Uneasily, Shir scooted to the edge of the bed and got to her feet, careful not to touch the bedspread with her sticky hand. Then she picked up her empty plate and tiptoed to the door. Easing it open, she found the hallway eerily quiet—no canned laughter coming from the TV, no caterwauling Celine Dion from Stella's room. The place felt like a tomb.

"I'm just going to use the can," she called into the silence and turned into the bathroom. Door closed, she turned on the tap to cover the sound of her urine so her mother wouldn't be able to figure out how much she had drunk. Then, avoiding the mirror, she sat down on the toilet and braced herself for the first painful rush. Head down, she waited the long process out. When it was finished, she washed her sauce-covered hand, picked up her empty plate, and headed down the hall toward the ominously silent living room.

Her mother was sitting on the couch, staring at the lifeless TV. "I'm just going to put my plate in the kitchen," said Shir.

Without looking at her, Mom nodded. Knees suddenly wobbly, Shir walked into the kitchen, set the plate on the counter, and returned to the living room. Still her mother didn't glance at her, just sat staring at the silent TV.

"Where do you want me to sit?' asked Shir, her body numb with dread.

"Not near me," her mother said tonelessly. "Not on the couch."

Shir's knees had never felt weaker. Walking to the far corner of the room, she slid to the floor and sat with her back to the wall. "Okay," she said, almost choking on her own voice. "I'm sitting."

Again Mom nodded without looking at her. Neither spoke, the silence dense and heavy, a lump in the throat. *Old*, thought Shir, watching her mother out of the corner of her eye. *She looks old for thirty-six. Heavy and gray, as if something is pushing down on her.*

Mom shifted slightly as if coming gradually awake. "I'm ready to give up," she said, her eyes still on the TV. "I don't know what to do with you. Every day, day in and day out, you're a misery to me and your sister. You don't do nothing except that it's for yourself, and I'm tired of you coming home drunk and staggering around like you own the place."

Taking a quick breath, Shir fought to rise above the fear that smashed in on her. "Mom—" she began, but the words died on her lips as her mother turned and looked directly at her.

"Don't *Mom* me," hissed Janice Rutz, rage deepening every line in her face. "The only time I'm your mom is when you want something or you're in trouble. Other than that, I just pay the rent. Well, I'm not doing that for you anymore. You're sixteen now, I don't owe you anything. If I want, I can call the Children's

Aid and get them to come fetch you, or I can just kick you out. The law can't do anything to me for that, not when you're sixteen. I don't even have to give you your clothes. I can kick you out and sell them at a thrift shop, get back a few bucks for all the money I've wasted on you. Then I'll be rid of you for good."

Wordless, Shir stared at the woman across the room. This wasn't the first time her mother had threatened to kick her out. It happened every few months. Once, when Shir was nine and they were living in a different apartment, her mother had gone so far as to push her into the outside hall and lock the door, then leave her out there, bawling and screaming for twenty minutes before letting her back in. It was one of the many things she had done, so many, Shir couldn't remember most of them now. Sometimes her mother just seemed to have to let off steam.

But tonight felt different, quiet and considered, as if Janice Rutz had thought things through ahead of time, worked out her exact words in advance.

"It was a bad day," said Shir, suddenly desperate, the words dragging themselves up her throat. Lord knew she didn't want to talk about this, didn't want to have to drag it out of herself, kicking and screaming and covered in shame, to lay it flat and helpless before that cold, dull face across the room. But she had to try something. If she didn't, she could be outdoors tonight in sub-zero weather, knocking on Gareth's door and asking for lodgings.

"A boy wrote a poem about me," she said hoarsely, her eyes clinging to her mother's face. "A mean one. Then he read it to me in the cafeteria. In front of a bunch of kids."

Silent, her mother simply looked at her.

"It went like this," Shir said thickly. Slowly, the shame rising in her cheeks, she recited the limerick. Branded into her memory, it wasn't difficult to recall, but each word was a burr, sticking in her throat. When she had finally finished the last line—*for a dog to find*—she sat with her head down, waiting for her mother's response. But from the other side of the room came nothing. In the apartment to her right, Shir could hear a muffled TV, and downstairs, a child was crying, but in this room was only silence.

Sick with dread, her fear covering her like a cold skin, she looked up to find her mother watching her. The expression on Janice Rutz's face was odd—neutral, but at the same time, slightly curious, as if for the first time it had occurred to her to wonder what it would be like to actually be her daughter Shirley Jane. *The way you would think about a stranger*, thought Shir, staring back at her. *Someone you saw on the street.*

"That's why you got drunk?" her mother asked slowly.

"Yeah," said Shir, keeping her tone dull, without obvious hope.

Her mother nodded, her gaze still on Shir's face, looking at each part separately, then all of it together, as if adding up its collective misery. "Kids are mean," she said, "and they're meaner to you than most. Some of the things your teachers have told me over the years ... Well, there's no excuse for kids treating someone the way they treat you. But there's no excuse for your behavior, either. I won't have no more of it, Shir. I won't."

Shir nodded, a shuddery relief heaving itself up her throat.

"One more chance, then," her mother continued grimly, "but that's it. No more drinking. No more yelling at your sister. No more making me nag you to do your chores. And you go to all your classes and pass everything, you hear?"

"I'm passing," Shir assured her quickly. It was a small lie— there was only algebra, and she should be able to push that up to a D if she started paying attention.

"No more drinking," her mother repeated firmly. "No yelling. And you'll do your chores."

"Yeah, sure," agreed Shir, swift gratitude blooming in her chest. Never before had she realized how much she loved this apartment, with its tacky windowsill knickknacks and threadbare carpet. The couch her mother was sitting on, for example—right now, Shir felt as if she could sit and stare at it, *loving* it, forever.

"I'll do all of it, Mom," she gushed enthusiastically. "Everything you say—*everything*."

For a long moment, her mother looked at her. "You have been a real burden to me," she said finally. "You and your dad, for sixteen years, even though he's gone now—nothing but a burden."

Shir sat motionless, the blood thick in her cheeks. "Well," sighed her mother, picking up the remote control, "that's all I have to say, I guess." She switched on the TV, and, dismissed, Shir fought her way up past her wobbly knees and dragged herself out of the living room.

Five

The store was busy with the usual late-afternoon rush, kids coming in to buy an after-school Pepsi, adults stopping by on their way home from work to pick up something for supper. Both cashiers had lineups at their tills and Mr. Anderson was circulating the floor, checking with customers to see if they needed assistance. Alone in the storage room, Shir loaded several boxes of spices, salt, and baking soda onto a trolley, then pushed open the *Employees Only* door and glanced out to make sure no one was in the vicinity. In spite of her caution, two children dashed, squealing, around the end of the produce aisle as soon as she had wheeled out the trolley. Pausing to let them pass, Shir found herself tuning into a conversation two aisles over that was taking place between her boss and Mr. Hrizi, an elderly man who seemed to live solely on sardines, pickled onions, and tomato soup. At least, that was all Shir had ever seen him buy.

"Here, let me get that down for you," said Mr. Anderson. "It's a bit of a reach." The scrape of cans being lifted off a shelf followed, and Shir grinned knowingly. Tomato soup, she would bet her day's wages on it.

"And how is Sarge doing these days?" she heard her boss ask.

"Any improvement?"

Sarge was Mr. Hrizi's pet terrier. Two weeks ago, it had come down sick, leaving Mr. Hrizi to walk the several blocks to Bill's Grocer alone and at half his usual shuffling, seventy-something pace. The first time he had made the solitary trip, Mr. Anderson had noticed him come into the store without tying the terrier to the stop sign out front, and had asked about the dog. Mr. Hrizi had gone on at length, all about fevers and convulsions and dog puke on the carpet. Shir had had enough after the first ten seconds, but Mr. Anderson had stood there listening, as if the terrier was his favorite grandchild.

"Right as a penny!" declared Mr. Hrizi, and Shir could hear the smile in his voice. "He's begging for cookies again. That tonic you dropped off really did the trick."

"Well," said Mr. Anderson with a note of deep satisfaction. "It worked with my son's dog and he had some left over, so I thought, why let it go to waste? Will you let me carry that up to the till for you? And did you know we've got a sale on tomato soup today? I—"

Voices fading, the two men moved up the aisle, and Shir let loose with another grin. Sale on tomato soup? she thought, starting off with the trolley. Not that she had noticed, but, hey— Mr. Anderson could declare sudden sales for special customers any time he wanted. Steering the trolley into the baking aisle, she stopped next to the spice rack and began opening boxes. *Cinnamon, cumin, curry*, she thought, picking up a bottle and studying it. There was something about spices—just looking at their rich, vivid colors made her feel different, as if something warm and pulsing from deep inside the earth had entered her body, dissolving its customary heaviness. This particular spice was such an intense shade of yellow, it was like holding September in her hands.

As she took out several bottles of curry, the front-entrance bell jangled and the store filled with the sound of laughing male voices. Her attention focused on the spice rack, Shir didn't give it any notice. People came and went constantly at Bill's Grocer—some of them were cheerful; some of them weren't. But as the laughter progressed through the produce section, she found herself tuning in. One of those voices, she thought, tracking it carefully, was familiar. In fact, it was too familiar—at least since this past weekend. Those snorts and guffaws coming down the produce aisle belonged to Wade Sullivan, she was sure of it—Mr. Blind Love, Mr. Love-by-Braille for a toonie.

Panic swept Shir and she glanced quickly down the baking aisle. Would Wade notice her, she wondered, if he walked past the back end? Chances were he hadn't come in for baking supplies, but why hadn't he done the after-school usual—buy a chocolate bar and a pop up front, then head for the exit?

"Okay, bonehead," said the other laughing voice. "Mom said it had to be *red* maraschino cherries—red to match my hair. Last time I screwed up and bought green ones, so before I left today, she made me get down on my knees and repeat five times, 'I love my mother and I will buy *red* maraschino cherries.' If I screw up this time, she's going to dye my hair green to match."

Shir's heart plummeted. In Bill's Grocer, maraschino cherries were stored in one place and one place only—the baking aisle. A quick glance revealed the small plastic tubs that contained them stacked on a shelf one meter to her right.

"Don't sweat it, Ben," Wade said cheerfully. "Green looks good on you. But don't you think buying cherries for your mom is kind of perverted?"

"*You're* perverted," said Ben as they reached the end of the produce section. "Really perverted for even *thinking* something like that."

"Hey," said Wade. "A cherry's a cherry and I'm blind, right?"

An agreeable guffaw greeted this comment, and then, as Shir watched, riveted, a red-haired, nerdish-looking guy she vaguely recognized as one of Collier High's top math students entered the baking aisle, followed by tall, blond, good-looking, *grinning* Wade Sullivan. Frozen in front of the spice rack, her knees almost melting into her calves, Shir swallowed and swallowed her panic. For two days now, she had been keeping her eyes peeled for Wade, had even developed an extra set in the back of her head so she could maintain a constant 360-degree watch. More than once, she had reversed tracks when she had spotted him coming down a hall, and she had been strenuously avoiding the cafeteria and anywhere else he was known to hang out. But here in the store, she was trapped. She couldn't take off and hide in the storage room; she had a job to do. To make matters worse, in this store, Wade Sullivan was a customer, and Mr. Anderson would expect her to serve him with a smile.

The moment they entered the aisle, both guys fixed on her. Immediate glee leapt onto Ben's face. "Hey, bud," he said, slapping Wade's arm. "Talk about cherries. And she's your type exactly."

The glee in Wade's face wasn't as swift. For a second he seemed almost as frozen as Shir, his eyes narrowing, the grin fading from his face. But he recovered quickly.

"Hey, Ben," he said, getting a grip on his grin. "Got a toonie?"

"The only toonies I've got are for maraschino cherries," Ben said firmly. "*Red* maraschino cherries. Anyway, bonehead, you pay for your own love life."

"Cheapskate," said Wade. Fishing in his pocket, he pulled out a handful of change. "All's I've got is a quarter, a dime, and three pennies."

"So invest," grinned Ben. "You know—the layaway plan."

"*Lay*-away?" said Wade, cracking up.

Blood pounding in her face, Shir stood, gripping a bottle of curry. *Not here in the store*, she pleaded silently as the two smirking guys approached. *You can't do this to me in the store.* Because if anyone overheard their comments, if Mr. Anderson or any of the store personnel saw her being treated this way, Shir knew without a doubt that it would change things. They would know then how the rest of the world saw her, how she really was. And from that moment on, everyone at Bill's Grocer would deal with her differently. She wouldn't be part of the store team anymore but separate—someone embarrassing, something to feel sorry for.

"Look," she said, trying to keep her voice steady. "I'm at work, okay? Like, this is my *job*. So could you please just—"

"Hey," said Wade, holding up the quarter. "You allergic to people talking to you? Look, this is from me to you." Still grinning, he placed the quarter on the trolley. "For our future. *Lay*-away, like Ben—"

"Excuse me," said a voice behind Shir, and she turned, startled, to see a tiny elderly woman standing beside the trolley and peering up at Wade through her bifocals. It was Mrs. Duran, and from the way she was observing Wade, she seemed to think he was a kind of curious insect, something she didn't quite understand.

"I don't mean to interrupt your conversation, young man," she said in her ancient quavery voice, "but I need some assistance from this young lady, if you don't mind."

Wade's grin vanished. Expression suddenly ultra-polite, he stepped back, raised both hands and said, "Of course, ma'am. No problem. Just kidding around a bit, that's all."

Giving her a wide berth, he started down the aisle after Ben. But as he was walking past, Mrs. Duran reached out and picked up the quarter he had left on the trolley.

"Do you want this quarter, dear?" she asked, glancing intently at Shir.

"No," Shir managed, her voice hoarse. "I don't."

"Then I think, young man," said Mrs. Duran, taking hold of Wade's hand and pressing the quarter firmly into his palm, "that this belongs to you." For a moment, she remained like that, holding his hand and staring up at him as he stared back at her. Then, with a small shake of her head, she dropped his hand and turned to Shir.

"Now, Shirley," she said with a smile, "I've run out of nutmeg, and it was such a lovely day, I thought I'd walk over to the store. Have you got some for me?"

Beside her, Wade seemed temporarily frozen, standing stockstill and staring at the quarter in his hand. Abruptly, his head came up and he strode quickly down the aisle.

"Hey, what's with you?" called Ben, looking up from the label on a tub of maraschino cherries. "I've got to get red—"

"Yeah, yeah," Wade called back. "I'll meet you up front."

With a shrug, Ben headed after him, leaving Shir swamped by relief so dense she almost sagged under its weight. Finally, the buggers were gone, she thought, taking their kiss-my-ass attitude with them. And leaving her standing, she realized suddenly, locked into position with a bottle of curry half-tilted into the spice rack. Letting it slide into place, she slowly stretched her cramped hand. She had been gripping the bottle so tightly, her knuckles were cracking.

"Goodness," said Mrs. Duran. "Your arthritis is worse than mine."

Another brief wave of panic swept Shir, and her eyes flitted uncertainly across the spice rack's gleaming rows of bottles. She had been so relieved to see the butt ends of Wade and Ben that she had completely forgotten about the old lady. What in the world was she supposed to say to Mrs. Duran now, after what she had just seen?

Turning reluctantly, she met the elderly woman's gaze. Tiny dark eyes peered back at her, bright with knowing, *warm* with it. A gulping sensation took over Shir's throat and she looked away.

"Now, dear," said Mrs. Duran, and Shir felt a small withered hand take her own. "What I need is some nutmeg. I'm about to make banana bread, and that's what my recipe calls for."

Quickly, Shir got a grip. "Nutmeg," she blustered, extra loud to give herself something to focus on. "Sure, Mrs. Duran, we've got lots of nutmeg, and it comes in different sizes. D'you want a bottle or a tin? The tins are bigger."

"A bottle, dear. That'll be fine," said Mrs. Duran, letting go of Shir's hand and accepting the bottle she was handed. But instead of heading down the aisle with it, she stood staring at the label as if she had never seen one before. Finally, her eyes still on the bottle, she sighed. Reaching out, she gently patted Shir's hand.

"Thank you, dear," she said quietly. "It was lovely of you to take the time to help out an old lady." Without meeting Shir's eyes, she started off down the aisle, walking her careful, creaky steps.

"Any time, Mrs. Duran," Shir called after her, the words overly loud, almost harsh in her throat. "Any time, you know it."

"Yes, dear," quavered Mrs. Duran without looking back. "I do." And she continued her ancient, creaking way down the aisle.

It was 8:30, the store empty of customers, the second cashier off-shift, and only Cathy left on till. In the far aisle, next to the diapers and toilet paper, Shir was maneuvering a wheeled bucket along the floor while she swished a steaming mop carefully across the linoleum. It had been a busy shift. After she had finished filling up the spice rack, Mr. Anderson had sent her out on several deliveries, one of which had been, once again, halfway across town. It had taken her forty minutes to get back to the store but he hadn't complained, simply pocketed the van keys and asked her to mop the floor. And now, she thought with satisfaction, there was only a half-hour until closing time when she would be paid, then head over to the alley behind the liquor store to pick up a few overpriced beers. If she restricted herself to two and zipped them into her jacket pockets, it would be easy to sneak them into the apartment. After 9 PM, Mom was usually heavy into a TV drama and oblivious to the world. You could practically scream into her ear and she would just wave you off like a buzzing fly. Someone could die in front of her, not on the TV screen but in actual real life, and she wouldn't pick up on it until the next commercial. Maybe not even then.

A moment of doubt hit Shir and her mop slowed. What if, she thought, for some unforeseen reason, Mom took a night off from Hollywood? What if, horror of horrors, she temporarily decided to take motherhood seriously and check out her elder daughter upon her return from work? There wouldn't be anything yet to smell on Shir's breath, but Mom could always go through her jacket pockets. If she found the beer, she would kick out Shir for sure. After what she had said last night, there would be no backing down.

Stockstill, Shir stood staring down at the mop. Without warning, it had once again descended upon her—the sucking, sinking sensation of fear that had been with her, now and again, since the first time her father had taken off. The knowing: *Mommy doesn't love me; she says I have to sleep on the floor tonight.* And then a brief blurred memory of Janice Rutz, hissing, "I could get rid of you, kid. I could put you in a plastic bag and set you out for the garbageman. I could tie the bag real tight."

But for all that, Shir thought, trying to shake herself out of it, her mother had never followed through on any of her threats. Last night's talk would doubtless end up like all the others—part of a long pattern of warnings and ultimatums that never went anywhere. As usual, Janice Rutz hadn't been serious; she had simply been letting off steam. Tonight, when Shir got in, her mother probably wouldn't even remember their blowup.

And anyway, Shir could practically hear it—the first can of beer *calling* her name. All she had to do was let her thoughts drift, and she could feel the tab popping under her fingers and the smooth slide of liquid over her tongue. Inspired, she refocused on the mop and began swishing it up the aisle. If she got this done quickly and Mr. Anderson let her off ear—

"Shirley, there you are," said her boss, poking his head around the end of the aisle.

Instantly, Shir stiffened, almost coming to attention. "Yes, sir," she said. "I'm mopping the floor like you asked, before I go home."

"Yes, and you're doing a great job," said Mr. Anderson,

starting down the aisle toward her. "You're my best floor-washer, you know."

"I am?" said Shir. For a moment her mind blanked and she stood, just staring at him.

"Oh, yeah," assured Mr. Anderson. "Everyone else just swipes at the floor, but you pay real attention to the dirt. And I wanted to tell you—today, one of the customers stopped me as she was going out, and told me what a help you'd been to her. Told me several times before she left, to make sure I got the message."

A flush swept Shir's face and she ducked her head. *Mrs. Duran*, she thought nervously. It had to be. Who else would have gone to the trouble of stopping Mr. Anderson and telling him something like that? But what she really had to find out now was whether the elderly woman had said anything more. Mr. Anderson had been outside the store, greeting Mr. Hrizi's terrier when the incident with Wade had occurred, and the cashiers too busy at their tills to notice. Would Mrs. Duran have mentioned it?

"I gotta tell ya," said Mr. Anderson, beaming warmly at her. "That lady is a very good judge of character, too."

He seemed about to say more when the front-entrance bell jangled, turning him on his heel. As her boss started back up the aisle, Shir stood, mop in hand, watching him go. That hadn't been too bad, she thought in relief. From what Mr. Anderson had said, it didn't sound as if Mrs. Duran had complained about Wade and Ben. If she had, the evidence would have been all over his face; there would have been a kind of *knowing* in the way he looked at her. But he had been his usual beaming, grandfatherly self.

With a sigh, she got back to mopping the floor. So, she thought wryly, she was Bill's Grocer's premium floor-mopper. Well, that was fine with her. Here in the store, she didn't mind doing that kind of thing. As long as it wasn't *Stella's* feet walking across the linoleum, and as long as she was being paid for it, she could mop floors all day. Especially if it was for Mr. Anderson. He was, simply put, the best kind of boss to have. Right now, she could hear him up front, talking cheerfully to a customer who had just come in. And the voice that replied was also familiar, a husky, edgy girl's voice Shir was certain she had heard cutting loose at Collier High.

Glancing around the end of the aisle, Shir saw a tall, dark-haired girl standing beside the drinks cooler. *Yup*, she thought, frowning slightly. The kid was from Collier, all right. In her grad year, this girl could usually be seen hanging around the edge of school property with the smoking crowd. Shir had never spoken to her, but, all things considered, that wasn't unusual. Leaning on her mop, she racked her brains, trying to recall the girl's name. Ellenore? Evelyn? No, she mused, it was something weird. Like ... Eunice, but shorter. Eunie—that was it. The girl's name was Eunie Jahenny.

"And your mom?" Mr. Anderson was saying, as he propped himself against the counter. "How is she? Found a job yet?"

"Not yet," said Eunie, the look on her face almost professionally bored. "Still working on it, I guess."

"And you?" smiled Mr. Anderson. "How are you?"

"Oh ... thirsty," said Eunie, her eyes flitting across his face. "*Real* thirsty. So I thought I'd come in for a Coke."

At her response, Mr. Anderson's expression changed slightly, as if a bell had gone off deep inside his brain. "Ah, yes," he said casually. "A Coke." Reaching into the cooler, he took out a can of Coke and handed it to Eunie. "While you're drinking this," he added, "why don't you come to the back with me? There's something I'd like to talk to you about."

"No prob," shrugged Eunie, displaying not even a flicker of surprise, and they moved off down the produce aisle, speaking in lowered voices. Still leaning on her mop, Shir stood staring after them, then caught herself as she realized Cathy was watching her. Quickly she raised a hand and saluted, then started back down the diaper aisle. *Weird*, she thought, jabbing the mop into the bucket of water. What would Mr. Anderson have to talk about with Eunie Jahenny, of all people? And in the storage room, to boot? Had one of the cashiers quit? Was Mr. Anderson thinking—

Sudden fear swarmed Shir and she swallowed hard. Had Mr. Anderson finally realized he'd had enough of her, she wondered, and decided to hire a different delivery person? Heart pounding, she stared in the direction of the storage room, willing herself to see through the intervening shelves of canned and packaged goods. But no third eye opened up in her forehead, no mysterious vision revealed what was going on behind the *Employees Only* door. Nervously, she twisted the mop in the bucket's wringer, lifted it out, and swished her way up the rest of the aisle. Then, dumping the mop into the bucket, she started wheeling the entire contraption toward the till, en route to the storage room.

"What—done already?" asked Cathy. Leaning against the till, she was reading the blurb on the back of a video box. In her early twenties and a Brad Pitt addict, she was Mr. Anderson's only full-time staff.

"Yeah," said Shir, pausing beside the till. "I just have to dump this water."

"Oh," said Cathy. Absent-mindedly, she tapped a burgundy fingernail against an upper tooth. "Well, that's good. Real good."

With a nod, Shir once again started to wheel the bucket toward the storage room. But as she did, Cathy came abruptly alert and turned to her with a startled expression. "Wait a minute, Shirley," she said, glancing toward the rear of the store. "Um ... uh ..."

For a moment, she fell silent, as if lost for words, then pivoted to face the front window. "What d'you think of the spring display I put up?" she asked brightly, pointing to several large cutouts that had been affixed to the glass.

"Nice," said Shir, nodding agreeably. "I like the daffodils."

"Good, that's good," Cathy said breathily, glancing again toward the rear of the store. "Look, could you do me a favor and straighten those chocolate bars over there?" Leaning forward, she pointed to the candy rack at the empty till.

Confused, Shir scanned the candy. From what she could see, the chocolate bars were already neatly arranged. "Sure," she shrugged. "I'll just wash my hands. Let me take the mop to the storage room, then I'll come back and—"

"Um ... *well*," Cathy said emphatically, stepping out from behind the till. "Maybe we—" Abruptly her head snapped to the right, and an expression of relief crossed her face as the storage-room door opened and footsteps started down the produce aisle. "Never mind about the chocolate bars," she said dismissively. "They look fine. Sometimes I get freaky about neatness."

Before Shir could reply, Mr. Anderson appeared at the end of the produce aisle. "There you are, Shirley," he said briskly. "All done, then?"

"Yes, sir," said Shir, scanning his face for clues. Was she right? she wondered shakily. Had he decided to fire her and give her job to Eunie? Was that what Cathy hadn't wanted her to overhear? "I just have to dump this water," she added carefully.

"Don't worry about that, I'll finish it off," he said. "Now, how much do I owe you—five hours, right?" Opening the second till, he counted out Shir's wages and handed them to her. "You're off," he said with a grin. "Come in Friday, four o'clock. We'll see you then."

"Yes, *sir*!" said Shir, relief hitting her like a tidal wave. With an enormous grin, she ditched the mop and bucket, and headed to the storage room for her jacket. So, she wasn't about to be fired, she thought exuberantly. Even better, she was getting off work at ten to nine, a little earlier than usual. Eleven blocks north, the liquor store also closed at nine. If she booted it over there on her bike, she should be able to find someone still hanging around the area, willing to offload a few beers.

Pushing open the storage-room door, she removed her work apron and dropped it into the laundry bin. Then she took her jacket from its hook on the wall. About to pull it on, she caught sight of an unopened Coke, sitting on a nearby counter. *That's odd*, she thought, eyeing the can. It had to be the one Mr. Anderson had given Eunie, but why would she have left it here, unopened, if that was what she had come into the store for? And why had she used the back entrance when she left? Customers always used the front.

A bizarre thought hit Shir and she grimaced in disbelief. Was it possible Mr. Anderson was having a secret red-hot affair with Eunie Jahenny? Back here in the storage room? *Nah!* she decided. They had only been back here five minutes—what could you do in five minutes? And why would Mr. Anderson be interested in a seventeen-year-old metalhead? There had to be at least three decades between their ages. Besides, from what Shir had observed, Eunie was a bit on the wild side—for Mr. Anderson, that is. Of course, *anyone* would be on the wild side for Mr. Anderson.

At any rate, she thought, pulling on her jacket, she still had her job. Next to that, nothing mattered. Snorting under her breath, Shir pushed open the store's rear door and took off down the alley.

Six

Gym bag over a shoulder, Shir headed out Collier High's back entrance toward the school's practice field. It was lunch hour, and all over the school grounds, students could be seen in pairs and small groups, enjoying the warm weather. Reaching the practice field's outer boundary, Shir set her gym bag next to the fence, unzipped it, and took out her lunch and the can of Molsons wedged in behind it. Then she settled down for a long, undisturbed slurp, her butt planted firmly on her gym bag and her back cradled by the mesh fence that ran the length of the field.

As expected, her mother had been engrossed in a TV movie last night when Shir had returned from work, and Stella locked in her room doing homework. So there had been no one to notice as she had shuffled carefully to her bedroom, still wearing her winter jacket, no one to freak out or nag, as she had unloaded her two-beer booty onto her bed. But just as she had been downing her first gulp, a knock had come at the door, scaring her so badly that her arm had jerked, spilling beer onto her jeans. Luckily, she had managed to shove the can under her pillow before the door opened, and it had only been Stella, wanting to borrow her Toronto Maple Leafs sweatshirt. Still, the incident had left her with the shakes; she had double-bagged the empty before stashing it in her gym bag, then decided to save the second beer for tomorrow's lunch, when she could hopefully savor it without interruption.

That was the problem with having a legal drinking age, she thought as she popped the tab. It caused so much hassle. Parents, kids—*everyone* got upset over it. If they just got rid of the damn thing so there was no legal age limit at all, it would solve a lot of problems.

At the opposite end of the field, several guys started kicking around a soccer ball. This posed no immediate danger; she was sitting well away from them, and they didn't appear to have noticed her. That was why she frequently came to this spot to eat lunch—no one else ever did. Moments with no one else in them came too rarely in a school day, and she had learned to treasure them like the sensation of the magic fluid flowing over her tongue.

Idly, she watched the players. Most of them were in grade ten, guys whose names she vaguely knew and had never spoken to. At least, nothing that could be considered actual dialogue—just the usual, as in, *Hey, it's Dog Face. If she looks at you, she'll turn you into dog shit.* Or, *Hide up my rear, ass zit.* The kind of thing she had come to expect from the average kid.

The Molsons was now one-third gone, and she was halfway through her first cheese sandwich. The sandwich was dry, without mayonnaise or margarine, but the beer got it down just fine. *Eight* AM, Shir thought lazily as she surveyed the field, *is way too early to think about mayonnaise or margarine, or putting cheese between slices of bread. There should be a law that makes it illegal to force teenagers out of bed before noon. That would solve a whole bunch more problems.*

On the other side of the field, someone gave the ball a resounding kick, sending it skittering wildly toward Shir. Instinctively she tightened, drawing in her feet, even though the ball hit the fence ten meters to her right. A guy came running over, scooped up the ball, and glanced at her. Quickly Shir slid both hands around her beer, covering the label. *No way* was she sharing a drop of the magic fluid with any of those jerks.

"Hey," said the guy. "Dog Face."

Shir's eyes narrowed. Glancing down, she held herself tight and waited.

"Hey," repeated the guy, coming closer. "I'm talking to you, Dog Face."

Gritting her teeth, Shir considered. Sometimes, if she glanced their way once—gave them that much—they were satisfied and went away. Reluctantly, she slid her eyes toward the guy. Shaggy-haired, sweatshirt, jeans, runners—he was someone she had seen around, but couldn't put a name to. Tossing the soccer ball lightly into the air, the guy let it spin on a fingertip.

"Just wanted you to know," he said. "I voted for you."

Then he headed back to the others, kicking the ball ahead of him as he ran. Bewildered, Shir stared after him. *Voted for me?* she thought. What was that supposed to mean? There weren't any school elections going on that she knew of, and anyway, *she* would hardly be running for anything. *President Dog Shit*, she could just see it. *Treasurer Ass Zit.* With a snort, Shir raised her beer and sucked it to the dregs. Then she bagged the empty can and tossed it into her gym bag. A warm sun was riding high in the sky, beer was toasting her insides, and for the moment, no one was hassling her. *This is the life*, she thought, sighing. Stretching out her legs, she closed her eyes.

Within seconds, something smashed into the fence to her right, sending shock waves through the mesh. Jerking upright, Shir glanced to both sides, then twisted to look over her shoulder. There, on the other side of the fence, in the alley that ran this side of school property, stood a group of minor-niners. *Hotshots*, thought Shir, assessing them quickly. *The kind who are already going steady by November.*

"Hey, Ugly!" called one of them, a guy with his arm draped heavily around a girl's neck. A *pretty* girl, Shir noted, her eyes narrowing. Expressionless, she stared back.

Don't give them anything, she thought dully.

The pretty girl giggled.

"You're way ahead," said the guy, flashing her a broad grin. "Everyone's voting for you. The others have only gotten one or two votes."

"Probably their friends," said another guy.

"Nah," said the pretty girl. "They don't have friends. Their mothers voted for them."

"Yeah," agreed the first guy, "their mothers. Anyway, *everyone* else is voting for you, Ugly. You'll get first prize, hands down."

Turning, the group sauntered toward the neighborhood

convenience store, leaving Shir to stare blankly after them. *Everyone's voting for me?* she thought, confused. *Voting where? And why?* Uneasily, she took an apple out of her lunch bag, then sat simply holding it. No way could she eat anything now, not with this on her mind. A memory of a kid snickering at her earlier in the hall came back to her, followed by one of a grinning group in her algebra class. She had assumed it had been the usual, nothing she needed details on. No one had said anything about voting.

Voting for what? she wondered apprehensively.

Panic ants began swarming her skin. Something was going on, she could feel it—something brewing deep inside Collier High's two-thousand-plus minds, and it had to do with her. It always had to do with her. Awkwardly, she started to get to her feet, then sank back down again. *No point in moving,* she thought bleakly. Anywhere else on school property would bring her into closer contact with other kids ... *voters.* Dully, her gut in a queasy roil, she sat and stared at the school's rear wall until the first warning bell rang. Then, getting reluctantly to her feet, she started across the field.

The guys with the soccer ball had already gone in, and the students currently pouring into the back entrance paid her little notice. Hanging back, she waited to let the majority of them pass, then started up the stairs toward the doors. But as she reached the fourth step, a voice behind her shouted, "Dog Face, watch where you're going!" and a foot shot out, hooking her ankle. Arms flailing, she staggered into the guardrail.

"Too bad," said the voice, and a hand shoved her right

shoulder, hard. "That's where your face belongs, bitch," the guy added. "Planted." Then he took off up the stairs, laughing maniacally.

Shir didn't even bother checking out her attacker's identity. The guy could have been any one of hundreds; what did it matter which one it was exactly? Head down, she waited until the last few stragglers had passed into the school, then followed them in. Here, under the eyes of the security cameras, she was supposedly safer. Picking up the pace, she made the trek across the building to the languages wing, where she ditched her gym bag, grabbed her binder, and headed to English.

The afternoon passed in queasy five-minute lurches. Head down, her body rigid with anticipation, Shir sat through her classes, bracing herself for another comment about voting, an election, even candidates, but got nothing. If there was something brewing out there about Dog Face Rutz winning some kind of prize, the guy with the soccer ball and the hotshot minor-niners were the only ones who seemed to have heard about it. Gradually, centimeter by centimeter, Shir allowed herself to relax. Her fingers loosened their manic grip on her pen, her head came up slightly, and the invisible vise squeezing her brain let go. *Forty minutes*, she thought, glancing at the clock. Half an hour plus ten until Twentieth Century History ended and she was out of this place. Thirty minutes. Twenty. Ten, and she would be flying the streets on the Black, picking up a few beers from Gareth, and heading to Myplace. If the price of oil hadn't gone up again, that is.

The bell rang, freeing her from academic blah-blah about Vietnam and the Domino Theory. Instinctively, Shir waited in her seat, letting the rush of students precede her out of the classroom. Then she slowly approached the door. This was when she really had to be on her guard—after school, when kids were loose-ended and revved for any possibility. Cautiously, she started down the hall. The history department was on the second floor, half a building and several security cameras away from her locker—two endless corridors' worth of comments, jeers, and catcalls ... *if* she was lucky.

"Hey, what d'you know," a voice called abruptly on her right—a guy's voice. "It's Dog Face. Front-runner Fuck Face."

Head down, Shir picked up the pace.

"Oh, yeah," moaned a second guy. "For a toonie, I hear she'll make it Suck Face."

"Suck Face," said a third. "My kind of dog. Hey, Suck Face!" As a nearby security camera whirred, a hand grabbed Shir's arm, jerking her to a stop. Immediately, she kicked out, but was surrounded, hands grabbing and pushing her into the wall. "Hey, Suck Face," leered a looming mouth. "I hear it's hands down, you're gonna win."

"Yeah," grinned another mouth. "What're you doing on your feet, bitch? Don't you know winners like you *crawl?*"

"What's going on there?" bellowed a voice from halfway down the hall—a teacher-type voice, ringing with authority. Instantly, the hands mauling Shir withdrew. Recovering her balance, she butted out with her head, jabbed with her elbows, and took off. Corridors zoomed by in a blur, her combination lock was three short spins, and then she was jerking open her locker, ditching her books, and grabbing her jacket. Not for one second did she consider telling a teacher what had occurred; if she did, this afternoon's perpetrators might get into trouble, but they had a hundred buddies who would make her pay. No, better just to make tracks, she decided, and leave every Collier High kid eating her dust. Tears streaming down her face, swallowing and swallowing the bile that rose in her throat, Shir flew down the street on the Black, taking herself away from education, security cameras, the place they called *civilization*.

Someone was sitting on one of the bridge's support arches. *A guy*, thought Shir, staring up at him. It wasn't the arch she usually sat on; rather, it was the one opposite, on the east side, but still ... Gripping the Black's handlebars, she stood at the base of the footbridge and glumly observed the boy. In the four years that she had been coming here, she had only seen kids on the support arches twice, and each time it had been a pack of them, competing to see who could make it across first. A scattering of shouts and jeers, a mad scrabble of feet on concrete, and they had been gone, leaving her alone with her personal patch of sky and the slow-murmuring river.

But this guy had his butt planted. Around fifteen years old, with a black knit cap pulled low on his forehead, he was sitting completely motionless and staring out over the river, as if fixing to become a permanent part of the landscape. Resentment rose thickly in Shir's throat and she took a step forward, then checked herself. What was she supposed to say to the guy—*This is my bridge; you have to get off?* Nothing about this place belonged to her; neither the bridge nor the river had offered her ownership rights. Wasn't that what she liked most about Myplace—its solitary, independent hiddenness, the way it was sandwiched between busy downtown streets, yet completely separate, an in-between place?

Shir wanted to open her gym bag, take out one of the three beers she had just bought from Gareth, and huck it at the guy. Aim straight for that cool black cap pulled down over his forehead, she mused, watching him. On second thought, maybe not so cool. The kid was a bit on the skinny side for a hotshot, and from what she could see, both his jacket sleeves and pant legs were riding high. The guy needed a cash injection into his wardrobe allowance, and he needed it fast. Still, he wasn't getting any sympathy from her—not an intruder who was keeping her from a much-needed date with Molson Canadian. At $3.75 a can, too, Gareth having suddenly decided that he had obligations to the government to "tax" his financial transactions.

Grimly, Shir turned the Black and headed back to the street. Much as she needed it—her entire body crying out for the magic fluid, in fact—for the present, Molson Canadian was going to have to wait. No other location granted her the kind of privacy that Myplace did at this time of day, not with kids running everywhere, footloose and fancy free. And at home, there would be Stella, poking her nosy face into everything. No, Molson

Canadian was going to have to wait until later, when Mom was heavy into movieland and Stella finishing up homework in her room. That meant spending the next several hours in waiting mode—fidgeting, staring at the wall, and counting heartbeats until the moment of joy arrived. But that was what most of life seemed to be these days—just putting in time until she could pop open a tab, raise a can, and sluice a bit of golden happiness down her throat.

With a morose sigh, Shir swung a leg over the Black, pushed off from the curb, and headed down the street.

"What's with all the voting crap going on at school?" asked Shir. Standing in the open doorway to Stella's bedroom, she steadied her breathing, and forced herself to meet her sister's gaze. It was 4:30, the apartment quiet, and their mother not yet home from work. Stella, a stack of homework in front of her, was flipping through a copy of *Teen Vogue* at her desk. Oddly enough, she had left her door unlocked, and it had come open with a gentle push of Shir's hand.

"Why don't you knock?" countered Stella, turning in her chair to face the doorway. For a second then, Shir saw it—a flash of fear on her sister's face.

"Just tell me what I want to know," she said heavily. "I know you know about it. You always do."

Stella's gaze flickered uneasily. "Know about what?" she asked reluctantly.

"Oh, come on!" exploded Shir. Stella knew; Shir *knew* she

knew. "Voting," she said grimly. "All these kids keep telling me they're voting for me. Voting for what? I'm not in any election."

Again, just for a second, something flashed across Stella's face, but this time it looked more like sympathy. Instant fear roared through Shir's brain. Stella never showed sympathy. Not once during the two years that they had both been attending Collier High had she shown the slightest inclination to let Shir in on any of the various Dog Face plots and conspiracies cooked up by their schoolmates.

The sympathy—if that was what it had been—didn't last long. "Don't worry about it," Stella said, shrugging coolly. "Probably just a couple of kids being stupid."

"It wasn't just a couple," said Shir. Voice rising, she stepped into the room. "And they didn't know each other—it wasn't like two buddies cooking up something together. Something's going on and lots of kids know about it. Tell me what it is. C'mon, tell me."

This time, the fear on Stella's face was obvious. Jumping to her feet, she took a step back. "I don't have to tell you anything," she said shrilly, one hand fluttering to her throat. "Just because Mom's not home, you think you can come busting in here and throw your weight around. Well, you can't. This is my room and I don't want you in here. Get out! Just get out!"

Motionless, the blood pulsing dully in her forehead, Shir stared at her sister. "I'm not getting out," she said slowly, "until you goddam tell me what's going on. That's all I want—for you to tell me what's going on."

"Oh, it's just some stupid *joke*," Stella spat, taking another step back. "Just something some kids are doing. What does it matter? They're all crapheads."

"Agreed," said Shir. "So tell me why the crapheads are voting for me."

For a long moment, Stella stood staring at her, one hand clutching her throat. Shir could see it in her sister's eyes—the fear of telling. What could possibly be going on that was so bad, Stella was afraid to explain what it was? She was usually raring to gloat over bad news.

From the other end of the hall came the sound of the apartment's outer door opening. "Stella," called Janice Rutz, kicking off her shoes. "You home?"

Obvious relief swamped Stella's face. "Yeah, Mom," she called back loudly. "I'm in my room."

Taking a step forward, she raised both hands, palms outward, as if warding off a curse. "Get out *now*," she hissed, low-voiced, at Shir. "Or I'll tell Mom you barged in here without permission and were hassling me."

Helpless, Shir stared at the sister who stood locked against her, mentally shoving her out of her life. "All I *want*," she said slowly, "is to know what's happening to me."

"Get out," repeated Stella, making quick flicking gestures.

Wordless, Shir turned and left the room.

Seven

She found out how bad the possibilities could get the following morning. It was 10:15, during the break between classes, and she was coming down a hall en route from algebra to English. Ahead, to her left, a group of kids had gathered around a guy with a laptop, who was seated on the floor. As Shir approached, she noticed Eunie Jahenny standing at an open locker next to the group and casually observing the laptop screen. Curiously Shir scanned the girl, noting the rings piercing her left nostril and the small snake tattooed across the back of one hand. What in the world, she wondered incredulously, could Mr. Anderson have had to talk about with a seventeen-year-old metalhead snake goddess?

As Shir came abreast, Eunie abruptly closed her locker and turned to head down the hall. Quickly, Shir swerved to avoid her, but not before the two girls' eyes had met and she had seen Eunie's widen in surprise. Chalking it up to the usual, Shir began to skirt the outside of the group gathered around the computer whiz, and unexpectedly found her gaze drawn across the crowded circle to where she could see her sister peering over someone's shoulder. Immediately, Shir's eyes flicked away. It was an unspoken agreement between herself and Stella—they never,

never acknowledged each other at school. If one of them forgot her lunch or needed money for a pop, she was up Shit Creek as far as the other was concerned. In the halls, they passed like ships in the night. The few times someone had asked Shir if she had a sister, she had emphatically denied it. Without asking, she knew Stella did the same.

But today, something in Stella's face drew Shir's eyes back for a second glance. Though the other kids gathered around the laptop were grinning broadly, Stella was not. In fact, her expression was so markedly different, she could have been peering in at the scene from another dimension. Eyes narrowed and mouth sucked inward, her face seemed almost to be collapsing under a dull anguish. Momentarily, she looked twenty years older, a carbon copy of their mother.

At that moment, a girl standing at the edge of the circle noticed Shir. "Hey, look," she said, poking the guy next to her. "It's Dog Face."

As the entire group shifted to face her, Shir saw Stella turn and take off down the hall. Quickly, she took a step back, intending to reverse tracks and return the way she had come, but a guy stepped forward and grabbed her arm.

"Rutz," he said. "C'mere. Take a look at your total."

The group parted, giving her room, and she was pushed toward the guy with the laptop. With a smirk, he swiveled the screen to face her and she saw it: an enlarged image of her grade-ten school picture beside two others, both Collier High students—a guy who was currently in grade ten, and a girl in her grad year. Beneath each picture was displayed a number, hers the highest by several hundred. Across the top of the screen ran the question: *Who gets your vote as the ugliest kid at Collier High?*

Stunned, Shir stood staring at the laptop. So this was what all the comments had been about, she realized—a web site set up by someone from Collier High, where kids could vote for their favorite ugly. And she was winning hands down. The other contestants weren't even sniffing her tail wind.

Turning once again to escape, she blundered into a guy standing behind her. "Watch it!" he said, lifting an arm and elbowing her. Pain bloomed startlingly in Shir's left breast. Raising both hands, she slammed her binder into the guy's chest, then lunged out of the group, gasping and gasping for air.

"*Jesus*, Rutz!" said a voice behind her. "You don't have to freak about it."

Ahead, the corridor was full of kids coming and going. No one was looking at her; everyone but the small group gathered around the laptop seemingly unaware of its contents. But Shir wasn't kidding herself. From what she had just seen, at least 279 Collier High students knew about the web site—that was her posted total. And it would soon climb. She had gotten her first comment about voting yesterday, so the web site had probably only been up for a few days. If the voting continued at its current rate, Friday would see her winning by more than a thousand. That meant a thousand Collier High kids taking time out of their busy family-and-friend-packed schedules to log onto their computers and express their personal opinions about

Shirley Jane Rutz's face. *A thousand kids*, she thought helplessly. *A thousand!*

As Shir staggered forward into the oblivious crowd, she caught a glimpse of Eunie Jahenny to her right, standing motionless at her closed locker. On her face was the same professionally bored expression that she had given Mr. Anderson at the store; still, it was obvious that she was watching Shir. Not avidly, not even with what could be called apparent interest—perhaps the look on her face could have been described as mild curiosity, as if Shir was an interesting object, a rat in an experimental maze that had no way out.

Had Eunie logged onto the web site and voted? Shir wondered wildly. If she hadn't, she knew it existed—the awareness was all over her face, a slight gleam in those casual hooded eyes. But no sympathy, realized Shir with a sickening lurch. Nowhere in that slack, professionally bored expression, was there the slightest hint of warmth.

Ducking her head, she blundered onward down the hall.

Gym bag slung over a shoulder, Shir worked her way around the outside of the third pillar and stepped onto the peak of the arch. Seven meters below, water rippled quietly past; up and down the river, trees stood guard over an afternoon of dull blues, browns, and a faint lacy green. In every direction, peace stretched uninterrupted, without another human in sight. *Myplace*, Shir thought wearily. She was home.

Heaving a sigh, she slid her back down the pillar and settled her butt. Then she simply sat for a while, letting her gaze roam the budding trees, the mud-covered riverbanks, and the large stone houses opposite. Old and rich, that was what those houses were, she thought musingly. Owned by people who had made it in life. People with money to burn. What would it be like to live in a place over a hundred years old, with no one in the next apartment yelling or crying, and your own long stretch of lawn to laze around on?

Thoughtfully, she unzipped her gym bag and took out a can of Molsons. Just one, she had only the one this afternoon; not enough really, considering what she had been through today, but something in her hadn't been able to stomach the prospect of another backyard wrangling session with Gareth. It had been only twenty-four hours since the last one, and he was sure to have come up with a few new taxes, oil price hikes, or natural disasters to justify a raise to four bucks a can. *An earthquake in Peru*, thought Shir. *Something like that.*

With a snort, she popped the tab and downed her first swallow. It had been a long day and an ugly one. Word about the web site was spreading quickly and, though not everyone had clued in yet, those who had seemed determined to let her know that she had their vote. She hadn't been able to escape the comments anywhere. Even barreling through the halls at top speed hadn't stopped them. In spite of the overhead cameras, guys had stepped into her path, tripped her up, or gotten in their twisted one-liners by ducking under her lowered head and delivering them directly to her face. One guy had finished his off by spitting—the gob had missed her cheek but had landed, bubbly and slimy, in her hair. Not having a Kleenex, she had been forced to mop it up with her shirt. The stain of it was still there, the guy's gob now a faint gray smear on her sleeve.

Classes had been just as bad, kids passing her notes every time the teacher's back turned. Not that she had read more than the first few, just brushed them angrily to the floor, but still they had kept coming—comments about dog shit, rotting Halloween pumpkins, doing it with animals and corpses. None of it was new—Collier High kids all pulled their thoughts out of the same gutter; it was the amount of the crap that got to her. On an average day, she had to endure five, maybe ten Dog Face jokes, but nothing related to necrophilia. The web site, however, was gradually tuning more and more kids into the same brain wave; everyone seemed to be logging onto her face and refusing to get off.

Raising her can, Shir nursed another grim swallow. *Slow,* she told herself firmly. It was *slow* with the magic fluid today—she was on a very limited supply. And she also had to stop thinking about Collier High shit *now.* She was at Myplace, and she didn't want to contaminate its special holy beauty with that kind of garbage. Besides—

From behind her came the sound of a scrape, followed by a soft grunt. Startled, Shir froze, then peered around the outside of the third pillar toward her bike, but it was still standing, locked to the church parking-lot sign with no one in the vicinity. Satisfied, she settled back into place only to hear another scrape, followed by the unmistakable sound of a pebble rolling off concrete into the river. Cautiously, she leaned toward the inside of the bridge and peered around the pillar, but saw only stalks of dried grass along the riverbank, bending under a gust of wind. Still, she continued to lean, her body rigid as she stared around the pillar, willing the sound to have been a rat under the bridge, an angel skipping stones, or the church rector out for a walk.

Abruptly, a hand appeared, gripping the outside of the second pillar on the bridge's eastern side. Breath sucked in, Shir watched, riveted, as a leg and torso slid into view, then a boy's face, fiercely concentrated under a black knit cap. Taking a moment to reorient himself, the boy stood hugging the pillar, then crouched down and began the climb toward the third pillar and the peak of the first eastern arch.

Heart pounding, Shir retreated behind her pillar. It was the same guy, the one she had seen yesterday, sitting directly across from her usual spot. Obviously, he intended to do the same today. What should she do—crawl forward across the western arches, heading for the opposite bank, or work backward the way she had come and take off on the Black? But why should she, goddam it, she thought, suddenly furious, when she had gotten here first, and had only just started her beer? And besides, this was *Myplace*—the small private wonder-corner of a spot that the city, the planet, maybe even God Himself had set down on this earth just for her.

A hand slid around the pillar opposite, then a foot, and the boy began to edge himself onto the peak of the arch. Busy working himself into position, he didn't notice Shir until he had gotten himself completely around the pillar. "Oh," he said, holding onto it and blinking at her in surprise. "Hello."

"Fuck off," said Shir, her eyes darting out over the river.

"Thanks a lot," said the boy, sounding aggrieved. Silence followed, broken by a gust of wind, teasing the dead grass along the riverbank.. Grimly, her mouth set, Shir glared at a distant tree. There was no need to glance at the boy to see what he was doing; she knew from experience—standing with his mouth agape and ogling the massive distorted contours of her face. Convulsively her hand tightened on her can of Molsons, and it creaked loudly. *For Chrissake!* she thought wildly. All she wanted was to drink one can of beer privately, alone and in peace.

"Molsons," the boy said companionably. "Light or Canadian?"

"Fuck off," repeated Shir. "It's mine."

"Okay, so it's yours," said the boy, sliding his back down the pillar opposite and stretching out his legs. "I'm a Moosehead fan, anyway."

Rage erupted in Shir, savage, overwhelming. Necrophilia, bestiality, and now a moose head—here, in Myplace!

"Shut your goddam mouth!" she snarled, turning to glare directly at him. "I am *not* a moose head!"

Stunned, the boy stared back at her. "No," he stammered finally. "Not *you*. Moosehead *beer*. Y'know, the *label*. They make it in New Brunswick."

Shir's rage withered as quickly as it had surfaced. "Oh," she said lamely, her eyes drifting out over the river. "Yeah, I guess."

There was another long moment of silence. "*God!*" the boy said finally. "That'd be a great way to make a good first impression—calling someone a moose head."

"Better than what I get from most people," mumbled Shir. The hand holding her can of beer had begun to shake, and then her arm—quick tiny trembles that ran from her fingers all the way up to her shoulder. A long day, it had been a long, tiring day, she thought bleakly. And now *this*.

"Look," she said carefully. "I've gotten nothing but shit all day. So would you mind terribly much crawling back the way you came and leaving me alone? Like, just get the hell out of here?"

Another pause followed as the boy contemplated her suggestion. "Yeah, I would mind," he said calmly. "I like this place and I just found it last weekend. So I think I'll keep sitting here. But I won't give you any shit—I'm not into that kind of thing. And I promise not to beg, wheedle, or steal any of your beer off you."

Wearily, Shir stared down at her can of Molsons. "Why?" she asked slowly.

"Why what?" replied the boy.

"Why no shit?" she said.

The seconds ticked by without response, the water rippling benignly past, the wind rustling along the riverbank. Finally, Shir glanced warily at the boy to find him studying her. Immediately, her eyes flicked away.

"What d'you mean by shit?" he asked quietly.

"You know—*shit!*" she exploded. Who was this guy trying to

kid? One look at her face should tell anyone what kind of shit she meant.

Again silence inhabited the opposite arch. "I dunno," the boy said finally, hunching his shoulders against a particularly sharp gust of wind. "Would you come to a place as beautiful as this just to give someone shit?"

Something shifted inside Shir then—dull, thick, and surprised. A bit, just a *bit* of the tightness in her chest loosened. "Most days," she said bleakly, "it's hard to figure out why people do *anything* they do."

"Yeah," agreed the boy. "People are like mad, tight fists. Or scared fists. I figure I'm one of the scared fists. But in this place, it's different. You come here and the fist opens up."

This time it was definite—surprise, opening in her like breath. *Yeah*, thought Shir, looking out over the river. He had gotten it. The boy with the black cap had described this place exactly.

"So," she said, shooting him a sidelong glance. Eyes on the opposite bank, he appeared lost in contemplation. "How come you only found this place last week?"

"My dad and I moved here last summer," said the boy, still studying the river. "So I don't know this city well yet."

Swiftly, Shir scanned his profile, taking in the large-but-not-monster-sized nose, the narrow sloping face, and the tufts of dark hair sticking out from under his cap. Then the way his jacket sleeves rode up his wrists. Whoever this kid was, he didn't run with millionaires. "What school do you go to?" she asked casually.

"Stanford Collegiate," replied the boy. Turning to look at her, he ran his eyes carefully over her face. "You?" he asked.

"Collier High," said Shir, lifting her beer and gulping a few swallows to steady her nerves. She had to give the kid credit, she thought wryly. He had a good shock-absorption system. It had only been five minutes and there was no longer any double take in his gaze, not even any lingering disbelief.

"Collier's a slag heap," said the boy. "At least, that's what I've heard."

"So's Stanford," Shir shot back. Stanford and Collier maintained an ancient football rivalry, so ancient it went back to the Dark Ages. Any self-respecting Collier student who heard the phrase "Stanford Sabers" made an automatic gagging sound, followed by a gesture that was nowhere near respectful. It was a matter of principle.

"Yeah," the boy agreed again, "but Collier's worse. Too many snotty little rich kids. Add money to a crowd and it gets ten times worse. Stanford's just your average slag heap."

"Maybe," said Shir, trying to ignore a sudden memory of Wade Sullivan's grinning face. "I don't particularly hang around with rich kids."

"Me neither," said the boy. "I don't particularly hang around with anyone."

"Why not?" asked Shir, glancing at him curiously.

The boy shrugged. "Too much going on inside my head, maybe. Too much no one else wants to hear about. What's the point of having a conversation with someone if it's about nothing? Most people just want to go on and on about nothing. *TV*," he enunciated in absolute disgust.

Raising her can, Shir downed the dregs. So her first impression of this kid, she thought with satisfaction, had been wrong. In spite of his dime-store appearance, the guy thought he was a hotshot. "What's going on inside *your* head," she asked suspiciously, "that makes it special?"

The boy threw her a wary glance. "It's interesting to me," he shrugged. "It'd probably be nothing to you. Anyway, I've got to get going. I just came by for a couple of minutes on my way home from school."

Carefully, he maneuvered himself into a crouching position, then rose to his feet, one hand on the pillar. "D'you come here much?" he asked, looking out over the river.

"Who, me?" asked Shir, immediately on her guard.

The boy glanced at her, a tiny smile riding his mouth. "No," he said, "the wind. Of course, you."

"Oh," said Shir, feeling a flush shoot up her face. "I guess."

"Well," he said, turning to work his way around the pillar. "I'll see you again then, I guess."

"Yeah," said Shir, straightening to watch him go. "Yeah, I'll see you, too."

"Just wait," said the boy as he stretched one foot around the outside of the pillar. "I'll let go of this thing or my foot will slip, and I'll fall into the river. Then *I'll* be a moose head."

Laughter bubbled unexpectedly through Shir. "Yeah," she snorted. "A drowned moose head. One hundred proof."

"One hundred proof," echoed the boy. Flashing her a grin, he ducked around the pillar. For a moment, all she could see was his hand and foot, and then he appeared on the other side, scooting down the incline on his butt. Intent, Shir leaned around her pillar, keeping him in sight as he repeated the process with the second pillar, and slid down the rest of the arch. With a wave, the boy jumped to the ground and took off up the riverbank. In seconds, he was out of sight.

Slightly stunned by what had taken place, Shir settled back against her pillar and let her eyes roam the river's rippling surface. A guy had talked to her, she thought, disbelievingly. *Really* talked. Not like someone talked to a dog or a piece of crap you don't want to get stuck to the bottom of your shoe—it had been a real conversation, with listening and back-and-forth comments.

But maybe it had been just another nothing-conversation to him, like most of his conversations seemed to be. Catching her breath, Shir considered. *No*, she thought slowly. Before he had left, he had asked if she came here much. And then he had said he would see her again. People didn't do that when they were bored with you. She had listened in on enough Collier High conversations to know when a kid really wanted to talk to another kid or was faking it, losing interest. And the boy with the black cap hadn't lost interest. At least, he hadn't seemed to. Unless he was a very good faker.

Opening her gym bag, Shir stashed her empty beer can and got to her feet. She was going to have to be careful working her way back along the arch, she thought, studying the way down.

The wind had picked up, and she was stiff from sitting so long in one position. One slip of a hand or foot, and she could end up in the river. Then *she* would be a moose head.

With a giggle, she slid her gym bag over a shoulder and took hold of the pillar. *A moose head*, she reminded herself smilingly, *like the beer label. They make it in New Brunswick.*

Sliding her foot around the outside of the pillar, she began to work her way down.

Eight

Settling in behind the wheel, Shir put the delivery van into gear and backed carefully out of its parking space behind the store. In the alley, there wasn't much room to maneuver, especially with an oversized vehicle, and today Mr. Anderson had parked his Honda Civic so close, she had been forced to ask him to move it. This had happened before, and the first time she had been so certain he would fly off the handle and fire her on the spot for incompetence, she had been trembling as she had confessed she couldn't move the van unless he reparked his car. But instead of getting upset, Mr. Anderson had simply smiled his usual amiable smile and reparked the Civic, leaving her a meter to spare. Today had been a repeat of that first incident, minus Shir's panic. Over the past few months it had come to her that there might have been a reason behind her boss's seeming carelessness—that he had intentionally parked too close in order to find out if she was a hotshot driver too big for her britches, or one with the sense to see that some things simply couldn't be managed.

Sneaky man, Mr. Anderson, in spite of the grandfatherly look, thought Shir, and if he had been testing her today for common sense, she had passed. The same could not be said about the algebra quiz that she had taken earlier in the day. Ms. Khan, her teacher, had sprung the quiz on the class without warning, just to make sure they had all been bright-eyed, bushy-tailed, and following everything she had said over the past week with bated breath. Unfortunately, Shir's breath had not been bated, and she had flunked royally. Now, if the quiz had asked a question about her current vote total as posted at a particularly nasty dot-com web site, she thought grimly, she could have nailed the sucker exactly: 392. It would have been impossible to get that answer wrong, since she had been receiving minute-by-minute updates from other students as long as she remained on school property. At lunch hour, someone had even tracked her to the parking lot behind a nearby convenience store to let her know the other two contestants had been declared officially out of the race, but an ongoing tally was being kept just for her.

Well, she decided, gripping the steering wheel firmly, she didn't want to think about that now. Now she was at work, where no one knew about the web site and she was treated like an actual human being. To top that off, she had eight deliveries to complete, seven to regular customers who always tipped. Casually, she switched on the radio, and shifted the dial from Mr. Anderson's talking heads to something that had a decent beat. Then she adjusted the rearview mirrors and headed down the alley, gearing herself up for two hours of Friday rush-hour traffic and a few hit-and-run conversations, delivered with the standard Bill's Grocer polite, professional smile.

As she turned onto 34th Avenue, Shir spotted Mrs. Duran moseying around her front yard, tying the still-leafless vine that hung down one side of her porch into place with binder twine. "There you are, Shirley," she warbled as Shir climbed out of the van with her order. "How kind of you to make my delivery first. My granddaughter and her children are coming over for dinner, and you've got half my recipe supplies in that box."

Setting down her ball of twine, she led the way to the back door, quavering on about her three great-grandsons while Shir followed with the box of foodstuffs, throwing in the occasional "Uh huh" and "That's real nice, Mrs. Duran."

"Now, do you have time for a cookie and some iced tea?" asked the elderly woman, peering up intently as Shir deposited the box on a small table inside the back door. Although she had known in advance the question would be coming, Shir hesitated. The house was already working its usual magic, the lace window-curtains quietly filtering the light and making each room feel like a cupped handful of peace. From the kitchen wafted the rich scent of nutmeg, and she could almost taste the first home-baked cookie crumbling on her tongue. However, eight deliveries was more than usual, and Mr. Anderson had asked her to be back by 6:30 because one of the cashiers had to leave early. In addition, she could feel the memory of last Tuesday afternoon's encounter with Wade and Ben hovering uneasily between herself and Mrs. Duran.

"Maybe not today," she said hesitantly, her eyes flicking away from the elderly woman's. "Mr. Anderson told me—"

"Yes, Mr. Anderson," interrupted Mrs. Duran, taking Shir's hand and patting it. "Mr. Anderson would certainly want you to have a cookie in your stomach to help you concentrate while you're driving."

Without further ado, she began steering Shir down the hall and into the kitchen, where an opened ice-cream pail of cookies stood on the table. "Help yourself," she quavered as Shir sat down. "Take a few extra to keep you going on the road."

"Thanks, Mrs. Duran," Shir said weakly. As she took several cookies from the pail, her gaze fell on the multitude of children's school photographs that had been taped to the front of the fridge—Mrs. Duran's great-grandchildren, every one of them beaming and cute as a button. On the wall above them ticked an antique clock, counting off seconds of tranquility.

"Um ... how old is that clock?" asked Shir, pointing to it with a thick peanut-butter cookie. If things went as usual, a question about the clock would get Mrs. Duran started on her childhood and the war, and then neither of them would have to think about Wade Sullivan, red maraschino cherries, or layaway plans.

"Older than I am," chirped Mrs. Duran, taking a pitcher of iced tea out of the fridge. "It belonged to my parents, you know, when they were living in Europe." And then she was off, warbling through stories about France and the war years, Nazi soldiers, and the underground movement that had taken her brother's life. "Seventeen," she said softly, stroking the lace doily that sat under her glass of tea. "Just seventeen. So long ago. So very long ago."

In response to her words, an image of Wade Sullivan's face flashed through Shir's mind. Wade also happened to be seventeen, but he was hardly part of any underground resistance movement. With his personality, mused Shir, he probably would have volunteered to join the other side. "Too bad kids today aren't like that," she muttered, half lost in her thoughts.

Across the table, Mrs. Duran sat silently, still stroking the doily. "Children today," she said finally. "Well, it's a different time, isn't it? A confusing time, when it's hard to find your way. The war ... is different now. Not outside ourselves, in uniforms, like it used to be."

Startled, Shir shot her a glance and found the elderly woman sitting with her eyes carefully lowered as if talking to the tablecloth. "Yes," Mrs. Duran murmured, folding her hands meticulously together. "Yes, today the war is different, more difficult to recognize. The war on terror, it is inside us, too. We go after each other for no reason. We forget ..."

Her voice trailed off, wobbly as ever. "We forget," she repeated almost aimlessly, then sat silently, watching a bead of water slide down the outside of her glass. The old clock ticked, children's faces beamed from the fridge, and Shir sat uneasily, cookie in hand and waiting for the elderly woman to bring her mind back from wherever it had wandered. Abruptly, the house quiet felt like a weight pressing down, and she had to get out of there. Blundering to her feet, she picked up the clipboard and handed it to Mrs. Duran.

"Thanks for the cookies," she said gruffly, keeping her eyes lowered, "but I have to get going. Could you please sign for the delivery?"

"Sign for the delivery," repeated Mrs. Duran, as if using the words to pull herself back to the present tense. Without looking at Shir, she took the clipboard and signed next to her address, the pen scratching gently across the page.

"Here you are," she said with forced cheerfulness, handing back the clipboard. "Now you can get on with your deliveries and leave this old woman telling her stories to the wall. Come along, I want to get you a tip."

Head lowered, Shir followed the elderly woman to the jewelry box by the phone and waited as she fished out a loony and several quarters. "Well," sighed Mrs. Duran, pressing them into Shir's palm. "It was lovely to see you again, Shirley. I always enjoy our chats."

With another pat of Shir's hand, she opened the door, and then Shir was stepping out into a brisk April afternoon, descending the three porch stairs, and heading around the small house to the street. After getting into the van, she sat for a moment, working her way back through the conversation and trying to shake the feeling of an invisible weight pressing down. Without warning, her eyes were swarmed with tears—heated, acidic, full of tiny pinpricks. *Crying*, she thought, brushing at her wet face. Why was she crying now, when she had yet to blink a single tear in response to the ugly contest web site?

Grunting in exasperation, she turned on the van and headed down the street. The next address on the clipboard was Joe's Pizza, then the seniors' home, a hotel kitchen, and several residential addresses. At the bottom of the list was the new customer, a pub located across town. *Better give it some gas*, she told herself—the drive there and back was going to eat up time. Over the next hour and a half, she worked her way through the addresses on her clipboard, making sure she was polite but efficient, and not stopping to dawdle as she had with Mrs. Duran. Still, it was verging on 5:45 when she finished the fourth residential delivery and headed off toward the pub. Double-checking the address on the clipboard, she frowned thoughtfully. As far as she could tell, the pub was on the other side of the Forest Heights district. Wasn't there a grocery store in that area of the city that made deliveries?

Eyes squinted against the low-lying sun, Shir drove steadily through a residential neighborhood, keeping out a sharp eye for skateboarders and kids on bikes, then turned onto 53rd Street. Within seconds, a small mall came into view and she pulled into it, scanning the various businesses. There it was at the mall's south end—a pub with a dark green sign called *The Fox and Brier*. And, she realized, breathing in sharply, seven doors down from it, a Sobeys, stocked with everything Bill's Grocer had on its corner-store shelves, and more. Far more.

Bewildered, Shir sat, her gaze darting between the Sobeys and the pub. Was it possible she had gotten the address wrong? she wondered. But no, she had double-checked, and besides, the name of the pub matched the one on the clipboard. *Weird!* she thought emphatically. The whole thing was weird, but so what? Her job was to deliver the goods, not ask questions.

Climbing out of the van, she opened the side door and reached toward the back passenger seat for the single remaining box. *One more delivery!* she told herself exultantly. Then it was back to the store and stocking a few shelves, mopping the floor, and heading out with her pay to pick up a few black-market beers. Carelessly, her mind on 9 PM and her first sip of the magic fluid, Shir took hold of the box and pulled it toward herself. But as the box slid over the edge of the seat, it unexpectedly tilted and slipped free of her grasp, crashing to the van floor and spilling its contents.

With a hiss, Shir began collecting cans of soup and tuna, then picked up the half-empty box to discover it wasn't the top that had come open as assumed, but the bottom. For some reason Mr. Anderson had taped the top of this box closed—something he did to the odd delivery order—and the pressure of the fall had broken the older tape across the box's base. Which meant, Shir realized, disconcerted, that she was going to have to repack everything upside down, then carefully replace the ruined tape with some packing tape Mr. Anderson kept stashed in the glove compartment. None of the box's contents had been affected by the fall; with luck, the customer wouldn't notice the damage to the bottom, and no one would ever have to know about her single brief moment of unprofessional, *unforgivable* carelessness.

Carefully, Shir rearranged everything, righting the cans that hadn't fallen out and straightening a bag of flour. As she was repositioning the latter, a small package slipped out from behind it. Curious, Shir picked it up and examined it. Wrapped in plain brown paper, the package had no label and flexed easily in her hands. At most, it weighed three, maybe four hundred grams.

Drugs: the thought hit Shir, sudden and so hard that she almost blacked out. When the shock cleared from her head, she found herself still sitting on the van's back passenger seat and staring at the package in her hands. *Cocaine!* she thought crazily. That was what this had to be. How many times had she seen TV-drama images of the white powder packed into small plastic bags? "Snow"—that was what they called it, wasn't it? And it always came as a powder that was laid out in a line, then snorted. She had never seen cocaine in real life—the most she had done was some weed and a few pills she had bought from a neighborhood pusher. The weed had been okay, but the pills had left her feeling dizzy and sick, and she had stayed away from them after that, even when a guy had offered her some for free, as a sample.

Cocaine, here in her own two hands, thought Shir. Or maybe ecstasy—did that come as a powder? Did you snort it? Heart thundering, she hefted the package again. If this really was the white powder, she thought with a sinking feeling, she was holding a lot of toonies in her hands. Had all of today's delivery boxes contained a package like this one? Had the box to Joe's Pizza? The hotel kitchen? Mr. Anderson had also taped shut the tops on both those orders. And, Shir realized abruptly, a box that had gone to one of the residential addresses. Come to think of it, the top to the Sunnyville Rec Center's order had been taped closed, too.

Not Mrs. Duran's, though, she thought, staring at the package. Or the other two residential addresses.

Dread thudded through her, a dull tolling bell. Imaginary police sirens wailed through her mind, she saw TV images of gunfights, a man's throat being slit, a dead body pushed into a river at night, a horse's head in a bed. How long she sat like that, staring at the unlabeled package, she didn't know, but abruptly the thought, *Don't be crazy!* came to her, and she found herself fervently shoving the mystery package back into its original position behind the bag of flour. Cocaine mixed in with a bunch of grocery supplies, she scolded herself angrily—it was insane. *She* was insane for even thinking it. What a crazy imagination she had. The unmarked package probably contained more flour, or maybe some icing sugar—something like that. The Fox and Brier had needed a bit of icing sugar but not a whole bag, and Mr. Anderson was giving them a deal, probably for free.

But then, Shir wondered suddenly, why was the package taped so securely—both ends were a mass of packing tape. For another endless moment, she sat staring at the delivery box's upside-down contents. Then, with an uneasy shudder, she shrugged the whole thing off. *Whatever*, she thought gruffly. *It's none of my business.* Quickly, she finished repacking the box, shifting the unmarked package so that it would sit underneath the flour. Then she folded the box's bottom closed, and resealed it with the packing tape and a pair of scissors from the glove compartment. Finally, pulling the box to the edge of the seat, she very carefully hefted it, right side up, into her arms.

Sure is heavy, she thought, stepping cautiously out of the van. Fortunately, someone was coming out of the pub as she approached the door.

"Thanks," she mumbled, ducking her head as the man held open the door. Once inside, she stood, letting her eyes adjust to the gloomy interior. As expected, on a late Friday afternoon, the pub was packed, several large TVs blaring from the walls as a bartender briskly took orders. Approaching the bar, Shir stood, holding the box and waiting for him to notice her.

"Excuse me," she said as his gaze fixed on her. "I have a delivery for Mr. Ninto."

"Huh?" barked the bartender, his eyes widening as they locked onto her face. Then his gaze flicked to the box. "Oh, yeah," he said, his expression growing careful. "Mr. Ninto's in the back. I'll let him know you're here."

Picking up a phone, he spoke into it, then set it down. "You can take it through those doors there," he said, pointing to a set of swinging doors on his left. "He's in his office—first door on the left."

"Thanks," said Shir, hefted the box higher in her arms, and pushed through the doors. The hall beyond them was narrow, a door marked *Office* a few meters in on the left. Bracing the box against the wall, she knocked. Muffled footsteps sounded, and then the door opened to reveal a middle-aged man in a polo shirt and jeans.

"Delivery from Bill's Grocer?" he said, pointing to a chair. "Put it over there."

"Yes, sir," said Shir and set down the box. Picking up the clipboard from the taped-over top, she held it out hesitantly. "I need your signature, sir," she said warily, wondering if this man was going to be a replay of Mr. Dubya. "Just to show you got your order."

"Signature?" asked Mr. Ninto. "Sure, sure. No problem." With a flourish he signed, then stuck his hand into his pocket and fished around. "Here you go," he grinned. "A tip. Spend it wisely." Unhurriedly, almost mockingly, he dropped two toonies into her hand, his eyes like a security camera taking in every detail of her face.

"Thanks!" exclaimed Shir, fighting off a flush. Pocketing the toonies, she turned to the door.

"And give my best to your boss," added Mr. Ninto, as she stepped into the hall.

"I will, sir. I will," promised Shir, turning back to face him, but he was already closing the door. Dismissed, she pushed through the swinging doors and made a beeline out of the busy pub. Deliveries were over for the day, she thought, relieved, and she was hauling her sorry ass back across town as fast as possible. Climbing gratefully into the van, she headed out of the mall's parking lot, her foot heavy on the gas. *Nope*, she decided, thinking better of it. *Ease off—might be a speed trap coming up.* The last thing she needed was a ticket, on today of all days.

After several blocks, she pulled onto a side street and parked. Then, leaning her forehead against the steering wheel, she let the shakes come. *Cocaine, ecstasy, crystal meth*, she thought miserably. Whatever had been in that package, it was the *mob* that did this kind of thing ... organized crime. While most of what she knew about the mob came from TV, she had also heard rumors over the years about things that went on in this city—beatings and disappearances. Almost by instinct, she knew which pawn shops were best avoided; keeping her eyes peeled had taught her which of the neighborhood toughs could be convinced to hire out their mean edge.

But, she thought helplessly, *Mr. Anderson? Bill's Grocer?* It was crazy, the whole thing impossible. Mr. Anderson was a nice guy, a family man with a wife, children, and grandchildren. Neighborhood kids knew him as a soft touch, someone they could depend on to support bike-a-thons and bottle drives. He even had a Neighborhood Watch sign posted in the front window of his house. *He* couldn't be a drug dealer, she thought miserably. The idea was *insane*.

Without warning, the memory of Eunie Jahenny's visit to the store flashed through Shir's mind, bringing back the manner in which the girl's manufactured boredom had contrasted with the intent look in her eyes as she had said, "Oh, thirsty. *Real* thirsty. So I thought I'd come in for a Coke." And then Mr. Anderson's studied casualness as he had taken a Coke from the cooler, saying, "Ah, yes. A Coke. While you're drinking this, why don't you come to the back with me? There's something I'd like to talk to you about."

All that talk about a Coke that Eunie had never drunk, thought Shir—a Coke she had ultimately left sitting unopened on the storage-room counter. And she had come in at 8:30 on a Tuesday evening, when it was practically guaranteed the place would be empty of customers. No, realized Shir, dismayed, what Eunie had actually come in for was cocaine, probably wrapped in a small unlabeled package. Not for herself, obviously—she didn't have that kind of money. She was probably a courier and the Coke a kind of code—a signal to clue in Mr. Anderson as to her real purpose for being there.

Now that she thought about it, there had been similar incidents, other customers Mr. Anderson had, apparently casually, fallen into conversation with, then taken into the storage room—not often, perhaps three or four times in the six months she had been working at Bill's Grocer. And, Shir realized, her thoughts racing, more frequently, there had been times she had walked in on her boss talking to individuals at the storage room's outer entrance. Had all these people come by for a "Coke"? She hadn't previously given them a second thought, but now she wondered if she had stumbled onto a pattern.

Would it be smartest to quit? she wondered heavily. But if she did, where would she get the money she needed to keep herself in beer? Mom had cut off her allowance when Mr. Anderson had hired her, and she expected Shir to buy her own clothes. She wouldn't look favorably on having to dole out extra cash again.

Besides, it would look suspicious, just up and quitting. And from this point on, Shir realized with sudden startling clarity, nothing could look suspicious—nothing she did, nothing she said, nothing she even *thought*.

Forcing a sob down her throat, she restarted the van and headed off toward Bill's Grocer.

Nine

S hir woke to an avalanche of sunlight pouring through her bedroom curtains and Celine Dion caterwauling across the hall. Blearily, she opened one eye, then closed it again. *The day*, she thought, poking around the grunge inside her head. *What is the day? Oh yeah, Saturday.* That had to be the reason Stella was running her stereo at top volume. Burying her head under her pillow, Shir let out a groan. Her brain felt like a throbbing, over-soaked sponge. Why, oh why, she thought miserably, didn't someone invent a beer that you could drink without getting hung over? It would sell like hotcakes; people would be lining up to buy it.

She had drunk seven ... maybe eight beers after getting off work last night, somewhere in a back alley, she couldn't remember exactly where. One after another she had poured them down her throat, so steadily that her gut had been sloshing like a washing machine as she had come staggering up the alley behind the apartment building, holding onto the Black to keep herself upright. *Yeah, the Black*, sighed Shir. No question about it—the Black was her trusted buddy, the one who had stood by silent and sympathetic as everything had gone suddenly vertigo one block from home, and she had heaved the entire contents of her stomach onto the pavement. *Wasted it!* she thought, cringing at the memory of all that good beer running smelly and acidic across the ground.

At least her stomach had waited to dump its contents until after she had seen the gang of kids tearing up and down an alley three blocks north, spray-painting graffiti onto the black garbage bins the city had placed behind each house. She had stopped to watch, standing inside a copse of trees to avoid being noticed, and had been impressed with the boys' efficiency. Swift and quiet, they had spray-painted their gang logo onto each bin, then gathered around one halfway down the alley and poured something into it. Next, they had tossed in several lit matches, watched as the bin's contents exploded into flames, and taken off at top speed.

Shir had taken off, too, in the opposite direction. Knocking on someone's door hadn't even occurred to her, past experience having repeatedly revealed that simply being in the vicinity of trouble meant getting blamed. A face that resembled a dog's hind end looked guilty to most people; it was that simple. *God,* she thought, touching her temples, *am I hung over!* Dark and heavy, her brain throbbed like a fresh bruise. Slowly, ever so slowly, she rolled over and peered at her clock radio. "Nine-forty," she moaned. That was early, *way* too early to have to listen to something as rage-inducing as Celine Dion. There should be a law against playing high-up screechers before noon. A person should be free to wake up in her own home without having her rage induced before lunch.

Centimeter by centimeter, Shir worked herself into a sitting position. Then she sat for a while, head in hands, as she stared at the floor. She had to pee like a racehorse, her bladder in a massive emergency state, but for some reason, she couldn't seem to get herself up and moving. Something—the part of her responsible for flicking the switch that got her legs going—wasn't flicking the switch. Eyes dull and unblinking, her brain in deep sludge, Shir continued to sit and stare at the floor. A minute ticked by, then another and another. The pain in her bladder worsened, the black throb in her brain deepened, and still she didn't move. Still nothing flicked the necessary switch.

With a rumbling belch, Shir glanced again at her clock. This time it stood at 9:56, which left approximately three hours until she was due at work. *I have to get moving,* she thought weakly. A lot of coffee was going to have to make its way down her throat before she cleared today's hangover. But though she repeated this to herself several times, the inner switch didn't flick. Slowly, soundlessly, her head sank back into her hands, and she returned to staring at the immense, vast nothingness of the floor.

A knock sounded at the door. "Yeah?" mumbled Shir.

The door opened and Stella peeked in. "Good morning," she said, smiling brightly. "How are you?"

Shir stiffened. Experience had taught her that the statistical odds on the possibility of her sister actually caring about how she felt ran at about one hundred to one. Stella wanted something. "Fine," she said shortly.

"Great!" Stella said cheerily. "Well, today's my walk-a-thon for cancer, remember? It starts at twelve. So, can I borrow your new runners? Y'know, your Nikes—the ones you bought a month ago."

"Nope," said Shir, without lifting her head.

"Why not?" demanded Stella, her voice rising a notch. "Our feet are the same size, and you'll just be standing around the store all day. I have to walk a long way. It'll take me hours. Your shoes are better than mine."

"Just can't, that's all," mumbled Shir. No *way* was she going to explain to Miss Saturday-morning-walk-a-thon that she had lost her runners last weekend because she had been too shit-drunk to find them in Dana Lowe's back hallway. Stella was just going to have to suffer through her walk-a-thon wearing her own runners—cute little pink ones with daisies appliquéd across the tips. You would never have trouble finding *them* in a back hallway.

"You can wear my runners to work if you want," wheedled Stella, taking a step into the room. "They'd look nice on you with my pink sweater. I'll let you wear that, too."

Of all the colors in the spectrum, pink was the one best designed to accentuate the limp, carroty-red shade of Shir's hair—especially with cute little daisies appliquéd across it. "Get out!" she roared, the rage erupting in her without warning so that she was suddenly lunging for her pillow and flinging it at her sister. With a squeak, Stella backed out of the room and slammed the door, and Shir sank back onto the bed where she lay clutching at her pounding head. Unfortunately, an imaginary monster happened to choose that particular moment to show up and begin kicking the left side of her head with steel-toed boots. Steel-toed boots, Shir realized incredulously, with pink daisies appliquéd across the toes. And now the imaginary monster was pulling out a sledgehammer and pulverizing her brain with it. A pink sledgehammer, of course, and it was repeatedly slamming her brain in the same spot. The *exact* same spot, she thought, dozing off. The *exact* ...

When she woke again, it was 11:30. Except for the sound of the TV, the apartment was quiet—Stella had obviously left for her walk-a-thon. As soon as her eyes opened, Shir realized that she had to pee like three racehorses. *No*, she thought, groaning, *three brontosauruses*. Brontosauruses that were about to go extinct if they didn't let loose soon.

Taking the utmost care not to jar her bladder, she eased herself off the bed and started toward the door. *Easy now*, she thought soothingly. *Easy does it.* One heavy step, she knew from experience—one that was made too quickly or came down not exactly right—and her bladder would erupt, bursting at the seams. Cautiously, she opened the door and stepped into the hall. *Ten steps to the can*, she thought, projecting ahead. *Nine, eight.* From the living room came a surge of melodramatic music, then a scream and some half-shouted dialogue, but Shir kept herself frantically focused on the bathroom door. *Three steps to go*, she moaned silently, *two, one.* Fortunately, the door was open. Once inside, she didn't bother to flick on the light, nor did she check to ensure the door had latched behind her. Her legs simply bolted for the toilet, her hands jerked down her pj bottoms, and she let 'er rip.

It took Rambo-like determination not to howl with pain, but after the first blast of urine, Shir floated in relief. *Yeah*, she thought dizzily, *this is ecstasy, this is bliss.* And not bad for eight beers—holding them all without a single trip to the can until 11:30 AM, even if the three or four she had upchucked were subtracted from the total. No matter what her mother said, she, Shirley Jane Rutz, could hold her own with any guy when it came to handling the bottle. Yeah, Shirley Jane Rutz really had things under control. She was managing fine, she was *laughing*.

When the steady stream of urine had finally trickled to an end, Shir flushed the toilet and stood up. Then she flicked on the light and peered hesitantly into the mirror. A low moan followed as she assessed the pouchy, bloodshot eyes gazing balefully back at her. She looked, she realized in dismay, like death warmed over. On second thought, forget the warmed-over bit. She was death in deep-freeze.

Popping a few Tylenol for her headache, Shir opened the bathroom door and started down the hall. The next thirty seconds, as she well knew, were the important ones—if her mother didn't start nagging right away, she wouldn't bother. Cautiously, Shir edged forward, wide-eyed with apprehension as the living room couch came into view, revealing a pair of fuzzy blue slippers, the plump rise of her mother's hip, then her face. Eyes closed, her mouth sagged dully open, Janice Rutz was lying flat-out comatose as the TV buzzed aimlessly on the other side of the room. Collapsing against the nearest wall, Shir stood staring at the scene. So, she hadn't been the only one hitting the sauce last night, she thought wryly. And with the way her mother looked, she wouldn't be coming out of this one for hours. Which gave Shir enough time—more than enough—to pour several cups of coffee down her throat and get herself out the door. By the time she returned from work, she would have recovered enough to look somewhere near normal, and Janice Rutz would never have the slightest inkling about her elder daughter's latest binge.

An opened package of English muffins sat on the kitchen counter, but Shir's stomach lurched at the sight. Plugging in the kettle, she boiled some water and made herself a cup of coffee. Then, sitting down at the table, she sipped it slowly, yawning as her body's sluggishness began to recede. With a sigh, she glanced at the clock above the sink. *Eleven-fifty-five*, she thought. That left forty-five minutes before she had to leave for work, a full hour before she had to walk in the door of Bill's Grocer. Sixty minutes before she had to smile at Mr. Anderson and—

Shir's eyes shot wide open and she remembered: the unlabeled package in the Fox and Brier order, the taped-over boxes, Eunie Jahenny's Coke. *Drugs!* she thought in a wash of fear. *Mr. Anderson, the mob, organized crime.*

Stop it! she shouted angrily inside her head. Jumping to conclusions like that—it wasn't fair. After all, she hadn't actually opened the unlabeled package. And just because one taped-over delivery box had contained a package like that didn't mean they all did. It wasn't right to assume bad things about someone, especially someone who had treated her decent. *Yeah*, Shir thought fiercely, Mr. Anderson treated her *decent*. Out of this whole goddam city, he was practically the only person who treated her okay. *He* wasn't a drug dealer; he couldn't be.

Savagely she brushed away a tear. She wasn't crying, she told herself firmly. No, she *wasn't*. She was just ... tired, that was all—tired because she had drunk one too many. Well, okay—maybe three or four. But Mr. Anderson would understand that. Just last month during a quiet spell in the store, he had told her that he had been a wild kid way back when—sowed his own reckless oats. "It doesn't pay, Shirley," he had said sadly, gazing out the front window. "All that craziness—it catches up to you in the end."

Had it caught up to him? she wondered, staring out the kitchen window. Was that why he was sending her across town to deliver unlabeled packages in taped-over boxes to hotels, pubs, and rec centers? Lifting her mug, she drank steadily, then set it down empty. "Time to get up now," she told herself in a bright, peppy, Stella-type voice. "Time to get up and moving. Time to head off for work. Yeah, time to go to work."

Still nothing flicked the switch.

When she walked into the store fifty minutes later, Mr. Anderson was waiting for her—not in an obvious way, and not in a manner anyone else would have identified as waiting, simply standing beside Cathy at the till nearest the door and chatting up a customer as he bagged her purchase. Normally, Shir wouldn't have thought anything of it; normally, she would have felt only a rush of pride as her boss turned to her with his customary smile and said, "There you are, Shirley. Early as usual, I see."

But today, as Mr. Anderson handed the customer her bagged purchase and turned to face Shir, she was hit with a gut-surge of panic. Taking a frightened step backward, she bumped into a small display table of oranges and had to grab at the stack of fruit to keep it from toppling over. Instantly, Mr. Anderson was at her side, breathing quickly as he helped steady the wobbly produce. For five, ten seconds they stood side by side, clutching at the orange pyramid, and the stack of fruit held.

"That was close," said Mr. Anderson, straightening. "Lucky you're fast on your feet, Shirley."

"Yes, sir," mumbled Shir, lowering her eyes. This was more difficult than she had thought it would be. Last night hadn't been too bad—the store had been continually busy after she had returned from her round of deliveries, and her only direct interaction with her boss had been at quitting time when she had been paid. Besides, last night he hadn't known about her accident with the Fox and Brier delivery box. Today he did. It was obvious; no one had to come out and say it in so many words— the evidence was written all over the way he had stiffened the moment he had laid eyes on her. Mr. Anderson knew about her and the box, that it had come open and that she had seen. And now he was going to fire her, banish her from the store for knowing something she wasn't supposed to know.

"I need to talk to you," said Mr. Anderson, catching one last orange that was escaping down the side of the stack. "Come to the back room with me."

Dread oozed coldly up Shir's spine. "Yes, sir," she whispered. Ducking her head, she trailed along the produce aisle after her boss, even when he slowed his pace to match hers.

"How are you, Ned?" Mr. Anderson nodded at a man with two young children. "Find everything you're looking for?"

"So far," Ned smiled back. "If I need help, I'll holler."

"You do that," said Mr. Anderson, then continued down the aisle and pushed through the *Employees Only* door. On his heels, Shir made a beeline to the opposite side of the storage room, where she stood with her head lowered and her back to the outer door. A short silence followed. Motionless, Shir stared at her feet and counted heartbeats.

"How are you today, Shirley?" Mr. Anderson asked finally.

"Fine," mumbled Shir.

"Really?" asked Mr. Anderson. "You look a little ... tired."

Panic leapt through Shir. Here it was, she thought frantically—a reason he could fix on to fire her. The problem was, she couldn't lie about being tired. She looked like a dog's breakfast.

"I am a little, I guess," she admitted reluctantly, keeping her eyes fixed on the floor. "But I can still do my job. I'm not sick or anything."

"Oh, sure," Mr. Anderson said easily. "We all have our tired days. I'll try not to run you off your feet. How's that?"

Startled, Shir shot her boss a glance and found him studying her intently. Dropping her gaze again, she mumbled, "That's ... fine, sir. I'm sorry I'm tired, sir."

"Don't worry about it," said Mr. Anderson. "That's not why I asked you to come back here. What I need to talk to you about is the Fox and Brier delivery you made yesterday."

Shir's stomach plummeted like a lead weight. *Here it is*, she thought. *It's coming.*

"Yes, sir?" she whispered.

"The customer called me about it," Mr. Anderson said slowly. "Said the bottom came open when he picked up the box. Nothing was damaged, he was able to catch it on time, but a corner of the box was torn. Did it fall off the seat while you were driving?"

Shir took a shaky breath. "Not off the seat, sir," she said, thinking rapidly. "But it did flip over when I moved another box. The bottom came open a bit, but I fixed it up right away. It wasn't ..."

She faltered, her eyes darting across Mr. Anderson's face. He was watching her so closely, he was practically breathing in every word. "Well," she continued nervously, "it wasn't a *major* flip, sir. Nothing fell out, or anything. I didn't think anything was broken, so I didn't look inside."

The relief that crossed Mr. Anderson's face was unmistakable. "Ah," he said, louder than necessary. "No need to worry then. Nothing was broken, nothing damaged. Like I said, the customer caught it on time. So you didn't ..." He hesitated, then added, "...

open the box?"

"No no no," gushed Shir, desperate to reassure him. "I didn't *open* it, sir, because it just tilted over a bit. Just a *bit*, sir. Y'see?"

Mr. Anderson's eyes shifted to the wall above her head. "Well," he said quietly, "that's good then. No problem, no problem at all."

"No, sir!" Shir said emphatically. "No problem at all!"

"Okay," Mr. Anderson nodded. "That's okay then." He sighed noticeably, then beamed at her. "The next time something like that happens," he said, "make sure you let the customer know so he won't get caught by surprise. And here," he added, pulling something out of his shirt pocket. "I want you to carry this cell phone with you from now on when you're in the van. If a box gets damaged again, or you get caught in traffic, call and let me know. The store number is on the back."

"Yes, sir," said Shir, accepting the phone as if it was a grenade about to go off.

"Have you ever used a cell?" asked Mr. Anderson.

"Yes, sir," said Shir. "I used to own one." She had, in fact, purchased a cell soon after starting work, but not having anyone to call, had ended up trading it away for a few Pilsners.

"Well," said Mr. Anderson. "Fine! Now, how about I let you take off your jacket and get organized. I've got five deliveries for you today, but they can't go out until after two. Until then, I'd like you to check the shelves and make a list of what needs restocking."

"Yes, sir," said Shir, nodding so enthusiastically her neck

cracked. "I'll get right on it, sir."

"All right, then," said Mr. Anderson, and she could hear the smile in his voice. "But Shirley, you don't need to call me 'sir' every three words."

"Yes, sir," Shir said quickly, then flushed and added, "I mean, yes, Mr. Anderson."

For a moment, her boss just looked at her, his eyes warm, the smile still on his lips. He liked her, it was obvious. For some inexplicable reason, this man really *liked* her.

"You take your time taking off your jacket," he said gently. "And when you're ready, I'll see you out on the floor."

"Yes s—" Shir started to say, but managed to catch herself. "I'll be right out," she added carefully, then stood motionless as the door swung shut behind her boss, watching it whisper back and forth until it settled silently closed.

Ten

It was the following afternoon and another warm day, so that birds were chirping everywhere and the slight breeze, when it came, was a breath of sun into the lungs. Face uplifted, her throat in a quiet hum, Shir balanced herself high on the Black's pedals as she coasted down the hill behind the Anglican church. *Myplace!* she thought with satisfaction, heading across the parking lot toward the bridge. After four long days, she was finally here again, at the shy, quiet center around which the rest of her life revolved. The only drawback was that today she was beerless—when she had knocked on Gareth's door ten minutes earlier, there had been no answer. All things considered, it was probably for the best; her stomach was still giving queasy lurches at the thought of popping another beer tab. Friday night had been a binge to remember, or rather, one to forget. From now on, five beers at one sitting was her limit.

As Shir approached the base of the bridge, she saw the boy seated on the first eastern support arch, jacket unzipped and legs outstretched as he contemplated the scene. Getting off her bike, she stood motionless and observed him. Unlike Wednesday afternoon, today she wasn't upset to see him; in fact, she had wondered on the way over if he would be here.

Now, as she stood watching him, memories of their last conversation flashed through her mind, bringing with them the calm steadiness of the boy's voice and the way he had given words to her so easily—as if it was simply part of who he was, a normal, natural thing to do.

At that moment, perhaps feeling her eyes on him, he turned and glanced toward her. Instinctively, Shir's gaze flicked away, and she stood staring so intensely across the river that her eyes hurt.

"Hey," called the boy, "you're here! I thought you might show today."

Startled, Shir's eyes flew back to his. Grinning—the boy was actually *grinning* at her. "Yeah," she called back, abruptly almost breathless. "I thought maybe you'd show, too."

Hands shaky, she locked the Black to the *Church Patrons Only* sign. Then, doing her best to look nonchalant, she walked over to the bridge. Pausing at the base, she hiked her gym-bag strap further up her shoulder. A quick glance showed the boy still peering around the third eastern pillar; hesitating, Shir sucked at her lower lip. She had never before climbed the arch with anyone watching, had never had to consider how she looked, scrambling up the steep concrete incline with her butt hiked into the air. It was that, however, or continue standing on the riverbank with last year's dead grass. *Screw it*, she told herself grimly, ducked her head, and began to climb. Fortunately, a recent rain had washed away most of the grit, and scaling the incline was easy. In under a minute, she had reached the third pillar, and was stepping around it and onto the peak of the first western arch.

"You're good at that," commented the boy as she settled into position. Brief relief sang through Shir and she shrugged, trying to fake casual. "Done it enough," she said. "Over a hundred times, I bet."

"How long have you been coming here?" asked the boy.

"Years," said Shir. "Since junior high. Grade seven."

"Lucky you," the boy said thoughtfully. "You've had it inside you for eons, then."

Curious, Shir shot him a glance. Across from her, the boy was sitting calmly, his gaze wandering the opposite bank. In spite of the warmth, he was wearing his black knitted cap.

"What d'you mean?" she asked.

"It's a theory of mine," he said, continuing to study the scene before him. "Places where you spend a lot of time grow *inside* you. Can you feel it?"

Shir thought about it, considering the locations she frequented most, and gradually she sensed what the boy meant. There, in the middle of her chest, sat a tight, dull lump that felt like home. Directly below it, in her gut, was Collier High, spinning like a black vortex. Then, abruptly, she felt Bill's Grocer, a clear sunlit space inside her forehead, murmuring with voices, and smelling of bananas and oranges. Last of all, she discovered a high, hushed arc of peace hidden behind everything else—Myplace.

"Yeah," she said wonderingly. "I've never thought about it before, but they do. Different places even live in different parts of you."

The boy nodded enthusiastically. "You do feel it!" he exclaimed, turning a wide grin on her. "I've told other people the same thing, and they don't get it at all. A place is just *outside* to them—somewhere they go to and come back from, and then it's completely gone for them."

Reaching into his pocket, he pulled out a package of Hostess Twinkies and opened one end. "No Moosehead today?" he asked, grinning slyly, and pulled out a cupcake.

"Nope, no Moosehead," replied Shir, flushing at the memory. "My main supplier wasn't in."

"Who's that?" asked the boy, nibbling a neat circle around the cupcake's upper rim.

"Some derelict welfare case who knows how to make a buck," Shir said bitterly. "One and a half years until I'm eighteen, and then I don't have to kiss ass with that loser anymore."

The boy nodded sympathetically. "Yeah," he said, "it's two years for me. Then it'll be 'Bye bye Twinkies,' that's for sure. Are you hungry?"

Instantly, Shir was on her guard. It had been over a year since anyone other than a family member or Mrs. Duran had offered her something to eat; the last time, she had bitten into the proffered Oreo cookie to find a dead worm curled into the center of the icing. "Depends," she said cautiously.

"Depends on a Twinkie?" asked the boy, holding up the package with the remaining cupcake. "Can you catch?"

Without waiting for a response, he lobbed the Twinkie, and Shir found herself lurching awkwardly forward to catch the gently arcing package. Disbelieving, her heart in a massive thud, she sat cradling the chocolate Twinkie. "Thanks," she managed finally, and eased it out of its package.

"No prob," said the boy. Tonguing the icing deftly off the top of his cupcake, he sucked it whole into his mouth. "By the way," he added casually as Shir took her first guarded bite. "My name's Finlay Cowan."

"Shirley Rutz," Shir replied automatically through a mouthful of intense sweetness. "Actually," she added after a thinking pause, "*Shir* Rutz. I like it better short."

"Okay," Finlay said agreeably. "Shir Rutz. As in sure. Like certain. Is that why? Are you certain about everything?"

The absurdity of the comment hit Shir splat in the face. "Hardly!" she muttered. Ducking her head, she took another cautious nibble of cupcake.

"Good," Finlay said easily. "I'm not crazy about people who are too sure about things. First person on my list of people who are too sure of themselves is God."

"God?" said Shir, glancing at him in surprise. "Isn't God supposed to be sure about things? Like, that's his job, isn't it?"

Finlay shrugged. "Is that what God is?" he asked. "A job? Or an attitude?"

Again Shir thought about it. *God—an attitude?* she wondered, staring out at the river. "My mom watches TV church a lot," she said slowly. "But if she's supposed to get some kind of attitude from it, it doesn't last long."

Finlay snorted. "I'm not religious," he said. "I don't believe in God. That doesn't mean I don't think there is one, but if there is, I don't think he would want me to waste my time *believing* in him."

An image flashed through Shir's mind of her mother seated on the couch and watching a TV preacher, her face slack and empty like a small child watching Saturday-morning cartoons. "What are you supposed to do with God," she asked carefully, "if you don't believe in him?"

Finlay stared thoughtfully across the river. "That's a good question," he said. "It makes me think." Silently he sat, apparently deep in meditation, and Shir sat just as silently, cupcake in hand and watching him. Whether or not her question was really all that good, Finlay was certainly working his way through it. His first few seconds of pondering stretched into several minutes and then several more, and still he sat, letting his thoughts play out inside his head.

"I think God is like what he made," he said finally. "Not what *we* made—not cities and concrete and *ideas* about God—what *he* made ... like this river, and those trees, and the birds. That bird there," he added, pointing to the quick darting path of a swallow low across the water. "It doesn't believe in God, it just is. And that tree, it doesn't believe in God, either. It just grows and is beautiful, especially in the fall. Trees are just about my favorite things. Of everything, I like to look at trees the most."

"Uh huh," murmured Shir, her eyes tracing the delicate greenery on a nearby poplar.

"So that's what I think," announced Finlay with obvious

satisfaction. "God doesn't want us to *do* anything with him. He doesn't really care if we believe in him or not. We're just supposed to be ... y'know ... *alive* and full of life—like the birds and the trees. And this river, I guess."

Warm gentleness filled Shir at the thought, and she sat, watching another swallow zigzag across the water. Suddenly, without warning, the memory of her botched delivery to the Fox and Brier surfaced inside her head, shoving aside the peaceful scene before her. "Okay," she said, swallowing hard. "Maybe God doesn't care if we believe in *him*, but what about right and wrong? D'you think God wants us to believe in that?"

"Right and wrong?" asked Finlay with a frown. "Maybe. But don't you think right and wrong is something we made up?"

Slightly stunned, Shir sat silently for a moment. "What d'you mean?" she asked finally. "How can you make up right and wrong?"

"I think we've made up almost everything," announced Finlay, popping the last of his cupcake into his mouth. "Most of what people run around doing is just made-up stuff—stuff other people tell them it's important to do. But that kind of stuff isn't important *really*, except inside their heads. It's not *real* stuff, like this river and those trees. Rivers and trees are real because they just *are*. No one has to tell them how to be. And they don't have to think about right and wrong, either. I mean, trees never think about what's right, but do they ever do anything wrong?"

Confused, Shir sat staring at a tree opposite. In all her born days, she had never heard anyone talk like this. Still, she thought musingly, it was kind of interesting. And what Finlay had said was probably correct—trees never did anything *wrong*.

"But trees don't *think*," she said cautiously. "And they can't *move*. So how can they do anything wrong?"

"Okay," Finlay said amiably. "Birds move. Do they ever do anything wrong?"

"They do if you're a worm," said Shir.

For a second, Finlay seemed to freeze. Then his head tilted back against his pillar, and he closed his eyes and sighed. "Yeah," he agreed disappointedly. "I'm talking a lot of crap, aren't I? It's nice crap, but it's still just crap."

Surprised, Shir sat, waiting for him to lash out at her for disagreeing, or at least put her in her place with a quick taunt or jeer. But instead, Finlay simply sat with his eyes closed, listening to the breeze at play along the riverbank. Thoughtfully, she nibbled deeper into her Twinkie. *No worm yet*, she mused, probing it with her tongue. Once again, the memory of the Fox and Brier delivery box flashed, unwelcome, through her mind.

"You haven't really answered my question," she said tentatively. "About right and wrong—d'you think God cares about it?"

For a long moment, Finlay continued to sit, eyes closed and head tilted back against the pillar. "Right and wrong?" he said finally. "No, I don't think God cares much about that. But that's just because there isn't any right and wrong in what *he* made. Right and wrong only exists in what people make—the made-up stuff, y'know? But I guess God probably wants *us* to care about right and wrong, because right and wrong are ours. We made it, so we should care about it. Yeah," he said decisively, "*we* should care about it."

Opening his eyes, he glanced at her, and for a brief scattering of heartbeats, Shir found herself looking directly into his gaze. Blue, his eyes were pale blue like hers, but larger and more intense. Every part of this boy was intense, she realized, observing him. He was all over his face, burning in every fiber— the pale ongoing blueness of his eyes, the heavy dark eyebrows, even the large hooked nose.

Flushing, she looked away. "But what ... if it's something *you* didn't make?" she asked uncertainly, her heart quickening, a foot kicking warnings against a half-open door. "I mean ... well, it's not your fault, but somehow you're caught up in it?"

"Caught up in it how?" asked Finlay, frowning slightly.

Shir hesitated. Obviously she couldn't get into *exact* details— she didn't know Finlay well enough to be sure he could handle the information. At the same time, the Fox and Brier delivery box seemed to have jammed itself, dead center, into her brain and wouldn't leave. "Let's just say it's something someone else is doing," she explained vaguely, "and you happen to find out about it. Without meaning to, of course," she added quickly. "And there's nothing you can do about it, even though they're sort of ... using you to get it done."

Instead of responding, Finlay sat motionless and studied her. In the afternoon's lazy, hovering quiet, Shir could almost feel his eyes tracing out every line in her face, *touching* it. "*How* are they using you?" he asked pointedly.

She shrugged nervously. "They just are," she said gruffly, "*maybe*. I'm not sure, actually. But it's not me doing whatever's wrong, *if* there's something wrong going on—it's them. So that makes me sort of like a bird or a tree, just being alive and full of life, right? And *they're* the ones doing what's wrong—the made-up stuff that's only important inside their heads, right?"

Unsure if she was making sense, Shir shot Finlay a quick glance and found his intense blue gaze still fixed on her. She had obviously asked another good question, at least, one that required deep thought. Uneasily, she raised what remained of her cupcake to her mouth, then lowered it without taking a bite. What was it with this guy? she thought, abruptly irritable. Did he have to think about *everything*? Hotshot, too-good-for-his-britches, Stanford *Saber*. Stanford Saber *slag heap*.

On the opposite arch, Finlay took a long breath. "I don't know what you're talking about," he said, so carefully it was as if he was sending his words out along a tightrope. "So I don't really want to say much. But if it was *me* that someone else was using ... or *might* be using ... for something *wrong*, that is ... well, I would want to know for sure."

There didn't seem to be much to say after that. A sinking sensation took over Shir's gut, sucking at her from the inside until she was nothing but dull, cold fear. Turning to look out over the river, she saw a dark mass of clouds moving in from the west and shutting out the sun.

"Well," she said, shivering, "I'd better get going. I have a ton of homework, and Mom's been on my case about it."

Getting to her feet, she let her eyes sweep the river. With the approach of the western cloud bank, the swallows had disappeared and a brisk wind kicked up. Cautiously, just for a second, she let her gaze flick right to see Finlay hugging himself for warmth and watching her.

"Okay," he said, his eyes darting away, his voice defeated, almost mournful. "I'll see you, then. *If* you come here again—when I'm here, I mean."

"Yeah," said Shir, her voice equally defeated. "If you're here when I am, I guess. Thanks for the cupcake."

"No prob," he replied, looking out over the river. For a moment longer, they remained frozen, each staring across the water as if suddenly, abruptly, alone. Then Shir got a good grip on the pillar behind her, swung a reluctant leg around it, and began to work her way down.

Eleven

Seated on a parking barrier at the edge of the student parking lot, Shir was eating a tuna sandwich and watching Eunie Jahenny. It was Monday lunch hour and another warm day, which meant the school grounds were swarming with students. Here in the parking lot, there were at least fifty, divided into the usual cliques—the jocks congregated at the center of the lot, tossing a football back and forth, the preps in a boisterous huddle closest to the school, and at the lot's opposite end, next to an overgrown hedge that skirted a low-rent apartment building, Eunie and her friends. Ensconced in the back of an old Chevy pickup, they were swigging a one-liter bottle of Coke and passing a cigarette.

Well, maybe *a cigarette,* thought Shir, running her gaze over them again. *And make that* maybe *on the pop, too.* Fifteen minutes ago, she had been walking past the parking lot, intending to spend the lunch hour at a nearby park, when she had spotted Eunie, and, curious, taken up her observation post. Since then, the group's initially rowdy conversation had grown decidedly languid. So had their body posture. And Eunie was just as languid as the rest. Slouched against the back of the cab, she was nuzzled in against a tattoo-obsessed guy, exchanging sweet nothings while the pickup's radio blasted Lady Gaga.

Whatever it was that Mr. Tattoo was whispering into her ear, however, it hadn't changed Eunie's perennially bored expression—she looked, mused Shir, about as excited as she had while talking to Mr. Anderson in the store. But that was probably due to the contents of the cigarette she was smoking. In contrast to the group in the pickup, every other student in sight was chattering, giggling, and roughhousing as if they hadn't yet seen the end of junior high. To Shir's right, someone let loose with a Pepsi-filled plastic bag, and the weapon sailed harmlessly past its intended target before erupting against the Chevy's rear fender. Glancing down at his Pepsi-spattered jeans, the guy sprawled closest to the pickup's open end shook out his pant legs in disgust. Other than that, no one in the Chevy even blinked.

Class, thought Shir, as she scanned the pickup's slouched inhabitants. *These guys have class.* Maybe they weren't Collier High's top students; maybe they couldn't be bothered with hauling themselves out of bed to run 6 AM laps around a school gym; but they knew when to take something on and when to ditch it. *Yeah*, thought Shir, running her gaze over the tranquil group again. *It's important to know when to ditch something, when to let things just be.*

Thoughtfully, she raised her sandwich and took another bite. Seated five meters over from the pickup, she was hidden from view by an ancient Volvo; as a result, she hadn't been noticed by Eunie, or, for that matter, anyone else. Realistically speaking, as far as every other student in the parking lot was concerned, she could have been nothing more than an odd bump growing out of the Volvo's front end. But that, thought Shir, snorting quietly to herself, was better than getting stuck in dialogue with any of the jerks currently bouncing around the vicinity. *The future leaders of society*, she thought, snorting again. *Civilization.*

A nearby voice brought her abruptly out of her ruminations. "Hey, Sullivan!" it called. "Look over there, behind the Volvo. Isn't that your toonie babe?"

Instantly, Shir was on red alert and turning toward the voice. The first guy her eyes landed on was no big deal—a grade-twelve nondescript getting into a Toyota directly across from the Volvo, who went by the nickname "Tombstone." But next to him stood Ben, the maraschino cherries expert, and next to him, Wade Sullivan. The second Shir's eyes focused on that familiar face, she was on her feet, nostrils flaring wildly as she assessed possible escape routes. Backing up was pointless—the hedge might still be in the budding stage, but its branches were too dense to break through—and any forward momentum would take her directly toward Wade. Cautiously, she began to edge around the Volvo's front fender, intending to force her way between the hedge and the row of parked cars until she reached the street, but the next vehicle—a minivan—was parked too close to the hedge to permit passage.

"Oh yeah, blind love!" moaned Wade as she turned desperately to face him. "Hey, Tombstone, move over." Leaning past the Toyota's apparent owner, he pressed the car horn and the sound blared across the parking lot, cutting off conversation and drawing the carousing students' collective attention. Quickly, Wade sent out a few more toots. Then, straightening, he faced the expectant crowd, a broad grin on his face.

"What d'you say, kids?" he called out carelessly. "Our Ugly Contest winner is right over here. C'mon, everyone who voted for her, and we'll show her what it means to win."

Trapped behind the Volvo, Shir watched riveted as myriad eyes zeroed in on her—speculative eyes, calculating eyes, the eyes of a pack. In the ensuing pause, a breeze gusted across the parking lot, rustling shirt sleeves and lifting locks of hair; still the eyes observed, dispassionate ... considering what to do, what not to do.

"What does it mean when Dog Face wins?" called a guy somewhere to Shir's left.

"What does it mean when any dog wins?" someone else replied.

A snicker ran across the parking lot; a third voice hollered, "Who's got a leash?" and they started to close in. Panic-stricken, Shir pressed against the hedge. *Not everyone*, she thought, counting the leering faces headed toward her. *Yet.* From what she could see, the girls seemed to be staying put, leaning against various cars as they watched, and most of the guys were also hanging back, several uneasily shaking their heads. This seemed, however, to be as much disapproval as anyone was prepared to offer, and it hadn't been enough to stop the seven or eight guys headed her way—guys she would never have put together at a party or even in a school-hall conversation, but suddenly, here they were, united by common interest.

"What d'you say, guys?" asked Wade, walking up to the Volvo's back end and eyeing Shir coolly. "Anyone got a toonie? A quarter?"

In the short distance that now separated them, Shir could see how his eyes had narrowed and his lips pressed in on themselves. Wade was so intent, so focused, so *rigid*, she could practically see the blood pumping through his veins. *What is it with this guy?* she thought frantically. *Why does he keep coming after me?*

Without warning, an ear-splitting rev erupted nearby. Startled, Shir glanced left to see the Chevy pickup, horn blaring as it backed out of its parking spot. Gears crunched, the engine gave another raucous roar, and abruptly, the pickup was turning and lurching toward Shir, forcing the guys closing in on her to scatter. With a blur of red paint, it barreled past, allowing a brief glimpse of several smirking metalheads in the back. Then the pickup was gone, but not before Shir had seen who was at the wheel—Eunie, with the third finger of her right hand raised and pointing emphatically at the street.

Get the fuck out of here! Shir didn't need to be told twice. As her would-be harassers stared in stunned astonishment after the gunning pickup, she darted out from the Volvo and took off, heart thundering, arms pumping, mouth gasping for air, sweet air, *freedom*. Behind her, no one made a move to follow. Prey that was trapped, terrified, at the back end of the student parking lot wasn't the same thing as prey with obvious predators in pursuit, tearing along the front of Collier High and the row of staff-room windows that traveled the building's south wall. Which meant that for the remaining fifteen minutes of the lunch break, she was safe. As long as she didn't go near the parking lot, Shir thought wearily. Or the practice field. Or the front lawn, the school halls, the ...

Slowing her pace, she crossed the street, walked a block east, and settled down with her back to a fire hydrant to finish the rest of her lunch.

As soon as afternoon classes let out, Shir headed for the bike rack, unlocked the Black, and took off. Jeers and taunts followed her down the street, but she ignored them, pedaling in a manic blur past chattering students, women with baby strollers, and parked cars. Jacket unzipped and gym bag hanging precariously from one shoulder, she flew, halfway between earth and sky, the contempt she had endured all day and the bliss that awaited her at the end of it. *Yeah, bliss*, she thought, pedaling furiously onward. A bit of the magic fluid pouring down her throat—that was what she needed. It had been three days since her last beer, three long, miserable days, and her body was crying out for a Molsons, a Labatts, even a goddam Moosehead ... from wherever the hell they made it.

Turning down the alley to Gareth's place, Shir locked the Black to a hydro-pole support wire and pushed open the backyard gate. With her first visit, she had started a practice of leaving the gate open behind her—*wide* open—and today, like always, she pushed it as far back as it would go before entering the yard. Next, she walked slowly toward Gareth's door, keeping her eyes peeled for anyone who might be lurking behind a tree or in the shadows at the side of the house. A few times she had seen other guys, losers like Gareth, sitting with him on the stoop, and then she hadn't come into the yard, just closed the gate again, and kept going. Even with no one here but Gareth, the place gave her the creeps, weird little ghosties hovering in the air. Old houses, she thought, shivering, that were decrepit and ramshackle should be torn down—no exceptions. Pulling her jacket closer, she took one last look around and knocked on the door.

Gareth answered immediately, opening the door just as she was jumping off the stoop. *Weird!* thought Shir, her heart pounding as she backed up several steps. On each of her previous visits, Gareth had stopped to peer through the venetian blind before opening the door. The guy creeped her out big time.

"Thought you might come today," he said, eyeing her blearily. As usual, he hadn't shaved, and his sweatshirt looked as if he had been sleeping in it. "Haven't seen you since Friday."

"Been sick," Shir lied automatically. "I need a couple of beers."

"Sure, sure," Gareth said easily. "I've got two here for you. Two Molsons. Right here on the kitchen table."

"Oh, yeah," said Shir, taking another step back. "And how much are you charging today?"

Before answering, Gareth slid his eyes slowly down to her

chest. "Four dollars and fifty cents per can," he said, clearing his throat. "Or maybe I could let you have them for two-fifty each, *if* you come inside to get them."

Stunned, Shir gaped at him. *Four-fifty a can!* she thought wildly. It was crazy—highway robbery.

"Might even make it to two bucks even," Gareth added carefully, his eyes sliding even lower, "*if* you sit down and chat for a bit."

Shir's throat tightened. That she needed a beer, there was no question; she was practically going into the shakes at the thought of her first slurp. And she had ten bucks on her, so she could afford two cans. But $4.50 each—the thought of it made her stomach clench.

"What do we have to talk about?" she asked warily.

"Oh, anything," Gareth said casually. "You make it up, I'll just listen."

"*Just* listen?" asked Shir.

"Yeah, yeah," said Gareth, stepping back. "*Just* listen. Promise."

Shir hesitated. She didn't like the thought of this—it gave her an ugly feeling, as if a dark, hairy monster was emerging from the back of her neck. On the other hand, it would save her five bucks ... six, if she sat down at the table and talked. Cautiously she ran her gaze over Gareth. He looked wasted, worse than usual, as if he hadn't slept in days. Which meant, she reasoned hastily, that he was probably not at his best, a bit slow on the uptake. Tired out like that, she should be able to beat him to the door if he tried anything. And anyway, what would five minutes' conversation hurt her? They could talk about the weather—it didn't have to get personal. Afterwards, she could put the six bucks she had saved toward replacing the runners she had lost at Dana Lowe's party.

"All right," she said reluctantly. "Just for a bit."

"Just for a bit," Gareth echoed blandly, holding the door open. "Come on in."

Sinkhole widening in her throat, Shir stepped over the threshold. Immediately, she was hit with the dense odor of moldy bread, garbage that needed to be taken out, and obviously overdue laundry. But there, sitting on the table as if waiting for her, were two cans of beer—Molson Canadian, the magic fluid.

"Go on," said Gareth to her right. "They're yours, two-fifty each—if you want them."

Shooting him a glance, she saw his hand resting on the doorknob. It looked casual enough, that hand, just sitting there gently, not as if it was about to pull the door shut or anything. Uneasily, Shir's eyes flicked back to the beer on the table. Just a few more steps, she thought longingly, and it would be hers—two cans of the magic, *magic* fluid. Again, she glanced at Gareth's hand on the doorknob, then back to the beer on the table. Choices, she thought bleakly. Life was made up of choices: magic fluid or no magic fluid. Swallowing hard, she started toward the table.

Instantly, Gareth slammed the door. Then he was on her, jumping her from behind and shoving her to the floor. But

Shir was ready for him, half-turning even as he tackled her, and the first thing she went for was his eyes, digging a finger deep into a tear duct and raking it across his cheek. Letting out a howl, Gareth clutched his face, and she stumbled backward, out of the stench of rancid sweat that surrounded him and up against the sink. Behind her something clattered loudly, and she whirled to see a large pot wobbling on the edge of the counter. Without stopping to think, she picked it up and thunked it hard against Gareth's head. Silently, his eyes rolling upward, he sank to the floor.

Blood thundering through her body, Shir stared down at him. *Is he dead?* she wondered faintly. *Did I kill him? No*, she realized, almost swooning with relief—tiny sounds were coming out of his mouth so he couldn't be quite dead, at least, not yet.

Which meant she had to get out of there, and fast. Darting to the table, Shir scooped up the beer and took off for the door. But when she turned the doorknob, the door jerked open a few centimeters, then caught on the chain-lock Gareth had slid into place. Swearing loudly, Shir slammed the door, undid the lock, and yanked desperately at the knob. This time the door opened easily, and there beyond it lay the outside world with its vast sweet air, sunshine, and beckoning gate.

Legs suddenly weak, Shir stumbled over the threshold and was halfway across the yard before she remembered: *$2.50*. Gareth had said $2.50 per can if she came inside, and $2 if she sat and chatted.

Well, she thought, continuing on grimly, *he doesn't deserve it. Not after what he did.*

But, the thought came back at her remorselessly, *he's your main supplier. You're going to need beer again, and soon. And you're going to have to buy it from him.*

Just inside the open gate, Shir came to a halt. Slowly she unzipped her gym bag, set the two cans of beer inside it, and placed the bag next to the fence. Then, heart in mouth, she tiptoed back across the yard and peeked through the open door. Relief flooded her as she saw, not a corpse, but a moaning Gareth, now seated slumped against the wall and clutching his head. A thick welt was rising on one cheek and his left eye swelling badly, but both were open.

Sensing her presence in the doorway, he turned his bleary gaze toward her. For three short breaths they remained like that, silent and staring at each other.

"Five bucks," Shir said finally, digging into her pocket for a five dollar bill. "You said $2.50 a can if I came inside, and I want them both."

Laying the money carefully on the stoop, she backed up, turned, and ran for her gym bag and the open gate.

Above the sink, the clock ticked. Across the table, Mom and Stella talked. Head down, Shir sat listlessly pushing a spoonful of macaroni around her plate as her sister regaled their mother with tales about her afternoon gym class. An affectionate smile on her lips, Janice Rutz nodded as Stella animatedly recounted her scintillating conquest of the box horse and parallel bars.

From the way she was describing things, Shir thought resentfully, Stella could have been first in line for the next Olympic gymnastics team.

Shir, on the other hand, had dropped Phys Ed as soon as it was no longer a requirement. Even though the classes were segregated, she had discovered way back in junior high that girls were as skilled as guys at getting in their digs. Without warning, locker rooms could morph into an obstacle course of elbows and stuck-out ankles, taunts and jeers that were all the worse when you were dressed only in a bra and panties ... and sometimes not even that. Shir hadn't taken a shower after gym since the time in grade nine when she had turned off the tap to discover her jeans and T-shirt stuffed down a nearby toilet. The toilet had been flushed so the water was clean, but the comments she had gotten as she had pulled on her sopping clothes had contained their own kind of filth.

Today, after escaping Gareth's kitchen, she had unlocked the Black and taken off at top speed in the direction of the river. But within ten meters, she had skidded to a halt, pulled one of the beers out of her gym bag, and popped the tab. A touch of the magic fluid, that was what she had needed—so badly, her hand had been shaking as she had lifted the can to her lips. But the moment the magic fluid had first touched her tongue had been heaven. There was no other word for it—that honey-golden glory had poured down her throat like absolute nirvana. As she had glugged the can nonstop, the memory of Gareth's vice-like grip on her arms had faded, and after sucking in the dregs, she'd had to stop herself from reaching for the second can.

Hold off, she had coached herself silently. *If you sit down to supper looking like Gareth, Mom'll be right onto you. Save it for later—bedtime, dream time, magic hour.*

Resolutely, she had dropped the empty can into a nearby garbage bin, then headed to Myplace for twenty minutes of solitary peace, which she had spent massaging the sore spots on her arms and watching the swallows fly low over the water. *Dumb*, she had thought to herself as she'd stared out over the quietly rippling water. Going in there had been *dumb*—even though the day had been ugly, even though she had needed the beer. Never again would she walk through Gareth's door, no matter how bad things got. *Never.*

"One girl," announced Stella, pulling Shir's thoughts back to the present tense. "Well, her name is Annie Cooper and she's a bit of a dweeb ... Anyway, she was jumping over the box horse and her foot caught. She went flying off to the side and landed smack on her head. Lucky the mats were down. You should've seen the teacher take off toward her."

"Was she hurt?" asked Mom, pausing with her fork halfway to her mouth.

"Nah," Stella shrugged carelessly. "She got up and walked away. Sat on a bench by the wall for a bit. I think she takes drugs—she's always half gone."

Irritation buzzed through Shir like a slow fly. Anyone, she thought sourly, who listened to Celine Dion had nothing to say about anyone *else* being half gone. "Maybe she *was* tired," she muttered as Stella paused to swallow, then froze, realizing her mistake. Drunk or sober, it was never wise to interject a comment into a conversation between her sister and mother. Instantly the mood at the table shifted; forks were laid onto plates, glasses of milk set down, and two pairs of matching narrowed brown eyes focused directly on her.

"Do you *know* Annie Cooper?" Stella asked slowly.

"Nope," said Shir, slouching down protectively in her chair.

"Well, *I* do," Stella said emphatically. "And I think you should keep your opinion to yourself, especially about things you don't know anything about."

In the ensuing silence, Shir could hear the whir of the kitchen clock, keeping pace with the buzz in her mother's brain as she honed in on her elder daughter, assessing, calculating. *One beer*, Shir reminded herself. *One beer doesn't cause side effects.* Still, something had to happen here, and fast—a distraction, a decoy, a temporary peace offering.

"Maybe," she said reluctantly, aiming for the kiss-ass tone Stella particularly liked. If Stella was happy, their mother was happy. "I just thought Annie might be having a bad day. You never know."

Keeping her gaze lowered, Shir held herself tensely and waited out the silence that had descended onto the room. To her right, Stella forked a spoonful of salad and began to chew, bits of celery crunching between her teeth. Abruptly she set down her fork with a clatter. "Is that blood under your fingernails?"

she exclaimed.

Shir didn't need to be told which hand, her eyes zeroing in on her right to see dried blood caked under the second, third, and fourth fingernails. When she had gotten home, she'd brushed her teeth to get rid of the smell of beer, but she hadn't thought to check her hands for blood ... *Gareth's* blood.

"I fell," she mumbled, shoving her right hand into her lap. A wave of nausea washed over her—thick, deep, and ugly. "It happened when I was on my bike, coming down 25th Avenue. My front wheel caught in the train track."

Warily, Shir darted a glance at Stella, then her mother, to find them both still narrow-eyed and watching her. It was something they did every now and then, the two of them together—just *stared* ... as if Shir was a talking lump, or a weird disease one of the kitchen chairs had suddenly developed. Finally, wearily, Janice Rutz let out a burdened sigh.

"So, Stella," she said, breaking the invisible log jam of silence. "What happened after your gym teacher helped Annie?"

Stella perked up visibly. "Well," she said, reaching for the bowl of carrot sticks. "I decided to work on some cartwheels ..."

Shir's shoulders slumped in soundless relief. She had been dismissed, which meant the moment of danger had passed, leaving her once again in the twilight zone, fingerprints of pain throbbing softly up and down her arms as she listened to conversation carried on by the rest of the human race.

Twelve

The store was the usual busy combination of voices, ringing cash registers, and the scent of citrus and Tide. Head down, Shir wove carefully around customers selecting oranges and cauliflower in the produce aisle, then pushed through the *Employees Only* door. Glancing around the storage room, she saw it was empty. With a sigh, she slipped out of her jacket and turned to hang it on one of several hooks Mr. Anderson had installed next to the door.

Behind her, the store's rear door opened. Whirling, Shir saw two figures standing in the doorway, backlit by the afternoon sun—Mr. Anderson and an unfamiliar man. The uniform the man was wearing, however, was very familiar. He appeared to be a cop, one currently on duty, and as he came into the room, he was chuckling with Mr. Anderson as if they were lifelong friends. Wide-eyed, Shir stood gaping at her possible drug-syndicate boss and his buddy, the police officer.

"Ah, Shirley," said Mr. Anderson, his chuckle broadening to a jovial smile as he caught sight of her. "Here early, as usual. Hank, I want you to meet Shirley Rutz, the most reliable delivery person I've ever hired."

"Shirley Rutz?" repeated the cop, holding out his hand. To

Shir's surprise, his dark eyes honed in directly on hers, then held her gaze steadily without the slightest trace of double-take. "How in the world did Anderson sucker you into working for him?" he demanded with a grin. "Pleased to meet you. I'm Officer Tursi."

"Pleased to meet you, sir," Shir said hesitantly, taking the proffered hand.

"Old friend of mine," Mr. Anderson explained as Officer Tursi shook her hand. "*Very* old friend. Though, for the life of me, I can't remember how he suckered me into it. Must've been because no one else would play with him. We go back to high school, eh, Hank?"

"Rugger team," agreed Officer Tursi, beaming. "I was first string, and you were—"

"Water boy," cut in Mr. Anderson with a laugh. "No need to remind me, Hank. Come into the store and I'll get you that Coke you wanted."

"Yeah, and a Caramilk," said Officer Tursi, following him through the door. "And don't give me one of your measly seconds, the ones you can't sell because you sat on them by mis—"

The door swung shut, cutting him off mid-word. Absolutely motionless, Shir stood at the center of the storage room, watching it settle gently into position. *A cop?* she thought, astounded. Mr. Anderson was friends with a *cop*? A cop who liked *Cokes*? Well, that settled it then—he couldn't be a drug dealer. Whatever it was that the Fox and Brier's unlabeled package had contained, it hadn't been cocaine or ecstasy, or anything else that was snorted, swallowed, or injected. Her best guess was still icing sugar, or something even more obvious. It was, after all, the obvious explanations that were most easily overlooked in this kind of situation.

Yeah, she told herself sternly, *the obvious explanations, as in* MR. ANDERSON IS NOT THE KIND OF GUY TO DEAL DRUGS.

Soundless and invisible, a colossal weight rolled off Shir's back. A deep breath lifted through her and an enormous grin took over her face—a grin that seemed to have no boundaries, stretching past her ears to the far corners of the room. What in the world had she been thinking lately? she thought, exasperated. What kind of loser paranoid brain did she have operating inside her head? One that had been drinking too much of Gareth's beer, obviously. Now *that* was a guy who was a clear-cut drug dealer. Put Gareth in a police lineup with Mr. Anderson, and he would be chosen as the suspect every time.

Still wearing an ear-to-ear grin, Shir tied on a work apron and headed out into the store.

It was 7:45 that evening and Shir was easing the van into the curb, about to make her last delivery before heading back to the store. Today's clipboard list had been long and the addresses spread out across the city, with several located on unfamiliar side streets. The map in the glove compartment had been helpful, but even so, she had been forced to call Mr. Anderson once on the cell phone for assistance. So it was with a decided sense of relief that she turned off the ignition and climbed out of the front seat, then pulled the single remaining box from the back of the van. Its top was taped shut like all the others, but today, even Mrs. Duran's had been sealed. *And Mrs. Duran*, Shir told herself in a firm no-nonsense tone, *does NOT take drugs.*

The address was residential, a two-storey stucco house set back from the street. A bit on the ramshackle side, Shir thought, assessing it, and the porch windows were blocked with what looked to be stacks of old newspapers, but the outside light was on and the yard reasonably well lit. Climbing the front steps, she braced the delivery box against the wall and rang the bell. Then turning, she retreated to the front walk, where she stood observing the closed door. For a second after she had rung the bell, that door had felt like the one that led into Gareth's place—kind of creepy, as if weird little ghosties were flitting right through it. Nervously, she took a step back and hefted the box higher in her arms.

Inside the house, a door opened. Footsteps crossed the porch, a chain slid out of a lock, and the outer door creaked open. Lit by the overhead light, a man leaned out. Swarthy and muscular, he looked to be in his mid-twenties. Swiftly, his eyes honed in on her face, then widened and made a second disbelieving scan before dropping to the box in her arms.

"Bill's Grocer?" he asked brusquely. "Hand 'er over."

"Could you sign for the delivery first, please?" asked Shir, nodding at the clipboard, which lay on top of the box. Without hesitation, the man signed, then slid the clipboard under her arm.

About to heave the box into the man's outstretched arms, Shir paused as a female voice inside the house called, "You got it, Manny?" Instantly, she felt herself tuning in—the voice was familiar, but not one she could immediately place. As she strained to identify it, Shir felt a quick shift in her brain, and was visited with the memory of an old Chevy pickup bearing down on several high-school bullies. *Eunie Jahenny!* she thought, startled, as Manny lifted the delivery box from her arms. Beyond his shoulder, she caught a glimpse of someone standing in a dimly lit hallway—a girl who looked to be around seventeen, with long dark hair and a Molsons T-shirt.

It was Eunie, all right. "Yeah, yeah," replied Manny as she came up behind him. Leaning on his shoulder, she observed Shir without a flicker of surprise. "Professionally bored"—there was simply no better way to describe Eunie's expression.

"Watch it," grunted Manny, shrugging her off. "This box is heavy. Anderson's loaded it up with canned tomatoes again."

"Gotcha," said Eunie, stepping back so her face blurred into the porch shadows. "Bring it inside, okay? I've got to get going."

"Yeah, yeah," muttered Manny, his eyes returning for one last scan of Shir's face. "No tip tonight, honey," he said gruffly. "No spare change." Turning to go back inside, he said to Eunie, "Get the door, would ya? My hands are full."

"The brain works," Eunie replied tonelessly, watching him retreat down the hall. Briefly, as she reached for the doorknob, her eyes flicked across Shir's. "Hi," she said, her voice still toneless.

"Hi," echoed Shir, riveted, her mind filled with the memory of yesterday's revving pickup. "Thanks," she blurted awkwardly. "For helping me out—with those guys in the parking lot, I mean."

Eunie shrugged and ran her gaze up and down the street. "Wade Sullivan's a prick," she said contemptuously. "I would've run him down, no prob, but he's not worth the jail time."

"Yeah," Shir agreed breathlessly. Then, before she could think better of it, she asked, "Hey, do you live here?"

"Here?" demanded Eunie, the boredom slipping from her face in a moment of definite surprise. "Nah, I'm just in the neighborhood. Y'know—visiting."

Visiting for a Coke? thought Shir, just as Manny shouted from inside the house, "I told you, Eunie—shut the door. We've got business here."

Something crossed Eunie's face, but in the shadows Shir couldn't tell if it was a slide into deeper boredom or fear. "The master calls," she said briskly, straightening. "See ya."

"Yeah," said Shir to the closing door. "See ya." And then she was alone in the deepening twilight, listening to the house's inner door close as she stared at the crazily tilted newspaper headlines that filled the porch windows: FRAUD AT THE U.N., TWO DIE IN CAR CRASH, POLICE MAKE MAJOR DRUG BUST. Abruptly the light over the door went out, leaving her in dense shadow. Nervously she glanced around the yard. Weird little ghosties were definitely on the prowl now, darting here, there, and everywhere. With a hiss, she turned and started down the front walk, forcing herself not to break into a jog. Looming under a streetlight, the delivery van felt like an old friend. The moment she climbed into its front seat and shut the door was enormous, relief collapsing in on her from all sides.

What in the world, she thought, staring down the street, was Eunie doing way across town in a house like that? Sure, she wasn't one of Collier High's top scholars, but it was a school night. And what had Manny meant by "business"? What kind of business—the kind that made you so thirsty you had to go out looking for a Coke?

Nah! Shir told herself angrily as she jammed the van keys into the ignition. *You're making up crazy things again. Weird little ghosties are taking over your brain.*

Still, her hands were shaking so obviously, she could see their trembling in the van's shadowy interior. Placing them on the steering wheel, she gripped and released several times, then turned up the volume on the radio, eased the van out from the curb, and headed carefully down the street.

When she got off work, she headed straight over to the liquor store on 23rd Street, zooming along the by-now familiar network of interconnected back alleys. Tuesday evening, the store closed at nine, but there was generally a scalper hanging around the neighborhood for another half hour, waiting to catch latecomers, especially expected regulars like herself. Upon reaching the store, Shir cut across the parking lot and out into the alley that ran along its rear wall; finding this empty, she rode over to the alley one block east and discovered it also to be uninhabited. Putting on the brakes, she stared around in consternation. What the hell was going on? she wondered, peering at the row of black garbage bins that stretched ahead of her. There was always someone here, parked somewhere along these alleys, when she arrived Tuesday evenings—one of several competing scalpers who rotated between the city's various liquor stores. It wasn't raining tonight, and the weather was relatively mild. Why wouldn't they have waited for her like they usually did?

Muttering under her breath, she pedaled the full length of the alley to make sure she hadn't missed anything, but discovered nothing—no car with an open trunk parked behind the first garbage bin, the second, or any of the others. Then, as she got to the alley's far end, she spotted a vehicle pulled into the shadows beside someone's garage, just far enough in so it couldn't be seen until the edge of the building had been reached. *Cops!* thought Shir, recognizing the car's familiar markings. In the dense shadow, there appeared to be two officers, sitting in the dark with their headlights off as they waited for scalpers and their underage customers who should be at home on school nights, working on algebra equations.

"Shit!" she hissed. Making a rapid U-turn, she burned rubber so quickly, she almost lost control and collided with a backyard fence. But she recovered in time, veering past the fence with centimeters to spare, and taking off again at top speed. Shoulders hunched, she listened for the expected siren to kick in behind her, but the night remained quiet; even the neighborhood dogs all seemed to be indoors. Halfway down the next block, she pulled into a driveway and stood with her head down, panting in time to her thudding heart.

Cops! she thought again, staring back the way she had come. For two years now, she had been coming to this neighborhood to buy beer, and in all that time, no one—not a scalper or another customer—had expressed concern over the possibility of being nabbed by the law. People joked about it, of course, and they were careful—she had never, for instance, seen a potential customer drive up to a scalper's car with a stereo blasting. But this was a community known for its hostility toward the police, and while the odd person might harass a scalper into moving on, everyone knew it was unlikely anyone would call in a complaint. So why, thought Shir, her heart kicking double-time in her chest, had the cops shown tonight of all nights—a mere five hours after Mr. Anderson's cop friend Officer Tursi had walked into Bill's Grocer and shaken her hand?

Was there a connection? But what kind of connection could that be? And why—why would the police suddenly be so interested in Dog Face Rutz?

For a long moment, Shir stood staring at the empty alley as her heart slowed and her breathing quieted. If the cops were interested in her, she thought finally, coming out of her panic, they had an odd way of showing it. The officers in the hidden car must have seen her—for starters, her bike light had been on—and the way she had taken off would have aroused anyone's suspicions. But they hadn't followed her, so whoever they were waiting for, it wasn't a sixteen-year-old delivery girl from Bill's Grocer.

All in all, she had been extremely lucky, Shir decided, firmly dragging herself back toward common sense—she had almost landed smack-dab in the cops' laps and had gotten off scot-free. As for the encounter with Officer Tursi, it had been a coincidence, pure and simple. Coincidences happened all the time; they were a fact of life. Why waste time thinking about that when there were more pressing problems to deal with—like the fact her usual Tuesday-evening beer source had vanished, leaving no alternative except Gareth.

And Gareth, she thought heavily, was out of the question, at least for tonight. Which meant she was beerless until tomorrow evening, when she would be reduced to scouring the areas around the city's various liquor stores for a scalper selling the magic fluid within her price range. Heaving a sigh, Shir got back onto the Black and headed for home.

Thirteen

The school grounds were a cacophony of catcalls, laughter, and the occasional supersonic whistle. As Shir came around the building's south-eastern corner, she kept her head lowered and her eyes peeled for anyone casting more than a casual glance her way. Because this morning, all across Collier High, something murky was bubbling under the surface. The sense of it was vague, but she had become aware of it as soon as she had stopped at the bike racks to lock up the Black—a scattering of students tuning into her presence like bubbles rising in heated water. While it wasn't everyone, past experience had taught her that a pot coming to a boil initially displayed a few bubbles, then several more, and, ultimately, the pot's entire contents were cascading over the sides.

Whatever this latest threat portended, Shir was more than willing to bet that it was connected to a phone call she had received last night, soon after she had gotten home from work. Her mother had answered it, then handed over the receiver with a questioning glance, no doubt wondering who would be calling her social-reject daughter. Receiver in hand, Shir had stood alone in the kitchen, an ugly feeling oozing through her gut as she had waited for her mother to return to the living room TV. No one called Dog Face Rutz; no one, that is, except Mr. Anderson, and he only on Sunday afternoons. Cautiously, she had lifted the receiver to her ear.

The only sound she had heard coming from the other end had been breathing—not heavy breathing, as in late-night horror-movie hyperventilation, but calm and even. In fact the impression she had initially received was twofold—the person at the other end of the line was creepy, but also composed and rational, and that he appeared to be thinking his way toward some kind of conclusion. She could have hung up, but something had come over her, keeping her wordless and riveted, gripping the receiver and listening as the unidentified caller continued to breathe his way toward judgment. Then, just as she had been about to falter out a tentative "Hello," the guy had spoken.

"Dog meat," was all that he had said, quietly and clearly, and then he had hung up. His tone hadn't been angry and he hadn't slammed down the receiver; the whole thing had been closer to conversational than confrontational, simply a normal voice talking about normal things. "Dog meat"—what was the phrase, after all, but the average mundane judgment that the average mundane teenager would make upon seeing Shir Rutz's face for the first time?

The alarm bells set off by the phone call hadn't been due solely to the words "dog meat"—she had heard them before. But brief as last night's phone chat had been, the caller's voice had been familiar enough to reveal his identity—red-maraschino-cherries, mega-math-brain Ben. Which meant, of course, that the real force behind the phone call had been Wade. And Wade, as he had repeatedly proven over the past few weeks, had a grudge to pick with her ... several grudges, as he probably saw it by now. Throw in a few supportive buddies, and the situation began to take on the qualities of a pot coming to a boil. And so today, with her brain also approaching the boiling point, Shir had decided to avoid entering the school until the last possible moment, and was instead barreling along the building's southern face, knowing that at some point she was going to have to slow down; she was going to have to, in fact, come to a dead halt, and then they would be onto her.

It happened just as she reached a side entrance on the school's western flank—a sudden swarm of kids, laughter and commotion all around, and then abruptly she was jerked sideways, her head pushed back, and something wet and foul-smelling smeared across her face.

"Bull's eye!" a voice said hoarsely. "Got 'er."

Instantly, the crowd dispersed, footsteps stampeding in every direction as Shir bent double, gagging at the reek coming from her face. Without warning, the taste hit—a revolting ooze sliding in through her lips. Spitting wildly, she lifted an arm and rubbed at the stuff plastered across her skin. It came away easily, a slimy muck that took less than a second to identify—dog shit. What they had rubbed across her face was a fresh batch of dog shit. There at her feet was the empty plastic bag someone had used to transport a family pet's poop-and-scoop specimen to school.

The stuff was in her eyes; she couldn't see what was going

on around her, but she could imagine it—kids staring, a few tittering, every last one of them keeping their distance. No one currently in the vicinity had been involved, that went without saying, and perhaps one or two of them even felt sympathetic. Still, what these students were doing now was almost as bad— simply standing and observing as if she was merely an event in their lives, something that happened to other people, outsiders, never to *them*. Though she fought it, Shir's tears erupted then like a geyser, those of a ghoul phantom crouched howling on a rooftop while normal regular people huddled warm and dreaming in their beds below. Without a word, she turned and tore back the way she had come, barely aware of the kids scattering to create a path and a single teacher standing in a school exit, shouting, "Hey you! You there! Slow down! Don't you know how to behave in a civilized manner?"

She biked straight home, shoved the Black into the storage shed behind the apartment building, and ran up the back stairwell, taking the steps two at a time. Knowing the apartment would be empty, she began stripping off her clothes as soon as she got inside, and headed for the bathroom. The moment she turned on the tap and lifted her face to the sluice of hot water was like God reaching down to her, down through the muck and stench of civilization and saying, *This is my child; I have not forgotten her. This is my child; she belongs to me.*

It was a while before she reached for the shampoo. There under the nozzle, with liquid love pouring over her and heated vapor swirling, she didn't have to think, didn't have to remember, didn't have to be anything but clear, clean sensation—skin, the rush of warm water on skin, and the aching soundless cry that lifted free of the body, a transparent, beautiful angel returning to the god that had created it.

Gradually, the water began to cool, and memory to return in sick, twisted shapes. Though she washed her hair three times and thoroughly scrubbed her face, still the smell of dog feces clung to her skin. The guy who had done the actual smear job had zeroed in on her nose like a professional, instinct telling him that it would be the most difficult place to clear out, and he had been correct—though she held the shower nozzle directly to her nostrils and pointed the flow upward until she was gagging, still the reek remained, clinging like an invisible vampire and draining her of everything she needed to go on.

Finally, shaking and convulsing, she climbed out of the tub and sat on the side, hugging a thin towel around her shoulders. In the apartment's reverberating silence, water dripped from her tangled hair and air shuddered in and out of her lungs. Slowly, reluctantly, she allowed thought back into her brain. No question about it, she realized bleakly—school was over for the day. It would be simply impossible to go back. Tomorrow, perhaps ... *perhaps*. But as far as the rest of this morning was concerned, the weather was halfway decent and she had three cans of the magic fluid stashed in her underwear drawer—Miller Chills she had wheedled out of a neighborhood tough she had unexpectedly run into on her way home last night. That would be enough to get her through the next few hours, and as for what came after that, well, there wasn't much point in thinking about it now.

Still shaky, Shir headed down the hall to retrieve her clothes. As she picked her windbreaker out of the crumpled heap by the apartment door, she let out a groan. There on the right sleeve, stretching wrist to elbow, was a large slimy dog-shit stain. From the looks of it, Tide wouldn't be getting this one out, but after pulling on the rest of her clothes, Shir placed the three beers into her gym bag along with her lunch and descended to the basement laundry room, where she dropped the windbreaker into a washing machine and turned it on. Then she went out to the storage shed to fetch the Black. Coming back out, she almost ran into the building's caretaker, applying a fresh coat of red paint to the apartment-block's side entrance. A surly elderly man, he would have been certain to report her mid-morning presence to her mother, so Shir took off in the opposite direction, burning rubber down the alley and leaving behind the cantankerous old man, her shit-stained windbreaker, and everything else that went with civilization.

She stuck to her usual back-alley route and headed directly toward the river. As she neared the church, she turned into the driveway that led to the parking lot and locked the Black to the *Church Patrons Only* sign. Then she walked to the base of the bridge, taking care to stay out of the church-office window's sight line, even though the rector's car wasn't in its regular parking space. Climbing the first western arch to its peak, she got to work on a Miller Chill, popping the tab and letting the warm fluid ease down her throat. *Sip by sip*—that was how she was going to handle the magic fluid today, she decided. The morning was yet young, only 11:15, and the afternoon stretched relentlessly ahead with no foreseeable way to escape her thoughts. Once today was over, things would probably improve, the hurt not quite as fresh, a buried ache. At the moment, however, it was still new pain, and three Millers weren't enough to soothe it, not nearly enough. Since she wasn't up for another visit to Gareth yet, she had no choice but to take the first beer slowly, then sit for a while, letting the breeze play with her hair and the sunlight settle into her skin, telling her things about breathing and softness and the gentleness of air—how they all went together, how here, in Myplace, they belonged to her.

With a sigh, she opened the second Miller Chill and worked her way through it, drinking more intensely, in longer, deeper gulps. Halfway through the can, a warning surge in her stomach told her that she had better eat something, so, getting out her lunch, she munched a tuna sandwich, then climbed down off the arch and snuck behind a nearby shrub to take a private pee. By the time she climbed back onto the arch, she could feel her blood moving quickly and the heat pulsing in her face. *Fuck the bastards*, she thought grimly as she popped the tab on the third Miller Chill. *Think they can rub shit in my face and I just have to take it? Hah to that! Hah hah HAH!*

Lifting the beer, she drank it in one extended gulp, then drew back her arm and sent the empty can flying into the river. *The bastards!* she thought again, watching it float off on the current.

What she needed right now was a good old-fashioned tornado to deal with those dog-shit jerks. That was it—a huge, black, Kansas tornado that would come whirling down this river, pick up this bridge, fly it over to Collier High, and land it SPLAT! on top of Wade and all his bastard preppie friends.

Yeah, thought Shir with satisfaction— *SPLAT all of those bastards straight into the land of Oz ... somewhere over the rainbow!* Tilting back her head, she began to sing the familiar song—softly at first, in case the rector was within listening distance. But when she reached the chorus, caution deserted her and she started bellowing the words, repeating them over and over. On her fourth time through the chorus, it came to her that a bridge's support arch and a rainbow were the same shape; in fact, with a little imagination she could make believe that she was sitting on an actual rainbow. And down below, she thought grimly, *way* down below were all the bastards of the world, suffering in her shadow. Up here, so far above them, she was laughing—she was *laughing!* Inspired by a vision of Wade on his hands and knees, crawling around the rainbow's base and gazing pitifully upward, Shir bellowed even more lustily.

Abruptly, she broke off, thinking, *My god, what's WRONG with me? I'm on a RAINBOW and I'm singing "Somewhere Over the Rainbow," and I'm just SITTING here when I could be CLIMBING OVER THE RAINBOW to see what's on the other side!*

Eagerly, she got to her knees, but was immediately swept by such dizziness that she froze, clutching the arch beneath her and gasping. *Drunk*, she thought fearfully, staring at the river, which seemed to be doing a series of bellyrolls. *You are way too drunk to be climbing fucking rainbows.* Then, without warning, she was throwing up, chunks of tuna and three cans of the precious magic fluid spewing from her mouth. Wave after wave of the rancid gunk heaved up and out, spilling onto the concrete in front of her and streaming over the edge. Eyes blinded by tears, her brain in a dizzy drunken swirl, all Shir could do was cling desperately to the arch and let her stomach rule.

Finally, her gut eased up, and the blackness clenching her brain faded. With a wheeze, she opened her eyes and squinted into the blinding sunlight. There, just centimeters ahead, was a revolting smelly patch of the magic fluid. *So much for somewhere over the rainbow,* Shir thought dully, watching it slither downward. Carefully, making sure she kept a firm grip on the arch, she settled back against the pillar and closed her eyes. *Tired,* she thought helplessly, she was tired, her brain still buzzed and swinging back and forth like a pendulum. *And,* she realized with a sinking sensation, she had to pee ... enormously. Only she was far too drunk to even consider trying to make her way around the pillar and down the arch toward the riverbank.

Suddenly, Shir was shivering uncontrollably—deep great shudders that seemed to undo her from the inside-out. Then she began to cry, hot tears stinging her eyes and rolling down her face, even though she told herself that what had happened this morning was just another dumb joke, some moron's idea of a hoot-and-holler, and nothing worse, really, than anything else they had done. But the problem was that she could still smell it, the stench of dog shit clinging to her face as if it belonged there, as if it would *never* fade away. Relentless, the tears poured down Shir's face, and she could do nothing but let them continue, until her body grew tired of producing them and let her have some peace.

She had no Kleenex and ended up having to blow her nose on her sleeve. Then a painful stab in her groin reminded her once again that not all of the magic fluid had exited via her mouth. So, in spite of the fact that her brain was still rippling uneasily, she slung her gym bag over a shoulder, eased herself carefully around the third pillar, and started down the arch. When she reached the riverbank she didn't pause, but stumbled frantically behind the nearest shrub, where she barely had time to unzip her jeans before the stuff began pouring out. Whether she was throwing it up or pissing it out, she thought listlessly, the magic fluid was really doing a number on her today. Wearily, she pulled up her jeans and made her way back to the bridge. A glance at her watch told her it was 1:07, with several hours to go before school let out. A mild hangover was beginning to settle in, and even from here, at the base of the bridge, the odor of vomit tinged the air.

The rainbow is dead, she thought, turned to the first eastern support arch, and began to climb. When she reached the peak, she unzipped her gym bag and got out a bran muffin she had packed with her lunch. After nibbling her way through it, she simply sat, her head resting against the pillar as she watched the sun inch across the sky through half-closed eyes. Gradually, the bridge's shadow stretched east across the water and the air grew cool; in the distance, she could hear the city going about its business. Some time later, she didn't know how much, there came a soft sound overhead. Startled, she leaned out stiffly from the pillar and glanced upward. The sun had moved deep into the western half of the sky, and the blueness above her was now tinged with gray, forcing her to squint to make out the details of the face that leaned over the bridge's guardrail.

"Hey," said Finlay, grinning down at her.

"Hey," she managed to reply.

"I brought you a Twink," he said, holding a package of cupcakes over the rail. "Want me to drop it down to you?"

"No," she said quickly. "I'm drunk. Well, hung over. I'd miss it."

"Okay," he said casually. "I'll bring it down. Just a sec."

His head disappeared, leaving her blinking at empty sky.

Fourteen

S hir watched, her mind like dull sludge, as Finlay climbed the arch, then knelt and stretched an arm around the third pillar to hand her a Twinkie. "Hey," he said, flashing her a grin. "You're on my arch today."

Ducking her head, she angled the fall of her hair across her face before reaching for the cupcake. "I threw up on the other one," she mumbled, "so I moved to this one."

"Oh," said Finlay, obviously taken aback. "Well, I'll have to sit on this side, then. Shove over and I'll come around the pillar."

Panic blew, wide and heated, through Shir. If Finlay came around the pillar, she thought frantically, he would see. It would all be there, close up and personal—the regular day-in day-out ugliness *plus* the tears and hangover. For three thundering heartbeats she stared rigidly downward, then slid a meter from the pillar and swung her feet over the arch's east side. Filled with dread, her face turned desperately toward the opposite bank, she listened to Finlay work his way around the pillar and settle into place beside her.

"So," he said, his voice elaborately casual, "if you've been here long enough to get skunk drunk, you must've skipped the whole afternoon."

Eyes still glued to the opposite shore, Shir couldn't tell if Finlay was looking at her. But the warmth of his shoulder, now only centimeters away, felt enormous, and the breeze, which had been brushing her face for hours, suddenly seemed alive. Without warning, a heat flickered through her—soft and undefined, a gentle fire, touching her from the inside.

"All day," she mumbled, keeping her face turned away. "Decided to take it all off."

"Didn't miss much," said Finlay as he slid the second Twinkie from its package. "Today I learned about the Magna Carta and the proper way to make a basketball chest-pass. Problem is, I don't have a chest ... at least that's what I've been told. Anyway, that was my education for the day—the Magna Carta and the no-chest chest-pass."

Peeking around her curtain of hair, Shir flicked him a quick glance. Cupcake in hand, Finlay was studying it with a calculating grin, working out his plan of attack. He seemed awfully ... *chipper*, she thought, watching him. As if getting here with his Twinkies was a big deal. As if, on arrival, he had been expecting ...

At that moment, perhaps feeling her gaze on him, Finlay turned and looked directly at her. Instantly Shir's gaze darted away, but not before she saw the first second of shock widen his eyes. Immediate shame swallowed her, sick heated waves of it, and she turned to stare fixedly across the river. In the short silence that followed, everything pulsed—the air, her skin, the blood inside her skin.

Gently, tentatively, something brushed the side of her head.

With a gasp, Shir jerked away, so quickly she almost lost her balance. "Hey!" said Finlay, catching her arm and steadying her. "Hold still—just for a bit, okay?"

In spite of his request, she continued to pull away and, reluctantly, he let go of her arm. For one long, terrifying moment, they sat wordless, side by side; then in that vast uncertainty, Finlay reached out again. Shuddering, Shir tried to keep herself from whimpering as he lifted thin strands of hair from her tear-streaked cheeks. Slowly his gaze took in the tell-tale details of her face—the puffy eyes, the raw patches that underlined them, the tear smudges. And, if her nose was working right, the faint scent of dog shit still clinging to her skin.

"Whoa!" he said finally, his voice croaking. "What happened to you?"

"Hung over," she said weakly, trying for a shrug. "I already told you."

"Uh uh," said Finlay, withdrawing his hand. "I know hung over—my dad's permanently tanked. You're ..." He paused, searching for words, then added quietly, "Fragile. You feel fragile, like one of my granny's delicate china cups."

"Fragile?" Shir echoed disbelievingly.

"Yeah," Finlay said thoughtfully. "Something beautiful that you have to be very careful with, or it'll shatter."

Immediately, Shir's eyes filled with tears. "I'm not beautiful," she said gruffly, brushing at them.

"Of course you are," insisted Finlay, staring out over the water. "I could feel that about you the first time I met you.

You love trees. You can't love trees if you're not beautiful. You wouldn't even *know* about loving trees if you weren't beautiful."

Dumbfounded, Shir turned and stared at him. Calm and steady, Finlay gazed back over a large-but-not-gargantuan nose. *Beautiful*, thought Shir—it was the last word anyone sane would use to describe either of them. "Look," she said heavily, "let's just face it. On a beauty scale of one to ten, I'm a negative integer."

"Oh, that," Finlay said carelessly. "I'm not talking about bone structure. You want to worry about whether your cheekbones are a seven or a two, that's up to you. I'm talking about *beautiful*. You know—the way you think, the way you *are*."

Slumped into absolute weariness, Shir sat watching the water ripple gently past. "I'm a drunk," she said slowly. "A complete loser. My life is shit."

"Maybe," said Finlay. "But you're still beautiful. Like I said, I could tell that about you right away. Anyway," he added, his awkwardness obvious as he carefully patted her shoulder. "What happened to you? Why ... were you crying?"

Her breath was a hook, snagging her throat. The ugliness of what had been done to her that morning—she could feel it in her gut, heated, eating her from the inside. "Kids bug me at school," she muttered finally, fighting the urge to shake his hand from her shoulder. "Today was extra bad, I guess."

"What did they say?" asked Finlay.

"It wasn't what they said," she replied guardedly. "It was what they did. They ..."

She paused, swallowing.

"They what?" prompted Finlay.

Again she paused, the memory of the event coming at her so violently that, for a moment, Myplace vanished and she was back beside the school exit, bodies shoving in around her, panting, laughter, all that hate. Then the memory faded and Myplace moved in to surround her, a breeze nuzzling at her hair, the air opening freely outward.

"Well," she said, releasing a slow clutching sigh. "This morning some guy brought dog shit to school and rubbed it in my face."

Beside her there was only silence, not even the sound of breathing. Cautiously, Shir shot Finlay a glance and saw him staring at her, eyes wide with shock. "That's *awful*," he said, his voice trembling slightly.

More tears stung Shir's eyes. "I guess," she said, ducking her head. "They do a lot of stuff like that. They always have. But that was the worst that's happened to me, I think."

"Where were the teachers?" asked Finlay.

"It happened outside," Shir said hastily. "There were kids around, but the teachers were all inside."

"Didn't anyone help you?" pressed Finlay.

"No," said Shir. "They probably didn't want to get shit on themselves. Besides, it wasn't something one kid could stop. A bunch of kids swarmed me; it happened fast, and then they were gone. And, y'know, it doesn't really matter who they were, exactly. Something happens every day, and every day it's someone different. So, really, it's everyone. Not that everyone rubs shit in my face, I don't mean that. But no one ..."

She hesitated, considering. Never before had she told anyone this; she hadn't even allowed herself to *think* it. "Well," she said faintly, staring off over the river. "I guess no one is my friend, really. Not at Collier, and not at the schools I went to before Collier. Except for maybe a few kids I knew in the early grades—they were okay. They let me hang around, fool myself into thinking they were my friends. But it didn't last. In grade five, it all changed. And then it changed again, even more, in grade six. In grade six, no one would let me pretend anything. Somewhere over the rainbow was *over*. It's because of the way I look, of course. If I looked different, things would be different. *They* would be different."

"No, they wouldn't," Finlay said decisively. "They might treat you different, but they wouldn't *be* different. Not inside themselves. Not in their souls."

For a long moment, Shir stared off across the river, thinking her tired, aching thoughts. "Maybe not," she agreed finally. "I watch kids a lot, y'know—because no one talks to me and there's nothing else to do. And I see them doing to other kids what they do to me—not as bad, of course, but still ..."

She waited before continuing, trying to get an exact fix on what she was thinking. "It's as if there's something invisible above them all," she said pensively. "Some kind of huge, big mind that runs all of them, and it decides who's in and who's out. Y'know—who gets to be popular and noticed and the center of everything, or even just a *part* of things, and who has to sit on the sidelines and shut up. And most of it has to do with the way kids look. Bone structure, I guess, like you said. Kids who are a three or four on the bone-structure scale are allowed to be around and no one bugs them really, as long as they don't get any ideas about being center stage with the nines and tens. But the negative integers? The negative integers have to sit off by themselves, alone and drooling in a corner. There's no changing that, not if you're ugly. *Born* ugly."

From beside her came another immense silence. Listening to it, Shir swallowed hard, wondering if she could carry on, push deeper into it, go where she most needed to go. "I want to think life could be beautiful," she said softly. "I want to wake up in the morning, thinking I could be happy. But no one will let me. Everywhere I go, someone is always taking a chunk out of me. I feel as if they've stolen something from me. The people in my life, they've stolen who I am. And they've left me with something that I'm not. I don't know how to get myself back.

"But it's even more than that," she added helplessly. "Y'see, my mom hates me. She really *hates* me. So does my sister. Both of them, all the time, they hate me."

Beside her, the silence continued. Glancing warily to her right, Shir saw Finlay frowning intensely across the river. "Y'know," he said carefully, "every group needs somewhere to dump its shit. I figured that out in grade three, and I also figured out that a lot of the time, it was going to be me. The bone structure thing, y'know? And along with that, I figured out that I was going to have to make myself happen. Other kids had people to help them—their friends and families—but no one was going to do it for me. I mean, Dad's always drinking, and Mom ... Well, my mom's in a psych ward. Permanently. And Dad's always telling me I'm just like her. So it was pretty easy, really, to figure out that I was going to have to do it on my own."

With a quick breath, Finlay turned to Shir, his eyes so fierce she almost flinched. "You exist, Shir Rutz," he said fervently. "You're alive. Not just some *thing*, a piece of shit someone crapped onto this earth. And if you don't get that through your head—that you're beautiful, and worthy, and ..."

He faltered, searching for words, then burst out, " ... that the earth loves you, that the sky and air and *trees* love you ... then all you've got left is those kids rubbing shit in your face. But they're not everything, y'know. They're not everyone on this planet. Did you know there's a guy in the Czech Republic named Vaclav Halek, who's written over two thousand pieces of music—film scores, symphonies for orchestras, all kinds of things—and every one of them was inspired by listening to mushrooms sing?"

Absolutely dumbfounded, Shir stared at him. Not a thought budged in her head. "Pardon me?" she asked faintly.

"Yeah," said Finlay, his face flushed. "He's this guy who's so sensitive, he can actually hear mushrooms sing. He says each mushroom sings differently; they've all got their own individual songs. They won't sing them to just anyone, though—you've got to be someone they trust. So he's written down thousands of their mushroom songs, and arranged them into music for people to listen to. And, y'know, if he'd spent his time as a kid worrying about his *cheekbones* and what people *thought* about him, especially what they thought about him listening to *mushrooms*, he never would've written anything."

Open-mouthed, Shir gaped at him. Equally open-mouthed, Finlay gaped back. "Yeah," he repeated, his gaze darting out over the river. "Not one song—that's what he would've written. *Nothing.* But he didn't pay attention to what other people thought. He thought for himself. He made himself happen, and he happened. Thousands and thousands of songs is how he happened."

Side by side they sat, listening to the breeze, the sound of their own breathing. "This guy," Shir asked cautiously. "Vaclav—is he ugly?"

"I don't know about his bone structure," Finlay said emphatically. "But I know for sure that he's *beautiful.*"

Again Shir sat, listening to herself breathe. "The mushrooms," she said finally. "Do any of them sound like Celine Dion?"

"Celine Dion?" repeated Finlay, looking confused. "I dunno. I hope not. One of her is definitely enough."

"Yeah," agreed Shir. "Actually, I'd say one of her is more than enough." Lifting her Twinkie, she took her first bite. "Don't watch me," she muttered, angling her hair across her face as she chewed. "Make me feel like a goof."

"Not a goof," said Finlay, shifting his gaze politely to the river. "A moose head. A moose head from New Brunswick."

"Uh huh," grinned Shir, sucking half the icing from the top of her cupcake. "A moose head from New Brunswick." A sensation flickered through her as she spoke—lightness, happiness? The feeling was so unfamiliar, she couldn't place it.

"When I'm eighteen," Finlay said musingly, "I'm going to go to New Brunswick. I'm going to buy a lot of Moosehead beer and I'm going to drink it all, and then I'm going to go into the woods and listen to mushrooms sing."

"Huh," said Shir, trying to imagine it. "I'd come with you, except I don't know if I'll be alive that long. My mom's going to kill me when she finds out I skipped an entire day of school."

"Just tell her why," Finlay said quickly. "She couldn't possibly get mad if you told her what happened."

"Maybe," said Shir, letting the last sweet mouthful of Twinkie dissolve onto her tongue. The sugar rush was hitting her bloodstream, and in spite of her hangover, things were beginning to look up. "She said she'd kick me out of the apartment if I ever skipped again."

"She won't," Finlay said firmly, as if he had a private through-line to God on this one. "Not if you tell her why."

Shir took a long breath, letting air deeper into her lungs, *feeling* it. Sometimes Finlay sounded so sure about things she couldn't imagine being certain about. "Can you ...?" she started to ask, then hesitated, flushing.

"Can I what?" asked Finlay, his eyes intent, watching every moment of her face.

"Can you ... smell it?" faltered Shir. "The dog shit? Is the smell still there?"

Holding herself rigid, she tried not to flinch as Finlay leaned forward and snuffled dramatically at her hair and face. "Dove soap!" he announced triumphantly. "And Pantene shampoo, right? But nope, I can't smell the teeny tiniest whiff of dog shit."

A giggly sigh lifted through Shir, releasing a last faint bit of ugliness. It was gone. At least for the present, what had happened to her today at school was gone. Through his talking, and his Twinkies, and his snort-snuffling in her hair, Finlay had managed to reach invisible hands inside her and lift this morning's ugliness out and away.

"You're right," she said, studying an icing smear on her hand. "The whole world isn't like those kids at school. There's Vaclav and his mushrooms, and trees ..."

Shir paused, glancing sidelong at Finlay, then added, "And there's you."

A flush blew across his face, followed by the shy corner-hook of a smile. "Yeah," he said, his voice abruptly hoarse. "There's me."

Fifteen

It was the following day and Shir was sitting a block and a
half from Collier High, her back to a tree as she ate lunch.
The tree, which stood on the edge of someone's front
lawn, afforded a clear view for blocks; as long as she remained
on guard and kept her eyes peeled, no one was going to get near
her with a dog turd, a toonie, or anything else a sadistic teenage
mind could think up.

Sadistic teenage minds had already gotten at her today. The
encounter had taken place, not at her locker where she had been
on her guard, but as she had been motoring downstairs and
turning into the basement corridor that led to her homeroom.
Suddenly, there he had been, leaning against a wall and grinning
nonchalantly—blond, good-looking, grad-year Wade Sullivan.
Next to him had lounged Ben and several others. As soon as she
had caught sight of them, Shir had begun backing up, and had
been immediately rammed from behind as someone bumped
into her. Loud laughter had erupted from Wade and his friends,
the sound slamming Shir like an electric wave, a brutal body-wide
current of shock. Then, before she had been able to recover,
Ben had stepped toward her. Quietly, his face expressionless, he
had said, "Dog meat."

Without another word, the group had taken off down the

hall, but not before Shir had caught sight of the expression on Wade's face—calm and gloating, as if he had figured he could do anything he wanted to her, as if he had thought she *belonged* to him ... and his dog-catcher friends. The rest of the Collier slag heap hadn't been much better. While no one else had felt the urge to offload their comments directly into her face, snickers had followed her all morning, and the collective buzz inhabiting her classmates' brains had been almost audible: *Her entire face covered in dog shit! Stuff from a dog's ass on her face! From what I heard, it didn't improve the scenery much. Didn't make it much worse, either.*

If there was sympathy out there for her, reflected Shir, munching on an apple, no one was making it obvious. Not that this came as a surprise; last night when she had told her mother about the assault, Janice Rutz hadn't initially believed her ... or worse—hadn't cared. While Shir had stood hunched on the opposite side of the room, edging out her story in ragged bursts, her mother had sat staring at the dead TV screen, face sagging with weariness, but otherwise completely expressionless.

"I don't know what to do with you," she had said heavily when Shir had finally fallen silent. "It's always like this—another crisis. I'm ready to give up. It's not your fault, I know that, but it's not mine either, and I won't carry the load of it anymore. I won't."

Here she had closed her eyes and leaned back against the couch, face bleak and empty, as if speaking to the dead. "You'll never amount to anything," she had continued tonelessly. "You'll never make good, just like your father never did. You got everything from him—your looks, your personality. You're his kid, not mine. Go find him and get him to take care of you."

Blind panic had swung through Shir then, so intense she had almost blacked out. "Mom?" she had squeaked, swaying on her feet.

In response, Janice Rutz had opened her eyes and simply stared at Shir. "All right," she had said finally. "I'll write you a sick note. But I don't want to hear any more about this, y'hear? I just don't want to hear any more about it."

At that moment, from down the hall, had come the quiet but defined click of a closing bedroom door, followed by the sound of a lock sliding into place. If Janice Rutz had noticed, however, she gave no sign. Without further comment, she had written the note, handed it to Shir, and turned on the TV. That had been the sum total of her reaction—on the one hand, no sympathy, on the other, no eviction. As Shir had left the living room, she had almost been able to feel an invisible force pressing against her back, her mother mentally pushing her out of her sight, her mind, and, as much as possible, her entire life. To make matters worse, as Shir had come down the hall toward her room, she had been greeted by the sight of Stella's door, locked tight, with only silence behind it. There was just nothing between them anymore, Shir thought, letting the apple rest, uneaten, in her hand. Not with Stella, not with her mother. Everything was closed doors, locked faces. All things considered, a sick note was the best outcome to be expected from a woman who spent hours every day in front of the TV, worshiping bone structure. There simply couldn't be two more different people than her mother and Finlay Cowan. In a million years, Janice Rutz wouldn't be able to imagine something like a mushroom singing.

As Shir pondered this thought, her gaze fell on a small white object poking out of the grass on the other side of the yard. *A mushroom!* she thought, honing in on it with lazy interest. One of the season's earliest, it was nothing special-looking—at least, it didn't appear to be about to break into a rousing chorus. Still, she thought, observing it speculatively, it *was* a mushroom. And Finlay hadn't said anything about singing mushrooms having to be of a particular variety—with purple polka dots, for instance, or day-glow stripes. Which meant that if Vaclav-the-crazy-Czech-guy was right, this mushroom should be able to sing. *If* it trusted you, of course.

What kind of songs do mushrooms sing? she wondered, observing it, chin in hand. *Do they like one kind of music more than another? If there's a group growing close to each other, do they sing back and forth or work out songs together like a choir?* Getting to her feet, she crossed the yard and knelt before the mushroom. Close up, it appeared more beige than white, and its cap tilted slightly to the left. All in all, it seemed a rather unmusical mushroom. *But maybe*, thought Shir, observing it intently, *that's a disguise. After all, Vaclav said mushrooms don't trust most people.*

"Hello, mushroom," she said awkwardly. "I ... heard from someone that mushrooms like to sing, and I was wondering—"

At that moment, she became aware of a murky rumble vibrating the ground beneath her knees. Abruptly, a horn honked, and Shir shot to her feet to see a red pickup idling at the curb, its passenger door open. There in the gap, leaning across the seat and looking out at her, was Eunie.

"Got a sec?" she asked, her face deadpan.

For three deep-bass terrifying heartbeats, Shir stood frozen, her brain temporarily dysfunctional from shock. "Hey, come on," said Eunie, a tiny twitch crossing her face. "I'm getting a cramp here, holding the door open for you."

All thoughts of singing mushrooms vanished from Shir's head. Snapping out of her trance, she picked up her gym bag and climbed into the pickup, then sat, heart in mouth, taking in her surroundings—the crumpled McDonald's wrapper on the dashboard, the crumpled Pizza Hut bag on the floor, the crumpled Doritos package half-covering the gear shift. Eunie obviously ate on the run, and had the money to pay for it.

"So," Eunie said casually, letting the pickup idle at the curb. "What the hell were you doing out there—kissing Mother Earth?"

"Uh ..." stammered Shir, her mind blanking at the prospect of an explanation. "I was just ... looking at plants for my biology class. We're supposed to observe plant life. You know— mushrooms and weeds, things like that."

"I get ya," Eunie said tonelessly. "Mushrooms and weed. I've observed a lot of those."

"I wish!" said Shir, catching her meaning. "This was just a regular mushroom, but anything's better than hanging around school during lunch."

"Hanging around school or Wade Sullivan?" Eunie asked drily. "Mr. Prick of the Dicks—he's observed his fair share of mushrooms, but my guess is he was doing speed the day he came after you in the parking lot."

"Speed?" said Shir, glancing at her in surprise. "Wade does drugs? At lunch hour?"

"Monday to Friday," Eunie said coolly. "Tried almost everything, I bet—uppers, downers, inners, outers."

"Inners and outers?" repeated Shir, confused.

"Just an expression," shrugged Eunie. "It means anything that'll take you down the rabbit hole, like in *Alice in Wonderland*. Great children's classic—about a girl who takes drugs and has hallucinations. 'Eat me, drink me,'" she singsonged sarcastically. "Wade Sullivan eats and drinks a lot of things. He was probably circulating something in his bloodstream when he came after you yesterday, too."

Instantly, Shir was back in the memory, surrounded by heavy-breathing bodies as a voice grunted, "Bulls eye!" Ducking her head, she rode out an intense flush. "Maybe," she said hoarsely, staring fixedly at her runners. "I didn't see who it was—they took off too fast."

Beside her there was a brief pause, and then Eunie said quietly, "The word going around is that it was Wade who did the dirty deed. No surprise, really—he's one of the planet's primary shits."

Eyes still glued to her runners, Shir stopped breathing, her body completely motionless as she assessed the gentler note that had crept into the other girl's voice. *Sympathy?* she wondered, something twisting in her gut. *Or pity?*

"Yeah, well," she replied, her own tone hardening. "Next time I'll smell it coming."

Silence followed, and she glanced furtively sideways to see Eunie watching her, an appreciative glint in her eye. "You'll smell *it* or you'll smell *him*?" drawled the other girl.

"I'll smell shit," Shir said tersely.

"All right!" exclaimed Eunie, a brief grin lighting her face. Then, reaching into her shirt pocket, she pulled out a small ziplock bag. "For you," she said, handing it to Shir. "No mushrooms, just weed—of the shit-destroying variety. Because I know what a bad day can be like. Next time you have a bad day, smoke one of these and all the shit in your life will instantly vanish. If you like the feeling, come see me and I'll get you some more, okay?"

Stunned, Shir sat staring at the bag and the three hand-rolled cigarettes it contained. "Okay!" she echoed, flashing Eunie a grin.

"Okay," repeated Eunie, her voice abruptly toneless, the interest fading from her face. "Well, that's over and done with, and I gotta make tracks. Shit calls—you know how it is."

Taking her cue, Shir dropped the weed into her gym bag and slid out of the pickup. Then she stood, watching as Eunie gunned the engine and pulled out from the curb. Suddenly it came to her that she hadn't thanked Eunie for the gift, and she stepped forward, waving furiously. But if the other girl noticed, she gave no sign, and Shir slowly lowered her hand, watching as the pickup receded into the distance.

A girl making tracks, she thought admiringly. *A girl who never looks back.*

Later that evening, Shir was sprawled on her bed, the zip-lock bag on one knee. Beside her sat the kitchen phone, which she had plugged into a wall jack next to the bed. For over ten minutes, she had been playing with it, punching imaginary phone numbers into the keypad, picking up the receiver, and setting it back down again. It had been years since she had phoned anyone other than family, or, perhaps, a radio station with a song request, and the thought of calling someone up for the express purpose of extended conversation sent a wave of numbing blankness through her brain.

Hesitantly, she again picked up the receiver and scanned a phone number scribbled onto a small piece of paper. Her free hand hovered over the phone's keypad, retreated, returned to the keypad. Though she was alone with nothing but her thoughts, her palms were sweating and her heart kicking. *I am a zero*, she thought miserably. *Someone people do things to. That's never going to change. Why bother?*

For another endless moment, she stared bleakly at the phone, and then, with a gulping sigh, jammed the receiver firmly to her ear and punched in a sequence of numbers. Heart thudding, she listened to the phone ring at the other end. On the fourth ring, someone picked up.

"Hello?" said a voice.

"Hello?" replied Shir, her voice trembling. "Is ... Finlay there?"

"Finlay?" grunted the speaker. An older male, he sounded slurred, confused. "Just a sec, I think he's home." A loud clatter followed as the receiver was set down, and Shir heard him call, "Finlay!"

Almost immediately, there was the sound of footsteps, then the receiver being picked up, and a familiar voice said, "Hello?"

A tsunami of nerves hit Shir. Clearing her throat, she croaked, "Hi, moose head. It's me, moose head number two."

Instantly, Finlay's voice brightened. "Hi yourself, moose head!" he said. "I was wondering if you'd call. If you didn't, I was going to call you."

Giddiness swept Shir. "Hey, I talked to a mushroom today," she giggled. "I tried listening to it, too, but I didn't hear anything."

Finlay snorted. "I haven't been able to hear anything, either," he admitted. "I've tried listening several times, but I guess they didn't trust me."

Again Shir giggled. "I guess we're not the mushroom type," she said.

At the other end of the line, Finlay giggled back. "Nope," he said. "We're moose heads. Mushrooms probably get real nervous around moose heads."

"Yeah," said Shir. "Hey, y'know what? Right now, at this very minute, I am sitting on my bed with a bag of happy stuff, and I'm about to open it."

"Happy stuff?" asked Finlay, sounding confused. "What are you talking about?"

Glancing at her closed bedroom door, Shir dropped her voice. "Weed," she said quietly. "Someone gave me some today at school."

"Weed?" repeated Finlay, his voice sharpening. "Have you smoked it yet?"

"Not yet," said Shir. "I was planning to after I got off the phone with you."

A barely discernible sigh sounded at the other end, and then Finlay asked slowly, "Who gave it to you?"

"A girl named Eunie," said Shir.

"How well do you know her?" asked Finlay.

"Just a bit," said Shir. "I've seen her around school and we've talked ... well, once."

Finlay breathed in and out several times. "Does she do a lot of drugs?" he asked.

"Probably," said Shir.

Again Finlay breathed in and out, in and out. "I dunno, Shir," he said finally. "I don't know this Eunie, and I don't know why she would give you free weed when she doesn't really know you. But I've heard dealers give out freebies to get kids hooked. And some dealers lace weed with crystal meth without telling you, so they can get you hooked faster. Crystal meth does that—hooks you really fast—and it's hard to kick. It's not like weed; it runs you. Before I moved here, a guy I knew smoked some weed, thinking that was all it was, and got hooked on the crystal meth hidden inside. He was gone then; he was *nothing*."

A loud ringing in her ears, Shir stared at the zip-lock bag.

A voice floated into her head, Eunie's voice—cool, casual, professionally bored. *Real thirsty*, it said. *So I thought I would come in for a Coke*. And then, *Well, that's over and done with*.

What's over and done with? Shir thought suddenly. *What?*

Thin and tinny, as if coming from a long distance, Finlay's voice broke into her thoughts. "Shir," he said urgently. "Shir, are you there?"

"I think so," she mumbled, trying to get a grip. "Maybe."

"Are you going to smoke the weed?" he asked.

Shir breathed in and out, in and out. "What would it matter," she asked dully, "if I did?"

"It would matter," Finlay said quickly. "*You* matter."

"Maybe," she muttered, "and maybe not."

"You *do*," burst out Finlay. "You *do*, Shir. I *mean* it."

Alone in her room, Shir sprawled without speaking, staring at the bag on her knee. Without warning, she was so tired her eyes were going funny. The bedroom seemed to be reversing colors, light going dark and dark light.

"Okay," she said slowly. "I won't smoke it. I'll ditch it down the toilet."

"Promise?" asked Finlay, his voice cracking.

"Promise," Shir repeated obediently.

"Okay," said Finlay. "Do it now."

"Now?" whispered Shir. She felt so tired, her limbs so dense and heavy, she didn't think she would ever move again.

"I'm waiting," said Finlay.

She imagined him then, at the other end of the line, hunched over the phone, his odd face scrunched into a worried frown. *Intense*, she thought weakly. Finlay was so intense.

"Come on, Shir," said Finlay. "Do it now. *Right* now."

"Okay," said Shir. Numbly, she worked herself into a sitting position, then pushed the immense weight of her body up off the bed. Briefly the room swayed about her, light-dark, dark-light. "I'm up, Finlay," she said into the phone. "I'm going to put down the phone now, so I can go do it."

"Don't hang up," said Finlay. "Come back. When you've done it, come back."

"Yes," said Shir. "Yes, I will." Setting the receiver onto the bed, she walked out of her room, down the hall, and into the bathroom. There she opened the zip-lock bag and dumped its contents into the toilet. Dully, without a single thought passing through her mind, she flushed the toilet and watched the three hand-rolled cigarettes whisk out of sight.

Come back, she remembered Finlay saying. Turning, she walked back to her bedroom and picked up the phone. "It's done," she said into the receiver. "They're gone—all three of them."

"You mean it?" asked Finlay, his voice wobbling. "You're not pulling my leg?"

"Honest," said Shir. Slowly, sensation was coming back to her, the dark-light clearing from her head; she could feel herself breathe. "Finlay," she said hesitantly, "I'm glad."

"Me, too!" he exclaimed, gusting a sigh. "Yeah!" For a moment then, they remained silent, letting exhaustion ease out of them. "I'm sure glad we traded phone numbers yesterday," said Finlay.

"Just think what *might* have happened."

"Yeah," said Shir, breathing, just breathing.

"Well," said Finlay. "What are you going to do now?"

"I dunno," said Shir. "Algebra?"

"I'm reading this really cool story for English," said Finlay. "Want to hear it?"

"Okay," said Shir.

"I'll go get it," said Finlay. "It's in my room."

"Come back," said Shir, a tiny smile creeping across her mouth. "Come back when you've got it, moose head."

The grin that lit Finlay's face was so loud, she could hear it at her end of the line. "Promise, moose head," he said, and set down the phone.

Sixteen

The store buzzed with the regular Friday after-work rush. Pushing open the *Employees Only* door, Shir peered into the back aisle, then wheeled out a trolley loaded with boxes of canned vegetables. At the third aisle, she steered the trolley into position and got to work, shifting the cans that were already on the shelves to the front and setting new ones behind them—a practice designed to ensure nothing stayed on the shelf longer than its *"best before"* date. Though Mr. Anderson had been smiling when he had explained this system, she knew he expected her to follow it; several times since, she had seen him pick up a can from the front of a shelf and check its *best-before* date against those behind it.

As she slid cans onto the shelves, people came and went in the aisle, picking up tomato soup and kidney beans, rustling packages of pasta. After several minutes, a mother with three children came by, the youngest trailing behind and stopping to stare up curiously at Shir.

"Hello," she said, her eyes wide. "Are you a goblin from the deep, dark woods?"

Instantly, Shir froze, staring rigidly ahead as invisible heated waves swarmed over her. Then, inexplicably, they faded, and she found herself turning to the girl and saying, "No, not a goblin. I'm a moose head."

The child continued to gaze up at her, expression confused but intent, her eyes ... *Not mean*, thought Shir, studying the little girl's face. *Just curious. Honestly curious.*

"A moose head?" repeated the child. "What's that?"

Shir considered, a small smile teasing her lips. "It's sort of like a goblin," she admitted, "but not from the deep, dark woods. A moose head is from New Brunswick."

"New Brunswick," muttered the girl, frowning slightly. Then, appearing to lose confidence, she turned and ran after her mother, crying, "Mommy, Mommy—what's a moose head?"

A full-fledged grin leapt across Shir's face, and, taking a deep breath, she got back to work, slicing open a box of canned corn. But, just as she was lifting out the first few cans, a familiar voice broke into her thoughts. "Well, what d'you know?" it demanded from the front of the aisle. "It's Dog Face, stocking shelves in a store because it's her job. Hey, Dog Face—you know what? You're good at that. Real good. So good, I'm going to give you a toonie for it."

Shir's head snapped up and she turned to see Wade approaching, a fixed grin on his face. This time he seemed to be alone, without any sign of maraschino-cherries Ben, but still Shir stepped instinctively backward, bumping into the trolley and sending it rolling toward the rear of the store. Boxes of canned goods slid dangerously; letting out a cry, she chased after the trolley, but before any damage could take place, a man stepped around the end of the aisle and stopped the trolley neatly with his foot.

"I'm sorry," moaned Shir, coming to a halt beside him. "It was an accident, I—" Abruptly she fell silent, a new wave of panic hitting as she realized that the man thoughtfully readjusting the boxes on the trolley was Mr. Anderson. A carefully serious expression on his usually smiling face, he was looking past her, his gaze fixed on the approaching Wade.

"You here to buy something?" he asked, his voice neutral and contained.

"Um ... yeah," said Wade, coming to a halt and glancing at Shir with the same fixed grin. "Just looking for the maraschino cherries, sir."

"They're in the next aisle," said Mr. Anderson. "Halfway down, second shelf. You're welcome to buy as many as you'd like. But you're not welcome to come into my store and harass my staff. Is that understood?"

Slowly, Wade's grin faded. "Um ... yeah ... sir," he said, backing up a few steps. "I just so happen to know her from school. I wasn't harassing her—just saying hi, that's all."

"Next aisle," Mr. Anderson repeated tersely. "And then the till and you're out of here."

"Yes, sir," said Wade, turning and retreating up the aisle. Within seconds, the bell over the door announced his departure from the store.

"Good riddance," muttered Mr. Anderson, a grim look on his face. "I'll tell Cathy to keep an eye out and call me the next time she sees him come in."

Wordless, Shir stood with her gaze glued to the floor. "He wasn't *exactly* harassing me, sir," she faltered, not wanting her boss to think that what had happened would in any way interfere with her ability to do her job. "He was just—"

"I heard what he said, Shirley," said Mr. Anderson, placing a hand lightly on her shoulder. "That was definitely harassment, and I won't have it in my store—especially when it's aimed at one of my best staff. Come on now, I've got some deliveries waiting for you out back."

Turning, he headed to the storage room and Shir followed, blinking back a rush of tears. How had it happened, she thought fiercely, that someone like her had ended up working for someone like Mr. Anderson? He was simply the best boss in the world and she didn't deserve him—*really* she didn't. Hastily brushing at her eyes, Shir ducked through the door Mr. Anderson was holding open for her and saw a long row of boxed delivery orders sitting on a counter on the far side of the room—twelve, to be exact.

"Another full evening of deliveries," grinned Mr. Anderson, handing her the van keys and cell phone. "How about you start taking them out to the van while I finish taping these last two?"

As he spoke, he picked up some tape and began sealing the top of a box. Beside him, Shir reached for a different box, then hesitated. "Mr. Anderson, sir," she said slowly.

"Yes, Shirley?" he asked, smiling at her.

"Well," she said, swallowing carefully. "I was wondering why you're taping *all* the boxes shut these days."

For a second, Mr. Anderson seemed to freeze, and then he said casually, "Oh, well, we can't have another accident like the one you had at the Fox and Brier, can we?"

"No, sir," said Shir. "It's just that I remember that you used to tape some of the boxes shut, but not all of them. Why ..." Again she hesitated, then blurted awkwardly, "Well, sir, why did you used to tape only *some* of them shut?"

Before she had even finished her question, Mr. Anderson's expression began to change, his eyes narrowing, mouth tightening. Suddenly, the man Shir was looking at felt like a total stranger. Clearing his throat, Mr. Anderson said briskly, "It gets busy in the store as you know, Shirley. I'm constantly being interrupted. Sometimes I get all the boxes sealed, and sometimes I don't. Now how about you start carrying boxes out to the van *like I asked* while I finish sealing this last one?"

Shir stopped breathing and stood frozen, her hands in the act of reaching for a box. *Fear,* she thought, her mind racing. No question about it—what she had just seen on her boss's face was full-out fear, caused probably by the fact that she had noticed something she wasn't expected to, or if she did, was *not* expected to mention.

Head down, she whispered, "Yes, sir," and carried a box out to the van.

Having loaded the last few boxes, she put the van into gear and headed down 12th Street. The first three addresses on her delivery list were in the downtown core—a specialty coffee shop, a clothing boutique, and what appeared to be a consulting firm. Refusing to think about the obvious—why would any of these businesses require a grocery order, especially late on a Friday afternoon—Shir completed the deliveries with a smile and pocketed her tips. Then, climbing into the van, she hesitated only slightly before heading in the direction of the river. Within minutes, she was turning into the driveway beside the church and easing down the slope into the parking lot. A quick scan of the walking bridge brought a grin to her face, and she pressed one hand hard on the horn.

"Hey, moose head!" she called as Finlay's startled face peered around the third eastern pillar. "I'm making some deliveries for my job. Want to come along?"

"Sure!" he shouted. Scrambling to his feet, he worked his way down the arch and trotted over to the van.

"Put on your seatbelt," Shir said importantly as he got in. "And remember—whenever we stop for a delivery, you hit the floor. If someone saw you, I could get fired."

"Yes, boss," said Finlay. Clicking his seatbelt shut, he watched curiously as she drove up the driveway. "So what do you deliver?" he asked. "Pizza?"

Idling the van at the end of the driveway, Shir shot him a sidelong glance and a brief warmth flared in her face. Today, with Finlay, felt different. Their Wednesday afternoon conversation at the bridge, plus yesterday's phone call, had changed things. Now there seemed to be a kind of ... *energy* between them, she realized, confused—invisible but definitely present, as if the air was humming gently to itself.

"I work at a corner store," she explained as she steered the van into the street. "It's called Bill's Grocer. Part of my job is making deliveries. Well, actually, that's most of it these days. I used to stock shelves and sort produce, too, but lately, it's been pretty much just deliveries. There's one of my regular stops coming up now."

Turning the van into the alley behind a small strip mall, she parked and pointed to an open doorway. "Joe's Pizza," she announced. "That means it's hit-the-floor time until I tell you it's okay to come back up."

"No prob," said Finlay. "Hitting the floor now." Undoing his seatbelt, he slid to the floor and huddled, grinning, against the opposite door. With an answering grin, Shir climbed out of the van, pulled the order for Joe's Pizza from the back, and carried it to the pizzeria's rear entrance.

"Hello!" she hollered through the screen door. "Bill's Grocer, delivery." Within seconds, Lucille appeared, her plump face all smiles as she dropped a toonie into Shir's hand and accepted the box. *A taped-over box*, thought Shir, watching the woman carry it down the short hall that led to the kitchen. The tops of Joe's Pizza's orders had always been taped shut. Pocketing the toonie, she shrugged off the thought and returned to the van.

"Okay, it's safe," she said as she got in. "You can come up for air now."

"Up is good," said Finlay, returning to his seat. "Where are we headed next?"

Picking up the clipboard, Shir felt her heart kick once, hard, as she read the next address. "The Sunnyville Rec Center," she said, a sick feeling oozing through her gut.

"The Sunnyville Rec Center," repeated Finlay. "What's wrong with that?"

"Nothing," mumbled Shir, reaching for the ignition.

"Yes, there is," Finlay said quietly. A short pause followed, Shir sitting motionless, her gaze fixed dead ahead as Finlay studied every millimeter of her face. Abruptly, he asked, "This has something to do with what you said about someone using you, doesn't it?"

Panic hit Shir, acidic, intense. "No," she said tersely, turning the ignition. Then, bringing her foot down hard onto the gas pedal so the van lurched out of its parking spot, she added, "And I never said they were using me *for sure.*"

She headed down the alley and onto the street, the city flowing past, familiar and at the same time alien, like the face of a suddenly panic-stricken, lying boss. Silent, Finlay slouched opposite, knees propped against the dashboard as he observed the passing scenery. After several blocks, he ventured, "Okay, how do you think they *might* be using you?"

Again, Shir tasted acid, but the wave of loneliness that followed was worse. "Drugs," she said tightly. "In those boxes behind you. They put them in there and I deliver them—I *think.*"

Darting a glance at Finlay, she saw his eyes widen. "You're delivering drugs?" he demanded.

"I said *maybe,*" snapped Shir. "I don't know *anything* for sure."

Several more blocks went by, and then Finlay asked, "What makes you think it's drugs?"

Mind racing, Shir thought about what to say, what not to say. Then, hesitantly she began to explain—about the Fox and Brier unlabeled package, odd deliveries like the Sunnyville Rec Center and Manny's rundown house, and the coded way Eunie had asked Mr. Anderson for a Coke when she had come into the store. "I dumped the weed down the toilet last night like I told you on the phone," she said slowly, "so I don't know if there was crystal meth in it or not. But like you said, it's weird that Eunie would give me free weed, and she does know Mr. Anderson and Manny. If I am delivering drugs for them, I can see how they might want to get me hooked. I drink a lot ..."

Pausing, she stared out the window, then added, "Too much, I know. Way too much—all the money I make goes to pay for it. I've hardly done drugs, though—mostly because they're too expensive. If I got hooked on crystal meth, I'd need this job more than ever to pay for it." A sigh came out of her, long and shuddering. "The more I needed it," she said, her voice frightened, "the more they could be sure I'd keep my mouth shut."

A scowl crossed Finlay's face and he hugged himself, as if for comfort. "Do you think every box you deliver has drugs in it?" he asked.

"Not all of them!" exploded Shir, thinking of Mrs. Duran. "For sure some are just regular deliveries. No, they're using the normal delivery run as a cover for drug drop-offs, and lately, there've been more and more of them. At least, I *think* that's what they're doing. I *think*," she stressed heavily. "I don't *know*."

"Okay," said Finlay, turning in his seat to look into the back of the van. "Let's find out."

"Find out!" echoed Shir, her voice shooting upward. "What d'you mean?"

"The Sunnyville box," said Finlay, still gazing into the back of the van. "That would be the one to pick. If there is a box that has drugs in it, it would be that one, wouldn't it?"

"You're crazy!" gasped Shir, turning to stare at him. "We *can't* open a box—they'd be able to tell. I'd get into trouble for sure."

"They couldn't tell if we opened the bottom," protested Finlay. "Just stop at a store and we'll buy some tape to fix it up after we've checked what's inside. I've got enough money on me. Come on," he added reasonably. "If they're not hiding anything, it won't matter if we open a box, right? And then you'll know one way or the other. You'll know for *sure*."

A loud roaring in her ears, Shir clung, white-knuckled, to the steering wheel. *Open a box,* she thought, her hands shaking, her arms, even her legs, giving off quick shudders. *A box of the forbidden.* Several blocks went by as she thought about it some more ... all those boxes stacked in the back of the van, boxes of fear and knowing. In the distance, an Office Depot was coming into view; three blocks west was the Sunnyville Rec Center and Mr. Dubya-got-the-goods.

"Okay," she said shakily, turning into the parking lot next to the Office Depot. "But when you buy the tape, make sure it's good and solid. Packing tape isn't strong enough to hold the bottom closed."

"Sure," said Finlay and climbed out of the van. While he headed into the store, Shir drove to a deserted area of the parking lot, well away from other vehicles. There she called Mr. Anderson, and told him she would probably be held up by traffic for the next ten minutes. Then, crawling in among the remaining delivery orders, she located the Sunnyville Rec Center box, turned it upside down, and sliced the tape that ran along the bottom with the tip of a ballpoint pen. Taking a deep breath, she opened the flaps. Immediately, she saw what she was looking for—an unlabeled package like the Fox and Brier's, inserted between two cans of tomato juice.

The van's back door opened and Finlay climbed in. "Here," he said, extending a roll of wide transparent tape. "I asked a clerk for advice. This should do it."

Frozen into position, Shir was staring into the Sunnyville Rec Center box as if she hadn't heard. "Look," she quavered. Quickly, Finlay knelt beside her and peered into the box.

"That brown package?" he asked. "Between the two cans—is that it?"

Slowly, very slowly, Shir pulled out the package. Wrapped in brown paper and thoroughly taped at both ends, it felt as if it weighed about two hundred grams. "It looks just like the other one," she said hoarsely. "The Fox and Brier package."

"If it's cocaine," Finlay said softly, "it's a lot of money."

Wordless, Shir stared at the package. Her hands were trembling visibly. "I thought," she said hesitantly, "the last one might be icing sugar. Or baking soda. Something like that."

"I doubt it," said Finlay. "You could tell by the smell, though. Cocaine smells strong, like a chemical. Open it and we'll check."

"We can't!" gasped Shir, open-mouthed. "How would we wrap it back up? They would know for sure I'd opened it."

"I guess," Finlay said reluctantly. "But if it is drugs, shouldn't we take it to the police?"

A memory of Officer Tursi's grinning face flashed through Shir's mind. "No cops!" she spat, recoiling. "I just wanted to *know*, not get stuck in the middle of a drug war."

Silence filled the van as they stared helplessly at the package in Shir's hands. "Well," Finlay said finally, "now you know. It ain't icing sugar, and it sure as hell ain't baking soda."

"No," agreed Shir, jamming the package into its original position between the cans of tomato juice. "Hand me that tape, would you? I've got to get this fixed up and delivered *fast*. I called my boss and told him I was stuck in traffic, but we can't hang around here forever."

Closing the flaps, she took the tape from Finlay and resealed the bottom of the box. "Look in the glove compartment," she said. "There's a pair of scissors in there. I need to cut this tape."

"Okay," said Finlay. Getting to his feet, he opened the glove compartment and rummaged through it. "Shir," he said, his voice hesitant. "I don't see any scissors."

"Sure there are," said Shir quickly. "Next to the packing tape."

"There isn't any packing tape," said Finlay.

Heart thundering, Shir stared at him. Abruptly, it hit her—Mr. Anderson had removed the packing tape and scissors so she wouldn't be able to fix up another box if she opened it. "Oh my god!" she wailed. "How am I going to cut this off? I need scissors. You have to go back to the store and buy some."

"I don't have any more money," said Finlay.

Desperately, Shir stared at the roll of tape hanging off the upside-down box. "I don't have any on me either," she whispered. "What am I going to do? We don't have time to waste."

"Just a sec," said Finlay, turning back to the glove compartment. "There might be something else in here." Rustling, rummaging sounds followed as Shir stared at the box, trying not to lose it completely. "Aha!" Finlay cried triumphantly, holding a small object aloft. "This should work."

Returning to Shir's side, he handed her a penknife and she cut the tape. But as she examined the finished job, panic hit again—immense, overwhelming. "You can see!" she cried frantically. "Where I cut the original tape with the pen—you can see it through the new tape!"

Fists clenched, she was shrieking at Finlay, her brain a whiteout of fear. Wordless, he stared at the resealed box, a flush rising in his cheeks. "It's not that bad," he said uncertainly. "No one'll notice unless they look really close."

"Easy for you to say," hissed Shir. "They don't even know you exist." Repeatedly, she ran her fingertips over the bottom of the box, smoothing the surface of the tape. Maybe Finlay was right, she thought, trying to convince herself. The fix-up job wouldn't be obvious unless the box was turned over. And why would anyone turn it over ... unless they were getting suspicious and decided to check up on her.

"Well," she said weakly. Clambering to her feet, she was hit by exhaustion so extreme that all she could do was cling, whimpering, to the van's middle passenger seat.

"Are you all right?" asked Finlay, touching her arm.

Instinctively, she pulled away. "I guess we'd better get going," she whispered.

"I guess," Finlay said dully.

Without speaking, they took their seats and drove off toward the Sunnyville Rec Center.

Seventeen

Shir eased the van up to the curb and sat staring at the house to her right. Late into Saturday afternoon, this was the final address on her delivery list, and, unfortunately, it hadn't changed since the last time she had seen it—a two-storey ramshackle stucco, its porch windows blocked by stacks of old newspapers, and weird little ghosties flitting all around it. Even in broad daylight, the place gave her the creeps; just looking at it made her want to put the van into gear and burn rubber. But after yesterday and the *stupid* mistake she had made listening to Finlay, today had to go by the book. No question about it—she had to make this delivery, and she had to fake absolute normal while completing it.

Not that Mr. Anderson had given her any indication that he had found out about the Sunnyville Rec Center box. He had been distant when handing her the van keys and cell phone, but that had happened before. His mind had simply been somewhere else. Besides, Shir told herself reassuringly as she climbed out of the van, when the problem had come up with the Fox and Brier box, he had asked her about it immediately. That was the way he was—direct, straightforward, to the point. So if he hadn't mentioned the Sunnyville Rec Center order today, it was because he didn't know about it ... which meant that Mr. Dubya, the rec center coach, hadn't noticed anything wrong with the box.

Pushing the matter firmly from her mind, Shir pulled the last box out of the van, placed the clipboard on top of it, and headed up the front walk. For a Saturday afternoon, the neighborhood was quiet—no children playing in nearby yards, only a single dog barking at the end of the block. With a grim feeling in her gut, she placed one foot resolutely on the bottom step, rested the box on her knee, and knocked. From inside came the sound of footsteps, then the door opened and Manny looked out. "Bill's Grocer," he said, his face expressionless.

"Yes," said Shir, and lifted the box toward him. Quickly, Manny reached out as if to take it, but to her astonishment, instead of grasping the box, he took hold of her forearms. At the same time, someone moved in behind her, pressing against her back, and a male voice said, "Walk up the steps and into the house. Don't make a sound and you won't get hurt."

As he spoke, he shoved his left knee into the back of hers, bending it up and forward, and Manny pulled simultaneously on her arms, forcing Shir to stumble, stunned and silent, into the porch. Immediately, the outer door swung shut and she was pushed, still carrying the clipboard and box, into the house's front hall. For the second time, there came the sound of a door closing behind her, followed by a brief swim of darkness as her eyes adjusted to the interior light.

"All right," said the man at her back. "Take her down the hall."

His voice was familiar, but in her terror, Shir couldn't place it. Moreover, with the unidentified man still pressed to her back and Manny holding onto her arms, she couldn't run, and, carrying the delivery box, couldn't strike out. Besides, thought Shir, realization rolling in like a dead weight, this wasn't a backyard beer-bargaining session with Gareth—these guys were pros at everything she didn't want to know about, and they were coming down on her because they had found out that she had opened the Sunnyville Rec Center box. She had this coming, there was no escaping it, and her only option now was to get through whatever was ahead of her the best way she knew how.

"Put the box down," said Manny and she complied, then followed him along the hall, not daring to glance at the man on her heels. At the end of the corridor, a doorway opened to their right; without comment, Manny turned into it, and, hesitating only slightly, Shir walked in, too.

It began with a hard shove from behind that pitched her forward onto her knees. At the same moment, Manny whirled and launched himself, knocking her sideways so suddenly she didn't have time to brace herself, and came down hard on her head. Blackness rolled thickly through her brain, followed by pain as her right arm was jacked up behind her back.

She didn't cry out. Crying out wasn't going to get her anywhere in this place, any more than it had helped when she was five years old and it had been her mother coming after her. Instead, Shir hunched inward, sucking up the pain as her right arm was jacked further up her back and her head slammed a second time, deliberately, against the floor.

"What did you think?" Manny shouted into her ear. "We wouldn't notice? We wouldn't know you opened it?"

There was no point in denying the obvious. Whatever was waiting for her here, lying would only make it worse. "I didn't take any," mumbled Shir, her mouth rubbery with fear. "Nothing is missing—I didn't open the package."

"So what?" screamed Manny, his voice skyrocketing. "Was the box yours? Did you have permission to open it, bitch? Did you?"

"No, sir," whispered Shir.

Again her head was slammed into the floor; again black sludge rolled through her brain. "Deliver the boxes!" screamed Manny. "Deliver them, don't open them! That's your job, those are your orders. You open a box again and you're dead, you got it?"

"Yes, sir," whispered Shir, almost fainting under a massive wave of relief. *Not dead*, she thought, sucking in a sob. *Not going to be dead in this ghostie, creepy place.*

"Just remember, bitch," hissed Manny, breathing onto the back of her neck. "You open a box again and I'll kill you. I've done it before; I'm good at it."

Abruptly, he jerked her upward and into a standing position, Shir crying out as her right arm was once again jacked up behind her back. "That's good," Manny said quietly into her ear. "You're learning, bitch. I'm teaching and you're learning. Some of us are slow, but we all gotta learn somehow, don't we?"

With that, he pulled up her chin, and through the hair falling across her face, Shir saw they were standing in a small dilapidated living room. On a sagging couch to her left sat Mr. Anderson, his face carefully neutral. Face equally neutral, Eunie stood opposite, leaning against the wall, and next to her, huddled on the floor like a frightened dog, was Wade.

Before Shir could grasp the implications of what she was seeing, the unidentified man stepped out from behind her and sat down on the couch beside Mr. Anderson. For a long stretched moment, everyone remained motionless, watching as Shir stared open-mouthed at Officer Tursi. Bent forward, her right arm still jacked painfully behind her back, Shir couldn't keep her gaze from darting between her boss, Officer Tursi, and Wade. That Mr. Anderson was involved came as no surprise; neither was Eunie, or even Officer Tursi. *But Wade?* she thought, confused. How was Wade Sullivan, Collier High popular preppie, connected to a guy like Manny and a rundown crack-house halfway across the city?

And then she got it. *Uppers, downers,* she remembered Eunie saying. *Inners, outers. It means anything that'll take you down the rabbit hole.* Swallowing hard, Shir tore her gaze from Wade's ashen face and glanced furtively at her boss. Apparently indifferent, he gazed back, his expression so cold it was almost unrecognizable, but as she watched, she began to see something familiar—a softness, an inner weakness, a kind of cringing away from what was going on around him. Clearly Mr. Anderson wasn't here by choice any more than Wade, and just as clearly, he would do anything he was told to do. Whatever she was about to face in this place, there would be no point in looking to him for help.

With a quiet clearing of his throat, Officer Tursi began to speak. "It wouldn't take much," he said softly, his eyes like a hunting cat's. "Not much to put you away, girlie. D'you think we don't know you? D'you think we didn't assess you carefully before taking you on as a courier? Every detail, honey—we know every detail of your miserable, worthless life. Your sister Stella, for instance—she's one grade below you, isn't she? And the two of you don't get along. And she just so happens to take a Tuesday and Thursday evening course at the Y. Comes home around 8:30, alone, at night, with no one watching out for her."

Eyes widening, Shir gaped at him. *Stella?* she thought frantically. What did Stella and her self-defense course have to do with this? As she continued to stare, bewildered, Officer Tursi casually lifted the second finger on his left hand, and Manny immediately shifted her right arm further up her back. Hit by a sheer whiteout of pain, Shir screamed. Gradually, the pressure on her arm lessened, and she came, sobbing, out of her agony to discover Officer Tursi studying her, assessing what he had just seen. For a moment, he allowed her to watch him watch her, and then he continued.

"And there's your mother," he said, his voice weaving coolly through the raw rhythm of her breathing. "Cleans houses for a living, doesn't she? And she has a drinking problem that goes back years. Hasn't been much of a mother to you; knocked you around more than she should have. Still, *her* drinking problem is legal, and not as bad as yours. Nowhere *near* as bad as yours.

You're quite the beer-guzzler, aren't you, Shirley? Underage, back alley, black-market beer-guzzler. What would happen if your contacts behind the liquor store on 23rd Street decided to cut you off? Or Gareth Fenske—what if he decided to stop doing business with you? Poor Shirley—no more Labatts to guzzle, no more Molsons to pour down your ugly, stinking throat."

Eyes closed, Shir fought to get a grip. That Officer Tursi knew about her drinking and back-alley negotiations was a given after last week's police stakeout at the liquor store. But Gareth! she thought, beside herself. How had Officer Tursi found out about him?

She opened her eyes to find the police officer still studying her, a knowing smile on his lips. "Ah, yes," he said, almost singsonging. "We know you, Shirley—like an open book. And here's the most important thing we know—your favorite Bill's Grocer delivery stop. A Mrs. Duran, isn't it? Such a sweet little old lady. A *nice* old lady who invites you in for a lovely twenty-minute visit every time you make a delivery. Let's say, sometime soon, this nice old lady gets burglarized. It could happen while she's out, it could happen while she's home. If she's home, she might survive it, and she might not. Either way, Mr. Anderson would be sure to hear about it. And when he did, he would be duty-bound to notify the police that his delivery girl, specifically a delivery girl named Shirley Jane Rutz, made regular deliveries to that address. And because Mrs. Duran is such a *little* old lady, it's a sure bet she would have asked Shirley to carry those heavy delivery boxes into her house. Which means that Shirley Jane

Rutz is well acquainted with the house layout, and has the old lady's trust.

"That would be enough, girlie," hissed Officer Tursi, leaning forward to emphasize his point. "Enough to pin the whole case on you and your accomplice, Gareth Fenske. You're turning seventeen in a few months; the case would probably be bumped up to adult court. Armed robbery and break-and-enter—that could get you five to ten years. Murder is life."

Mind blank with shock, Shir gaped at him. *Murder?* she thought. *He's going to ... murder Mrs. Duran?*

"I ..." she stammered, dry-mouthed. "I won't ... talk, tell anyone. I swear, I swear. I—"

Face expressionless, Officer Tursi once again raised his second finger; on cue, Manny eased Shir's right arm further up her back and she cried out sharply. "Please," she whimpered as the pressure on her arm decreased. "I mean it. I won't tell, I—"

"No, you won't," snapped Officer Tursi. "You won't even *think* about telling anyone; you got it?"

"Yes, sir," whispered Shir.

"Yes, sir," repeated Officer Tursi, his voice mocking. Glancing at Mr. Anderson, he asked, "How many times does she say that to you on the average shift, Bill?"

Mr. Anderson jerked slightly, as if poked with an electric prod. Reluctantly, his eyes slid across Shir's, then away. "Yes, sir, no, sir," he said quietly. "About fifty times a week, probably."

"Fifty," mused Officer Tursi, his gaze shifting back to Shir. "Well, that tells me exactly how much it's worth—*zero*. 'Yes, sir, no, sir' to your boss's face, but opening boxes without permission behind his back and rooting through what doesn't belong to you. You're going to have to learn, girlie. You're going to have to learn the hard way what 'yes, sir' really means."

As he spoke, he unwrapped something from his wrist—a long metal chain with a leather handle at one end. Her mind exhausted and uncomprehending with fear, Shir watched dully. Even when the police officer dangled the object at full length, she didn't catch on.

"You've got a nickname at school, don't you?" he said evenly. "Something all the kids call you? 'Dog Face'—that's what they call you, isn't it? *Isn't it?*"

"Yes, sir," said Shir, her stomach lurching as she finally recognized the object for what it was—a dog leash.

"C'mere, boy," snapped Officer Tursi, and Wade scrambled shakily to his feet. Crossing the room, he stood, head lowered, before the police officer.

"You know Wade, don't you, Shirley?" Officer Tursi asked smoothly. "Wade Sullivan? Popular kid at Collier High, I hear. Smart, good-looking; a lot of kids like him. Yeah, with the face he's got, Wade used to have everything going for him, but unfortunately, he developed a big hunger. A big hunger for what he shouldn't be hungry for, and consequently an even bigger debt. And that, y'see, is how Wade Sullivan became our boy. Anything we tell him, he does. Am I right, boy?"

Eyes fixed to the floor, Wade nodded. A grim smile crossed Officer Tursi's mouth and he added, "So y'see, Shirley, hungry-boy Wade is going to be our eye on the back of your head. As you might have noticed, he's already been on your case, but from now on, it's going to get worse—a hundred times worse. Everywhere you go at school, every second of the rest of your miserable flunk-out year, he's going to have his eye on you, aren't you, boy?"

Convulsively, Wade nodded, and Officer Tursi handed him the leash. "Go on, boy," he ordered. "Put the leash on the dog and lead her around. Show her what 'yes, sir' really means."

For a moment, Wade stood transfixed, staring at the leash in his hands. Then, trembling visibly, he turned to Shir and slid the leash around her throat. "Down on your hands and knees, Dog Face," he said gruffly, pulling tentatively on the leash. "We're going for a walk."

Without warning, Manny shoved Shir violently, releasing her jacked-up arm and pitching her onto her knees. "*Teach* the bitch!" Officer Tursi roared at Wade, half-rising from the couch. "Teach her what 'yes, sir' means!"

"Yes, sir," stammered Wade, jerking the leash so it tightened around Shir's throat and sent her scuttling forward. "C'mon, Dog Face," he added hoarsely. "We're going for a walk. Keep your nose to my heel. That's right—*right* on my heel. Okay, now we're turning left ..."

Blinded by tears, her sore arm clutched to her chest, Shir crawled awkwardly wherever the tug on her throat dictated. On command, she turned this way and that, put her nose to Mr. Anderson's sandals and sniffed, even licked Officer Tursi's cowboy boots. Pain pulsed nonstop in her right arm, it danced and sang in the bruises on her head, but her only thought was to keep the tip of her nose to the back of Wade's runner, do what she was told, *survive*.

"All right," Officer Tursi said finally, a satisfied note in his voice. Beckoning to Wade, he took the leash, then grasped Shir's chin and forced it upward. "Now you know what 'yes, sir' means, don't you, bitch?" he hissed. "Don't you, *Dog Face*?"

"Yes, sir," whispered Shir, eyes lowered, tears running freely.

"And you'll remember what it means every time you say it from now on," added Officer Tursi. With a snort, he released her chin and Shir knew it was over, they had done what they had planned to do, taught her what she had needed to learn. "Get up, girlie," snapped Officer Tursi, and she worked her way carefully to her feet, trying not to wince at each fresh wave of pain.

"So now you know the way it'll be from now on," said Officer Tursi as she straightened. "At school, Wade and Eunie'll be keeping an eye on you. And when you're not there or at the store, don't be surprised if you see Manny around, also keeping an eye out, making sure you know that we know *everything*—what you do, where you go, what you think. Believe me, girlie—from now on, you'd better be careful what you *think*."

The very room seemed to go quiet then, catching its breath and waiting for what was coming next. Momentarily, Officer Tursi remained silent, letting his words sink in, and then he snapped his fingers. "You, girl," he barked at Eunie. "She can't drive with her arm like that. Take her home in the van, then return it to the store. And you," he added, pointing to Shir. "Dog Face. You will show up at work on Tuesday, ready to do your job like any good dog. Dogs are obedient. They do what they're told. They listen to their masters. Or they get shot."

"Yes, sir," stammered Shir.

Without comment, her face bored as ever, Eunie pushed out from the wall she had been leaning against and walked past Shir. Cradling her sore arm, Shir turned to follow, then froze as she caught sight of Manny standing inside the door. Something like a smile crossed his face and he continued to stand motionless, eyeing her; ducking her head, Shir forced herself forward, past the violence she could feel looming out of him and through the open doorway, where she followed Eunie's dark silhouette toward the front door.

Eighteen

Pressed against Gareth's backyard fence, Shir peered through the wood slats. From what she could see, the yard was empty, the house curtains drawn. Anyone unfamiliar with Gareth's habits would think no one was home, the house even without a tenant, but Shir knew better. Gareth's curtains were always drawn and his door closed, even on warm Sunday afternoons like this one. As far as he was concerned, sunny afternoons were the bane of his existence and twilight the point at which the day really began, when he no longer had to squint to get his bleary eyes into focus. No, Shir thought grimly, on a day like today, Gareth would be home, guaranteed—probably huddled at his kitchen table, planning various rip-off schemes.

Which was where she came in, obviously. It had been four days since she had shelled out money for his overtaxed beer; Gareth must have felt the financial effects of her absence and should be relieved to see her—so relieved he would be certain to toe the line. There wouldn't be any trouble today, she told herself, she was sure of it. Sure as her name was Shir, like Finlay had said.

Besides, she had no choice. After Eunie had dropped her off

yesterday, Shir had holed up in her bedroom all evening. With her sore arm practically dysfunctional, there had been no chance to take off on the Black as planned, and prowl the city's various liquor stores until she located a scalper. Four days was too long to go without a beer; she had a headache tolling like the bell of doom, her skin felt clammy, and she was getting flat-out twitchy. In addition, something dark and moody kept shifting through her—an alien, a vampire, an oversized virus. She felt possessed. No question about it, she needed a beer and she needed it quick.

This isn't crazy, she told herself as she locked the Black to the usual hydro-pole support-wire. *He doesn't know I'm coming; I'll catch him by surprise.* Nursing her still sore arm, she approached the gate, opened it, and started across the yard. Ten steps in, the sun slipped behind a cloud and the yard darkened noticeably, the air suddenly full of weird little ghosties coming at her from all angles. Hit by a surge of panic, Shir almost turned and ran, but forced herself to get a grip. *It's just the sun*, she scolded herself angrily. *You took him down last time. No way he'll come after you today.*

At the back stoop, she ducked quickly to the right, and checked to make certain no one was hiding around the side of the house. Then, swallowing hard, she shook the trembling out of her hand and knocked. Blood pounding in her ears, she stepped back and waited. Children's shouts erupted from a nearby yard; the sound of a bike passing in the alley startled her so vividly that she whirled, heart thundering, to see if someone was coming through the gate.

The gate stood empty, only a sparrow perched atop a gatepost and cheeping calmly. Breath rasping in her throat, Shir scanned the yard but nothing moved—not a shadow, not a delicate young leaf in the trees. With a relieved hiss, she turned to the door, then stepped back in alarm as she caught sight of Gareth standing in the open doorway.

He hadn't shaved, his T-shirt looked as if he had died in it, and his eyes were narrowed to dark-shadowed slits. Across one cheek stretched a freshly-inflamed scab, evidence of their last encounter. Briefly, Shir's gaze flicked across it and away.

"Beer," she said hoarsely. "Three cans. How much?"

Gareth studied her silently, then raised a hand and lazily scratched his chin. "Dunno," he said, yawning. "Have to think about that."

"Four-fifty," said Shir, taking a step forward. "That's what it was last time."

"Two-fifty," he corrected calmly, eyeing her. "*If* you came in and had a chat."

Shir's knees wobbled. "Four-fifty," she repeated, fighting the tremble in her voice. "Four-fifty for three cans makes $13.50, total. I've got that much."

Another yawn crept up Gareth's body, rising through his chest and mouth—a snake ready to strike. "I dunno," he mused. "Feel kind of like conversation today. You come in, I might just give them to you for free."

Shir's eyes bugged and she took a quick step back. "Five bucks," she blurted. "I'll buy two. That's ten bucks even."

"You come in," Gareth said quietly, "and it's nothing. Even."

Speechless, Shir gaped. Beyond Gareth's back, she could sense the kitchen's layout—dirty dishes in the sink, garbage rotting and waiting to be taken out, and five steps in from the door, the forty-year-old fridge, containing a cold six-pack of Molsons or Labatts ... maybe even some Mooseheads. In spite of her fear, Shir could hear the pop of the tab on her first can, feel the cool spray of beer it released onto her wrist. A minute of polite conversation, maybe two—if she cooperated, that was all that stood between her and a bit of the magic fluid, and today she needed it, *needed* it. If Gareth tried anything funny, she told herself uncertainly, she could handle him—even with her sore arm. She had done all right last time, hadn't she?

Sick with dread, she took a step toward the door. A tiny smile crept onto Gareth's mouth and he moved back into the kitchen, leaving the doorway empty. Hands raised, her fingers tensed and ready to scratch, Shir stepped up onto the stoop. From here she could see into the kitchen, its overloaded sink and garbage pail, and Gareth standing next to the table. There, beside him, only five steps to her left, was the fridge. One more step, that was all it would take, and she would be over the threshold and inside.

And then she saw it—a tiny movement in the venetian blind hanging in the open door's window, as if someone had just brushed against it ... probably one of Gareth's loser buddies, hiding behind the door. In a rush of terror, Shir glanced at Gareth and saw his expression change, the eyes widening and the mouth opening as if someone completely different had abruptly taken over his body and was rising through it, ready to reveal itself.

To her right the venetian shifted again, and there was the sound of a muffled cough. With a cry, Shir turned and ran full-out across the yard, her arms reaching desperately for the gate as if to pull it nearer. From behind, she heard a shout and the sound of someone leaping off the stoop, but she had enough of a head start and was through the open gate, then slamming it shut behind her before her pursuer was halfway across the yard.

And then she ran. Leaving the Black locked to the support-wire, she took off along the alley, arms pumping, head back, sucking in air, the sun, the universe, and whatever lay beyond it.

Hours later, she didn't know how many, she was out on the Black, careening down an alley toward home. Sometime earlier, she had retrieved her bike from the alley behind Gareth's place, then spent the rest of the afternoon aimlessly cruising until she had spotted a familiar face coming out of a convenience store—one of the back-alley liquor scalpers with whom she regularly did business. A quick exchange had occurred and she had retired to a nearby alley, where she had settled down with her back to a logo-painted garbage bin and downed three Molsons in quick succession.

Not having eaten since lunch, the alcohol had gone straight to her brain, and now she was weaving wildly on the Black, her stomach sloshing as she roared out the first verse to "Somewhere Over the Rainbow." Abruptly, two blocks from home, the sidewalk went vertigo and she swerved, smashing the Black's front wheel into a hydro pole. As she crashed to the ground, her stomach upended and there was nothing to do but surrender, gagging and heaving until the urge had passed. Exhausted, Shir sat slumped in the middle of the sidewalk, gazing dully at the puddle of vomit before her. *Pot of gold*, she thought morosely. *Magic fluid wasted, all wasted.*

Wincing at the renewed pain in her arm, she got to her feet and reached for the Black. Then she walked the rest of the way home, concentrating on placing one foot carefully in front of the other. When she got to the apartment block, she put the bike into the shed and wearily climbed the back stairwell. Empty and silent, the third-floor hallway stretched ahead of her, each numbered off-white door bringing her closer to doom. *Mom*, Shir thought bleakly as she approached the Rutz apartment. How in the world was she going to get past her guard-dog mother with obvious vomit dribbled down the front of her shirt? For a moment, she considered trying to pass off a story about a street drunk who had thrown up on her, but realized her mother would have to be comatose to buy it. No, thought Shir, her hand on the Rutz apartment doorknob, whatever was coming was coming. She was just going to have to face the music, no matter what tune her mother was singing.

Cautiously, she unlocked the door and stepped into the front hall. But instead of the expected sound of the TV, what she heard was Celine Dion, caterwauling from the living room CD player. A surge of hope hit Shir—Celine Dion was not a Mom sound. Was it possible her mother wasn't home? Or second best, had gone to bed early?

Creeping along the front hall, she poked her head into the living room. Immediately, Celine hit full force; squinting through the cacophony, Shir caught sight of Stella, eyes closed and arms raised, swaying dreamily to the music. Incredulously, Shir stared at her sister. How could anyone, she thought derisively, prance around tippy-toed to that kind of balderdash? Shit, her sister's head was crammed with it—I'm-a-beautiful-princess-waiting-for-my-Prince-Charming *shit*.

And, Shir realized in a surge of anger, dear little sister Stella, *pretty* little sister Stella was wearing a Toronto Maple Leafs sweatshirt—a sweatshirt that decidedly did not belong to her. Which meant she was wearing it *without* permission, had snuck on her beautiful-princess tippy-toes into Shir's bedroom and *stolen* it while Shir was out cruising the streets, her life in hopeless, bleeding tatters.

"You're wearing my shirt!" roared Shir, her voice so loud, it drowned out Celine and her entire back-up band. With a squeak, Stella whirled to face her, bug-eyed with fright as Shir launched herself. Then, unexpectedly, she darted forward, reaching for Shir with both hands. Suddenly, Shir found herself being pulled in against her sister's jutting hip, and thrust up into the air in a confused arc of arms and legs. As she thudded resoundingly to the floor, even Celine went mercifully quiet—awed, no doubt, by what had taken place. A second later, she kicked back in, screeching exultantly as Shir lay winded and gasping for air.

"Oh, my god!" shrilled Stella, staring down at her. "I can't believe I did that. Are you all right?"

Shir tried to focus through the pain in her arm. Above her, Stella's face kept shifting, splitting into two and snapping back together. *Unbelievable*, she thought grimly as she realized what had happened. Darling little sister Stella had just chalked up another stellar accomplishment—Cinderella-pretty, straight-A student, and now a black-belt self-defense expert.

"Fuck off!" she roared in renewed fury, clambering painfully to her feet and eyeing her sister who had retreated to the far side of the room. "Celine Dion!" she screamed, bending forward with the effort of her words. "Celine *Dumb* is over the rainbow! She's no better than a fucking beer!"

For a moment, the two sisters remained frozen and staring at one another, Stella's hands raised defensively, Shir's anger a monster, snarling out of the deep. Then, without thinking, without the slightest idea as to what she was going to do next, Shir turned from her sister. As she did, a door opened at the far end of the hall and Janice Rutz emerged; face enraged, she started full steam toward the living room. One second of her mother's expression told Shir all she needed to know, and bolting to the apartment entrance, she yanked it open and tore through it, slamming the door behind her.

Out in the corridor, she took off, fear like a wrecking ball inside her head, aiming for anything that moved. Blundering down the back stairwell, she tripped and fell the last few stairs, then dragged herself outside and stood leaning against the wall, holding her sore arm and breathing, just breathing. Over, it was over, she knew it without question—home, family, whatever that had been. No one, not even someone drunk as a stone, could have mistaken the message on Janice Rutz's face as she had erupted from her bedroom doorway: *Get out of my life, you SHIT!*

Making her way to the shed, Shir unlocked the door, flicked on the light, and glanced around. There, where she had left it, leaning against a wall, was the Black, and on the floor nearby, a can of paint left over from the caretaker's door-painting spree. As she stood in the shed entrance, staring blankly at the can, an image surfaced inside Shir's mind—a gang of teenage boys with spray-cans moving along a row of back-alley garbage bins. Quickly, she scanned the shed, but seeing no sign of a paintbrush, hissed in disgust. It was just like the old man to leave out the paint and put the brush under lock and key, afraid someone might steal it.

Again, her eyes returned to the can of paint, and she replayed the image of the gang spray-painting their logo. Abruptly, she stepped forward, picked up the can, and slid its handle onto the Black's right handlebar. Then, wheeling the bike into the alley, she closed the shed door and stood shivering in the cold night air, the mess of her fucked-up life like a sinkhole closing in around her. *Over*, she thought again, blinking back tears. *It's all over—home, job, school … me.*

Desolately, she climbed onto the Black and started off down the alley. Guided by the odd garage security light, she could see well enough to negotiate bumps and potholes; what creeped her out as she pedaled along was the vastness of the Sunday-evening hush—no dogs barking, back yards deserted, and virtually no traffic ... as if the end of the world had snuck up on her when she wasn't looking, leaving her alone on the planet, everyone dead and gone except her. Putting on a burst of speed, she watched 12th Street come into view, Bill's Grocer looming on the corner, its alley parking spots deserted. Nearby businesses were equally deserted, the houses in the area locked-up for the night. Along 12th Street, the odd car was still traveling past, but the avenue at the store's side wall remained quiet. Hesitantly, Shir dismounted and leaned the Black against the usual stop sign, then set down the can of paint and levered off the lid with her apartment key. A sigh escaped her as she saw it was one-third full. Too bad she didn't have a paintbrush, she thought, grimacing, but what the hell.

Cautiously, she inserted her right hand into the paint and mushed it around. When she pulled it out, her hand looked black, but holding it up to the streetlight, she saw it morph into the expected red—thick and dense as blood. Without warning, she was hit by the shakes and had to kneel, slumped inward until they had passed. Everywhere inside she could feel it—blood racing, running, *pounding*.

Getting to her feet, she approached the wall that faced the avenue. Her right arm was throbbing heavily, but she could manage, she thought grimly. She had to. Tentatively, her hand visibly trembling, she reached above her head and slid her paint-covered palm carefully down the concrete. *Not too big*, she thought. *You don't have much paint*. Gently, she hand-painted another downstroke, then linked the two lines with a crossbar, lifted her hand free, and started the next letter. *ANDERSON,* she spelled out in trembling red-black letters, the breath jagged in her throat. With a half-sob, she again dipped her hand into the paint and wrote furiously, the words leaping from her palm— *IS A DRUG DEALER.* Finished, she stood exhausted, swaying on her feet and staring at the five-word sentence, its massive, gut-grinding truth exposed for all to see.

Not enough, was all she could think. *It isn't enough.* As she continued to stand, wide-eyed and staring, Mr. Anderson's face surfaced in her mind, smiling its familiar jovial smile as he told her once again that she was the best delivery person he had ever hired. *Super Boss,* she thought, the sobs heaving out of her, *I loved you.* Alone on the darkened street, she bent double, the silent scream like an inner knife. *I loved you like a daddy,* came her thoughts, *but you were never my daddy. No one was ever my daddy.*

With a groan, she leaned down and dipped her hand into the remaining paint. Then, feverishly, she wrote *liar,* and again, *Liar,* and one last time, *LIAR,* wild and sprawling across the concrete. When she had finished, a wave of dizziness descended onto her, and she pressed, gasping, against the wall to wait it out. Then, clutching her sore arm, she backed up to the curb and stood, reading and rereading her dimly-lit message. Tilted and haphazard though it was, the words were legible, their meaning clear. In the morning light, they would be impossible to miss. The world would see and it would know.

But her work wasn't complete, she thought, turning to her

bike. One more person had to be warned. Slinging the near-empty can of paint onto the Black's right handlebar, Shir set off for 34th Avenue and the familiar yellow house. By bike, it was a five-minute trip, the house windows dark upon her arrival, the doors locked tight. On her knees, she levered off the paint-can lid and assessed the small puddle at the bottom. There wasn't much, she was going to have to be concise. Carefully, she smeared her palm in the sticky fluid and crouched, studying the sidewalk that ran the front of Mrs. Duran's house.

DON'T SHOP, she wrote in mid-size letters, then stopped to replenish the paint on her palm. *Come on!* she thought, jamming her hand desperately along the can's sides to get every last bit. *Give me enough for a few more words.* Pulling out her hand, she managed a much smaller AT and BIL before running completely out of paint. DON'T SHOP AT BIL, she thought, staring at the truncated phrase. Whether or not it made sense, it was clearly legible—the elderly woman should notice it the next time she was out and puttering around.

Bright-eyed and bushy-tailed, thought Shir with a rush of fondness. *The cookie fairy.* Stiff and shivering, her right arm fiery with pain, she got to her feet and clambered back onto the Black. Then she stood a moment, fighting the dead weight of her legs, a sky-wide hopelessness pressing down upon her. Lifting a foot, she pushed heavily against a pedal and got herself moving, one more bit of darkness rolling through the greater dark. When she arrived at Myplace, she locked the Black to the *Church Patrons Only* sign and walked over to the bridge. Behind her loomed the church, a single security light on over the rear entrance; across the river, a few house windows glowed. In the night quiet, the water rippled calmly, traveling toward wherever it was going. As she stood watching it, Shir became aware of a painful throb in her lower back. She had hit the floor hard when Stella had thrown her. Poor old Mrs. Melville, who lived downstairs, would never recover.

Abruptly, Shir's knees gave out, and she sat down with a thump. A whimper came out of her, and though she tried to bite it back, another followed, and another. *Get a grip*, she told herself weakly. *Wash the paint off your hands. Do something.* Slowly, she crawled to the riverbank, slid her hands into the water and splashed them around. Then, drying them on the new grass growing along the shore, she sat staring at the water, its dark ripples moving like thought across her brain. Breath harsh in her throat, she considered; several years ago, she had heard of a woman who had done it by filling her pockets with rocks and walking into a lake. With the fatigue and shakes currently convulsing her muscles, it wouldn't take long, and the water looked gentle enough. This was a place that knew her; it probably wouldn't be bad.

It would solve everyone's problems, she thought dully. Mom, Stella, Mrs. Duran—no one would bother going after them if she was dead. And, finally, they would be rid of her, Mom and Stella—could go on to live their lives without having to worry about some drunken slob staggering around, messing things up. She hadn't been much of a daughter, that was the truth, and she had been an even worse sister. How many times, when they were younger, had she gone and beaten on Stella after Mom had finished whaling on her?

It isn't just my face, Shir thought miserably. *No matter what Finlay says, I'm ugly through and through.* BORN UGLY, LIVED UGLY, DIED UGLY—that would be her epitaph. They wouldn't even have to put her name on the tombstone, just her final score from the Ugly Contest and everyone would know.

Breathing, just breathing, Shir sat, letting her thoughts ripple past, alone and quiet at the end of things.

Nineteen

She woke to the sensation of something brushing gently against her forehead. "Shir?" said a voice. "Shir, are you all right?"

Groggily, she opened her eyes to see Finlay leaning close, his narrow face tense with anxiety. Beyond him, in the distance, the sun hovered near the horizon. It appeared to be early morning. "Yeah," she said hoarsely. "I'm okay."

Relief flooded his expression and he backed away, allowing her to sit up. Stifling a groan, she straightened slowly. Her arm, not to mention every muscle, ached, her throat burned, and her chest felt as if someone was standing on it. She was coming down with something, probably pneumonia.

"Why are you here?" asked Finlay, his eyes skipping uneasily over the vomit stains on her shirt. "Without a jacket?"

"I ... slept here," croaked Shir, covering her face with her hands. "I couldn't go home, I ..." Convulsed by a body-wide shudder, she hugged herself.

"Here," said Finlay, handing her a cup of take-out coffee. "I came here to drink this before school."

"Thanks," whispered Shir. Gratefully, she began to sip, moaning aloud as the heated fluid slid down her throat. On his knees beside her, Finlay shrugged off his knapsack, opened it, and pulled out a bag lunch.

"Chicken salad," he announced, handing her two sandwiches. Without a word she tore into them, and when she had finished, Finlay silently removed his windbreaker and draped it around her shoulders. Warmed by his body heat, the jacket settled against her. Tearfully she pulled it closer.

"Thanks," she whispered again, and he nodded.

"Okay," he said, watching her closely. "Now tell me why you're here."

Another shudder hit as the enormity of the situation rushed over her, and then, haltingly, Shir began to talk—about the second delivery to Manny's house, her drunken attack on Stella, and her hand-painting spree on her boss's store wall. "Whoa!" Finlay said wonderingly when she had finished. "No wonder you didn't want to go to the police."

"I can't go home," Shir said bleakly. "I don't have a job. And after what I painted on the store wall, they'll come after me. I'm a dog, and bad dogs get shot. My life is over. There's nothing left—nothing."

"Yes, there is," said Finlay, a stubborn look crossing his face.

Wearily, Shir glanced at him. "And how do you know that?" she asked. "Did a singing mushroom tell you?"

Her words weren't mean, just empty; in response, Finlay simply shrugged. "There's got to be," he said, his gaze darting across hers. "There's just *got* to. I mean, think, Shir—just *think* for a minute. What d'you want to do more than anything?"

Head aching, her chest a dull, congested weight, Shir sat slumped. *Nothing*, came the thought. *Nothing ever again.* Then, almost imperceptibly, she felt something stir within herself— deep, blurred, and alive. Straightening, she met Finlay's eyes. "Collier," she said hesitantly. "The slag heap. But I don't have any more paint."

Finlay frowned, pondering, and then his face cleared. "I've got a magic marker," he said. "Black, and it's indelible. It wouldn't work on an outside wall like at the store, but inside your school ..."

He paused, waiting as she considered. Slowly, she nodded, then, looking at her watch, said, "What about your school? Don't you have to get to Stanford? It's 9:30."

"Not today," he said firmly. Holding out a hand, he helped her to her feet, and together they walked over to the Black.

"I can't," she said, after unlocking the bike. "My arm is sore, and I'm too stiff. You'll have to pedal, and I'll just sit on the seat."

It was a fifteen-minute ride to Collier High; they arrived to find the playing field occupied by a gym class and the rest of the grounds empty. "It's almost ten," said Shir, again glancing at her watch. "Everyone will be in class. Come on."

Leaving the Black at the bike rack, they entered the school's south door. "This way," said Shir, heading down a main-floor corridor. On the way over, she had been considering various sites for her message to Collier High—it had to be a busy hallway, if possible, the one with the most traffic, and her communiqué had to be written, not on a wall, but on the floor. *Yeah*, she thought grimly, a message from her, Shirley Jane Rutz, would have to be inscribed onto the lowest position possible—the floor under everyone's feet.

"Here," she said, stopping partway down a hall. Around the corner was the Guidance Office, and next to it, the front office. Five meters to her left, an overhead security camera whirred quietly, taking everything in. This had to be done quickly. "Have you got it?" she asked Finlay. "The marker?"

Hastily, he shrugged off his knapsack, rummaged through the contents, and handed her a large black marker. "Indelible, like I said," he assured her.

Getting down on her knees, Shir stared at the scuffed, stained linoleum. Off-white with a faded brown pattern, it would display a black-marker message well enough. With a jerk, she pulled off the marker's cap. As she leaned toward the floor, the words came to her, seemingly without thought, as if rising directly out of her gut. *I AM DOG FACE*, she wrote in feverish slapdash letters, each movement of her arm sending pain shooting through it. *YOU WALK ON ME*. To her left, Finlay watched silently; she didn't glance up to gauge his reaction. *I AM DOG FACE*, she wrote again. *YOU SHIT ON ME*. For a moment here, she faltered; the last phrases felt enormous, as if they would have to be torn out of her. *I AM DOG FACE*, she wrote for a third time. *I KISS YOUR ASS. DOG FACE—I KNOW WHAT I AM. BUT WHAT THE FUCK ARE YOU?*

Finished, she knelt, staring at the message she had written, each letter so large, together they took up two-thirds of the corridor's length. Blood pounded in her ears and she felt herself breathing from some deep, raw place; as if from a great distance, she heard Finlay start to say something, and then the end-of-class buzzer went off, followed by the sound of classroom doors opening all over the building.

"Shir," said Finlay, "they're coming. We have to get out of here."

Lunging to her feet, Shir took off down the hall. At the corner, she turned and raced toward the school's main exit, which stood between the Guidance and front offices. "Come on," she called to Finlay as she pulled open the heavy oak door, then froze as her gaze fell on a man standing at the bottom of the outside stairs and talking into a cell phone. At that moment, the man looked up, their gaze met, and she saw his dark eyes narrow. *Manny*—in spite of the sweatshirt hood pulled over his head, Shir recognized him instantly, and as his right hand darted into a sweatshirt pocket, she retreated frantically through the open doorway, bumping into Finlay and forcing him back into the corridor.

"It's him," she hissed. "Manny. I think he's got a gun."

Instinctively, she turned toward the front office, but the press of students coming from that area was too dense, and so, followed by Finlay, she took off in the opposite direction—past the Guidance Office and the hallway where she had left her message, and on toward the school's west wing. All over the building, students were on the move, intent on a bathroom break or a quick smoke before their next class. Racing along the corridor that led to the languages department, Shir kept thinking, *A gun. He's got a gun and he wants to shoot me.* The most obvious way to keep safe was to ensure that she was surrounded constantly by other students—Manny wasn't likely to shoot if there were ten or twenty kids in the way.

And then it came to her—a school shooting. If Manny took her out along with ten or so other students, no one would think to question her individual death; she would be simply one of many, indeed the one least mourned or missed. In a fresh rush of fear, Shir glanced back and saw Manny entering the corridor she was now halfway along; though he was taller than anyone in the vicinity, with his sweatshirt hood up, he could pass for a grad-year student, and no one was giving him a second glance. Ditto for the security cameras; if anyone in the front office was currently monitoring them, they hadn't picked up on his presence. Then, glancing upward, Shir realized there were no cameras in this short secondary corridor—they were positioned, for the most part, in the school's main halls and exits.

Behind her, Manny's pace had been slowed by the press of students; she could see him talking into his cell phone as he scanned the surrounding crowd. He didn't appear to have noticed her further down the hall, and as far as she knew, he had never seen Finlay before; at the same time, she realized it was unlikely he would have chosen this route if he hadn't seen her head this way.

Seven meters ahead, the corridor divided into two staircases, one descending to the business department, the other traveling upward to the languages classrooms. Halfway up the ascending staircase, the steps leveled off into a platform and the wall made a ninety-degree angle to the right, creating a small corner. Without hesitation, Shir headed up the ascending staircase and ducked into the corner. A second later Finlay joined her and they huddled together, peering out at the passing crowd.

"School shooting," hissed Shir. "I think that's what he's got planned—me and anyone nearby."

Finlay's eyes widened. "We've got to get out of here," he said. "Where's the nearest exit?"

"He'll still come after me," said Shir. "One way or another, he has to get me."

Overwhelmed, Finlay gaped at her.

"He won't shoot unless he sees me," continued Shir, her thoughts so intense they hurt. "He doesn't know you at all. Go down the stairs and walk in front of him. Slow him down as he gets to just about there." Raising her hand, she pointed straight across the small platform to the handrail that ran along the outside of the stairs. For a moment, Finlay simply stared, and then he nodded—a fellow bridge-frequenter, he understood what she intended to do.

"You sure?" he whispered, and the look in her eyes told him all he needed to know. Wordlessly, he stepped out into the stream of students and walked down the stairs. Pressed to the wall, Shir peered around the corner, bobbing up and down to see through the crowd that continued to pour past. Approximately ten meters away, Manny was walking quickly but cautiously, his eyes darting between the two flights of stairs ahead. The choice seemed to have him perplexed, but as Shir watched, a thin dark-haired boy appeared to Manny's right and brushed against his arm, causing the man to instinctively shift left, away from the ascending set of stairs. "Not too far," Shir whispered in alarm; as if Finlay had heard, he dropped back behind Manny and moved around to his other side, where he gently herded the man toward the handrail that ran along the outside of the ascending set of stairs.

As they drew close, the rising staircase began to block Shir's view, and she had to move out from her hiding place to keep them in sight. But Manny had made his choice and was keeping his gaze focused on the descending set of stairs, nowhere near the straggly, carrot-haired girl easing up to the handrail above him, her breath held in and watching the stream of people below, the way she had so often watched the river flow under the first western support arch ... so often, she knew exactly how long it took a ripple to shift from one trajectory to another, then pass by and out of sight. And so she knew from years of practice how to calculate Manny's speed and direction, knew the exact moment he would draw abreast, still three meters from the point the descending staircase began, how she would then need to swing her legs up and over the handrail, letting go of life the way she had so often thought about doing it at Myplace—dropping down toward the smoothly rippling water, the void, the end of it all. As she went over the handrail now, shouts broke out behind her, but the distance of her fall was too brief to give Manny time to react; angling her hip, Shir hit his head straight on, and carried it directly to the floor. There was a resounding crack, she felt his tensed body splay, and then she landed beside him, taking the shock of impact on her right shoulder.

She was still alive, Finlay immediately at her side, grabbing her arm and trying to pull her upright. "Not that arm!" gasped Shir, as a searing pain shot through her right shoulder. "The gun—get his gun."

But the need for panic appeared to be over. As Shir clambered painfully to her feet, she caught sight of the blood pooling under Manny's head and the dull blank look in his eyes. "I think he's dead," Finlay said hoarsely, staring down at him.

A cold, sick feeling washed over Shir. "Get his gun anyway," she rasped, clutching her sore arm. "It's in his right pocket."

"Gun?" demanded a nearby voice, and abruptly she became aware of the hundreds of eyes fixed on her. From one end of the hallway to the other, traffic had come to a halt, students riveted and ogling the body on the floor. Here and there, they were talking into cell phones; a few appeared to be filming the scene.

On his knees, Finlay was fumbling awkwardly inside Manny's right pocket. "I've got it!" he cried. Withdrawing his hand, he opened his palm and displayed the weapon—small and snub-nosed. *Not a machine gun*, thought Shir, swallowing hard, *but enough to take out more than me.*

At that moment, there was a movement in the crowd, and Shir glanced past the body at her feet to see Officer Tursi push his way through to the front line. Dressed in casual clothes, he wasn't identifiable as a police officer; most of the students present probably assumed he was a substitute teacher, putting in a shift at Collier High. As his eyes darted from Manny to Shir to the gun in Finlay's outstretched hand, Shir could almost read the man's thoughts, and she kicked Finlay's foot to get his attention.

"Put the gun down," she said. "On the floor. Then back away."

Uncomprehending, Finlay stared at her. "It's Tursi!" she said frantically, pointing at the police officer. "He probably has his own gun and he wants to shoot! Put your gun down!"

Mouth open, Finlay whirled toward Officer Tursi, giving the police officer the excuse he needed. But as the man's hand darted into his jacket pocket, the crowd erupted behind him; suddenly his knees buckled and he pitched forward, a blurred figure clinging to his back.

"Come on!" shouted a familiar voice, and Shir, astounded, recognized her sister, struggling to pull Officer Tursi's arm behind his back. "Someone help me keep this guy down!"

A horde of students piled on, just as Principal O'Donnell and several teachers managed to push their way through the crowd. "What is going on here?" demanded the principal, his mouth dropping as he surveyed the scene. Voices broke out around him, students shouting explanations, and then Stella got to her feet and silently handed him the gun she had found in Officer Tursi's pocket. As Mr. O'Donnell accepted it, Finlay also gave him Manny's gun. Aghast, the principal gaped at the two weapons, then turned to one of the teachers and snapped, "Call the front office and get them to put out a lock-down order.

Then call 911."

The teacher pulled out a cell phone, but it was hardly necessary—several students had already called and distant sirens could be heard, their mechanical cries interweaving as they headed toward the school. Trapped under a mound of determined students, Officer Tursi wasn't moving—playing dead, thought Shir, or working out the bullshit he planned to lay on his buddy cops when they arrived.

But whatever happened, and whomever the police ultimately chose to believe, today's intended catastrophe had been averted. As this realization hit, Shir's knees dissolved; seeing her stagger, Finlay ran over and slid an arm around her.

"Are you all right?" he asked, but her exhaustion and shock had finally overcome her and she broke into sobs, covering her face with both hands. Quickly, Finlay slid his other arm around her and they huddled, weeping, as someone behind Shir patted her back and the shattered world began to piece itself together again.

Twenty

I t was late the following afternoon. Earlier in the day, the police had come and gone, their interrogation kept to the minimum due to Shir's head and chest cold. Initially apprehensive, she had given measured responses, wondering if her allegations about Officer Tursi were likely to offend, but the two officers had been neither skeptical nor supportive, simply businesslike—clarifying some details and challenging others. To her relief, she had learned Officer Tursi had been denied bail due to a kilo of cocaine that had been discovered at his residence. Traces of the drug had also been located in the storage room at Bill's Grocer, and Mr. Anderson and the cashiers brought in for questioning, but in their cases, no charges had been laid yet. Wade and Eunie were at the Youth Detention Center, pending their first court appearances.

Now that the police had left, Shir was seated on the living room couch, cocooned in her bedroom quilt. Across the room, her mother was ensconced in an armchair, and Stella had taken up position cross-legged on the floor. That morning at breakfast, Janice Rutz had announced the need for a meeting, and had asked her daughters to think about what they wanted to say to each other. To Shir, this had the sound of a death sentence, and she had spent the hours since shrouded in dread. Now that they had gathered, all three seemed to be waiting for someone else to begin speaking, their eyes lowered, even their breathing uneasily quiet. Finally, with a heavy sigh, Janice Rutz cleared her throat.

"I've been thinking all day at work," she said slowly. "This has been a hard decision to make. Crazy weekend, but it's always crazy living in this place. Never, in all my born days, did I think I'd see the likes of something like this."

Raising her eyes, she looked accusingly at Shir. "You're not changing," she said. "You promised no more drinking; you'd go to all your classes; and you'd stop fighting with your sister. And then you went and attacked her in this very room."

Silently, Shir stared at her mother, each pound of her heart an inner mouth, eating her alive. Her mind was blank; there was nothing she could think of saying in response to these accusations—they were all facts, the plain undeniable truth.

"Mom—" broke in Stella, but her mother lifted a silencing hand.

"I *know* what's been going on, Stella," she said harshly. "But that's not an excuse. She's been like this from the day she was born—acting like a wild animal, never considering anyone but herself. And instead of getting better as she grows older, she gets worse. Drug dealers, criminals—could've gotten us all killed."

Eyes filling with tears, Shir pulled the quilt tighter. Too sick to protest, all she could do was watch the inevitable descend. From the beginning, she and her mother had been wrong together, and now it was time to face up to the fact and make the break.

"Wait a minute," Stella cut in shrilly. "Just hold on a friggin' second."

"Hold on for what?" demanded Janice Rutz, her eyes abruptly alive and flashing. "I've been holding on for years. I'm tired of holding on."

"Well ..." faltered Stella, her gaze dropping. "What I mean is ... well, I live here too, don't I? And I was the one who got jumped. So I think *I* should get to be part of the decision."

"Last I noticed, *I'm* the one who pays the rent," Janice Rutz snapped angrily. "So *I'm* in charge, and *I* make the decisions about who lives here."

"Okay, okay," said Stella, backing off. "You pay the rent and you make the decisions. But at least think about it, Mom. This is a big thing here, kicking Shir out. It's going to wreck her life, and her life is already pretty wrecked. And, let's face it ..."

Biting her lip, Stella hesitated. In the slight pause that followed, Shir saw her sister swallow hard. "Well, part of the reason her life is wrecked is *you*," Stella blurted finally, her eyes glued to their mother's face. "It's true, you know. It *is*."

White-faced, Janice Rutz sat gaping at her younger daughter. "What *exactly* do you mean by that?" she hissed.

"All the beating you did on her while she was growing up," replied Stella, her words hesitant but determined. "I mean, I know Shir's always been kind of an angry lump, bumbling around everywhere and rubbing everyone the wrong way, but you've got to think about *why*, Mom. Every day, there you were, whaling away on her because she doesn't look like you, and when you were finished, she would come and whale away on me. And the whole time, growing up, I was just so shit-scared that some day you'd stop liking me and start hating me the way you hated Shir—not because I *didn't* look like you, but because I *did*."

Janice Rutz's mouth opened, but nothing came out. Blinking rapidly, Stella took a deep breath and continued. "That's the way it's been since I was born," she said, her voice quavering, "and that's the way it still is. I've spent my whole life scared of you both, and I finally got so sick of it, I went out and did something about it. I learned how to defend myself, and now I know I can take either one of you any time, probably together, if I wanted. So I'm not scared of *you* anymore," she announced, pointing dramatically at Shir. "And I'm not scared of *you*, either," she added, shifting her finger to their mother.

"Stella," faltered Janice Rutz, but Stella, not yet finished, ignored her.

"It was never the way you looked," she said, turning to Shir, her eyes filling with tears. "That wasn't the problem. I just wanted a sister, but you were always, like I said ... this *lump*." Pausing, she rubbed her eyes like a small child. "I know it's been hard on you, Mom," she said hoarsely. "Two girls to bring up, and no husband around to help with anything. But it's been hard on us, too. I don't want to live in a house of enemies anymore. Can't we just figure out how to get along?"

Shir was crying openly, hot tears pouring down her face. "I'll stop," she gulped, drying her face on the quilt. "Drinking, I mean. I want to now. Before I didn't, but now I can see that's why Mr. Anderson chose me—partly because I didn't have friends, but a lot of it was because of my drinking. Drinking and drugs—they're the same, really, like a dog leash jerking you around. Everyone at Manny's house that day—Wade, Eunie, all of us, even Tursi—we were all on dog leashes. Theirs were invisible, but they couldn't take them off, either.

"I'm still trying to figure out everything that happened, why Wade did this and Cathy did that; how a nice person like Mr. Anderson got stuck in the middle of all that crap. Some of the stuff they did was just to keep me believing in him—Mr. Superboss, you know? I've finally figured out why he hired me, but I still think, all along, he really liked me. It's confusing, but I do know one thing—I don't want to end up like him. I want ..." She paused, searching for words. "I want my life to be clean," she finally blurted. "I want other people to look at me and know who I am. And I want ... a mother and a sister. I want to want to come home."

For another long moment, all three sat, their eyes lowered, submerged in thought. Then, reluctantly, Janice Rutz said, "A.A. You will start next week, as soon as you get over your cold."

Wordless, Shir nodded.

"And if it comes to it, summer school," added her mother. "I talked to one of your teachers last week, and you're probably going to fail at least one course. If you do, you'll make it up this summer, and no arguments."

Something akin to horror washed over Shir, but she nodded a second time. For several minutes, it was quiet, just the sounds of sniffing and snuffling. Then, with a resigned expression, Janice Rutz said, "Well, that casserole's probably warm enough to eat now," and went into the kitchen.

Taking a Kleenex from a box on the coffee table, Shir blew her nose long and hard. "House of enemies," she muttered, shooting Stella a glance. "I guess. I mean, I'll try if you'll try. If you hadn't taken out Tursi, I'd be dead now."

"I didn't know he was a cop!" Stella exploded. Pulling out her own Kleenex, she dabbed delicately at the tip of her nose. "But I saw you jump Manny, you know—I was coming toward you from the other end of the hall when you went over the rail. And Tursi pushed right past me, trying to get to you. So when Finlay held up Manny's gun, and you said that about Tursi wanting to shoot ..." She shrugged.

"They were talking on cell phones while Manny was looking for me," said Shir. "My guess is, after Manny shot me ... and whoever else was around ... they were probably supposed to meet up somewhere. Then I think Tursi planned to kill Manny, and maybe even Eunie and Wade, but they hadn't figured that out." A shudder ran through her, deep and wrenching. "God," she whispered. "It felt like the end of the world, the end of everything. I didn't know what was going to happen when I went over that rail. Now all I can think about is the sound Manny's head made, hitting the floor. The blood. And what they wanted to do. It's so *sick*."

"You saved the school, Shir," Stella said quietly. "No one got shot, and Tursi's in jail. Everyone knows what you did and they're all talking—about how you jumped Manny, and what you wrote on the floor. It'll be different when you come back."

Another shudder ran through Shir, and, exhausted, she rested her head on the back of the couch. "Maybe," she said quietly, unconvinced.

"You'll see," said Stella, a set expression on her face. "Like you said, you never know what can happen. You can change; I can change. So can Collier High."

Standing high on the Black's pedals, Shir coasted down the driveway beside the old Anglican church. Ahead lay the familiar haven, with its quietly rippling river and concrete walking-bridge, washed clean by a recent rain. And yes, when she checked, there he was, seated on the first eastern support arch and leaning around the third pillar, grinning at her—Finlay.

"Hi, moose head!" she hollered.

"Hi, moose head!" he hollered back. Dismounting, she locked the Black to the *Church Patrons Only* sign, then crossed to the base of the first western support arch and scaled it carefully. Though it was now Saturday, her sore arm healed, and her chest cold almost gone, the odd moment of weakness could still catch her by surprise, and so she waited a moment at the second pillar, standing and surveying the scene before completing the climb to the arch's peak and settling down with her back to the third pillar.

"Did the police come back and talk to you again?" Finlay asked immediately. "Since Wednesday, when you called me?"

Shir nodded. "Yesterday," she said. "They waited until I was feeling better, and then they really grilled me—I had to think of every little detail. I'm not supposed to talk to you about it, though."

"I know," he assured her. "They told me that, too—we might end up changing our stories to make them agree, and it would contaminate the evidence." Shooting her a lighthearted grin, he added, "Don't worry, Shir—I won't contaminate you."

She smiled tentatively, the week's events still pressing on her. "Mr. O'Donnell came to our apartment Thursday and talked to me," she said slowly. "He's our school principal—the man you gave Manny's gun to. He wanted to know why I wrote what I did on the floor, and what the other kids had been doing to me. I told him about the dog shit ..." Abruptly, it came to her that she had never told Finlay about the Ugly Contest, and she added lamely, "... and some other things." This afternoon, with its balmy sunlight and vast shimmering greens, didn't feel like the time to go into it. "He got pretty *mad*," she said wonderingly. "Not at me, though. Stella said he was on the PA Friday morning, and he gave the entire school a long lecture about it. They were all late for their first class." She sighed uneasily. "I dunno."

"You dunno what?" asked Finlay.

"Well," she said, "going back after *that*. It was already bad enough, but now I have to face two thousand kids who had to listen to Mr. O'Donnell bawl them out about *me*."

Finlay stared off thoughtfully. "Yeah," he said. "That's pretty grim."

"He said I would have to clean up what I wrote," Shir added. "Because I put it there, and that was vandalism. But he also told me a couple of girls came into the office Tuesday morning, and they volunteered to do it. He told me their names, and I don't even know who they are. So they're going to help, and Stella said she'd help, too. It shouldn't take long."

"You should have help," Finlay said staunchly. "And it should be those guys who rubbed that shit in your face."

"No, thanks," Shir said hastily. "I think I've smelled the last I ever want to smell of them."

Finlay snorted and they fell briefly silent, caught by the beauty of the scene before them. "I'm sure glad the one thing Tursi didn't know about my life is this place," Shir said casually, cradling her head against the pillar's warm concrete. "Y'know what I used to call it?"

"What?" Finlay responded idly.

"Myplace," said Shir. "That was before I met you here, of course. At first, I was really mad at you, busting in here and taking up my private space."

"Oh, well," Finlay said carelessly. "Lucky I had the Twinks, eh? Want one?"

Instead of answering, Shir flushed. She had told herself that morning to bring a couple of muffins from the dozen Stella had baked the previous evening, then had forgotten and left without them. *Next time*, she told herself firmly as she caught the cupcake Finlay tossed to her. Sliding it out of its package, she observed the chocolate icing affectionately. *No worms here,* she thought.

"Thanks," she said, and started nibbling.

"Everything's changed," Finlay observed as she ate. "I haven't been here since last weekend—it's been so busy, what with talking to the police and all. The leaves are all out now, the breeze is warmer, and it smells ... *greener*. Even the water is moving different—quicker, as if it's waking up."

"Yeah," Shir said contentedly. "This place is like a person, almost—always changing. In a month, you'll hardly be able to see those houses over there because the trees will cover them. And there'll be a lot more birds."

"Huh," said Finlay. "I bet the mushrooms will be singing so loud, even us moose heads will be able to hear them."

Shir laughed, the glad, clear sound lifting out of her. "Long as I don't sing back," she said. "That'd shut them up for good."

They fell silent again, their eyes roving over the scene, absorbing dappled shifts of light, lush shades of green, and the gleam of the bridge's support arches stretching out ahead of them. *Peace*—Shir felt it lapping through her body, a gentle inner river.

"I always thought ..." she began slowly, then stopped, flushing.

"What?" asked Finlay, turning toward her.

"Well ..." said Shir, her thoughts stumbling. "I thought this was a place to be alone, I guess. It was the one place I felt okay; no one bugged me. I wasn't ... *ugly* here.

"But now when I think of this place," she continued, "when I'm not actually *here*, I mean ... I think about talking. Talking about weird things, different things—things I would never think about on my own. This place is still nice; it's the most beautiful place in the world, really, but when I think about it now, I don't think about the way it looks anymore—I think about talking to you."

Shyly, she glanced at Finlay to see a huge smile take over his face. Without speaking, he simply sat and beamed at her. "What?" asked Shir. Taken off guard, she ducked her head and stared fixedly at her knees. "Why are you looking at me like that?" she mumbled.

"I like looking at you," said Finlay. "It makes me happy."

Astonishment exploded softly inside Shir's head. "Oh!" she said, then burst out with a long "Geeeeeeez!" Never, in all her born days, had she expected to hear anyone say something like that. When she finally got up the nerve to look at him again, Finlay was sprawled contentedly opposite, watching a pair of nearby chickadees. "Do you like cookies?" she asked hesitantly.

"Cookies are good," said Finlay, turning to smile at her.

Quickly, Shir glanced away. "I know this little old lady," she said. "She's, like, eighty or ninety, and she's got a zillion grandchildren, and she makes the best cookies in the universe. And ..." She hesitated, thinking, then added, "Well, I think the two of you would get along."

"Does she live near here?" asked Finlay.

"Pretty near," said Shir. "We could get there on my bike. Want to go visit her?"

"Sure!" said Finlay, straightening. Then, with a grin, he added,

"Sure, Shir!"

"Come on then, moose head," said Shir, getting to her feet. "I'll pedal, and this time you can sit back and relax."

They climbed down their individual support arches and walked over to the Black. Unlocking the bike, Shir swung her leg over the crossbar and stood gripping the handlebars as Finlay climbed onto the seat. For a moment longer, she stood gazing at the river, a tiny smile on her lips. "It is *so* beautiful here," she said finally. "It's a nice place to have inside yourself."

"Yeah," Finlay said quietly.

Then, his hands resting on her shoulders, she pushed down on the pedals, and they set off together into the world.

Epilogue

Handlebars gripped tightly, Shir turned the Black onto the street that led to Collier High. To either side, chattering students filled the sidewalks; as she pedaled past, the hood of Stella's best sweatshirt pulled over her head, no one gave her a second glance. A block and a half away, the school loomed ominously—a dense lump of dread drawing ever nearer. Quickly, the distance shrank to a block ... half a block ... and then she was pulling reluctantly into the curb and dismounting.

For a moment, she stood, head down and simply breathing. It had been eight days since her drunken attack on Stella—eight days without a beer and she was twitchy like she had never felt it, the sensation like fine sandpaper rubbing everywhere against the inside of her skin. More than anything, she wanted to ditch what lay ahead, take off for the nearest liquor-store scalper, and barter away Stella's sweatshirt, the Black, *anything* for a bit of the magic fluid pouring down her throat. Breathing, just breathing—Shir stood with her head down until the urge passed, then glanced guardedly around. No one appeared to have noticed her; slowly, ever so slowly, she began to wheel the Black toward the bike racks.

Earlier at breakfast, Stella had suggested they walk to school together, but Shir had said, maybe tomorrow, their relationship still too raw, and this first day back something she needed to face alone, on her own terms. Sidestepping a group of gossiping students, she edged the Black's front wheel into the nearest bike rack. Incredibly, no one had yet recognized her, but then, as she bent down to click her bike lock shut, she heard a voice say, "Hey, it's her! Do—"

The voice cut off abruptly, as if its speaker had been elbowed in the ribs, and Shir straightened to find everyone in the vicinity gone quiet, the usual catcalls and laughter evaporated into thin air. Raising her eyes hesitantly, she saw a crowd of fifty or so students, standing motionless and staring, their expressions as tentative as her own. To her left, a girl stepped forward, smiling, as if about to speak, but was suddenly interrupted by several loud whistles. Startled, Shir glanced beyond the group immediately surrounding her to see students all over the school grounds coming to a halt and watching, and then, without warning, piercing whistles exploded on all sides.

Someone began to clap and others took it up, eddies of applause rippling through the throng, and finally, in a burst of unleashed enthusiasm, a wave of cheering broke forth, her name "Shirley! Shirley!" lifting simultaneously from hundreds of throats toward the early morning sky.

Interview with Beth Goobie

This is a tough, powerful story about victimization, exclusion, and the abuse of an ugly girl—and sometimes it's quite painful to read. Can you say where the idea for this story came from?

Everything I write is ultimately an exploration of my life experiences. In junior high, I was targeted by a group of classmates for pretty much unremitting abuse. They were from upper middle-class families; mine was low income. Although my physical appearance was average, my mother dressed me funny—I was still wearing my grade-three cat-eye glasses, and two pairs of polyester pants that were so short in the leg, a brocade ribbing several inches wide had been sewn around the bottom. One pair was mustard yellow, the other rust red; the ribbing was psychedelic. You get the picture—social disaster. I didn't get my first pair of jeans until well into grade eight. To round things out, I also had prominent buck teeth and braces.

I did have one supportive friend, and there were a few classmates who remained neutral, neither contributing to the abuse nor defending me from it. But the majority were vicious, and, gradually, much of the school joined in. The limerick read to Shir was read to me (and remains burned into my memory), and

I have had feces rubbed in my face, although under different circumstances. One of my coping mechanisms was a beautiful spot I found in my hometown of Guelph, that contained the walking bridge described in *Born Ugly*. I called it "Myplace" and spent many hours there, always alone.

When I moved from junior to senior high, the abuse gradually lessened because I was no longer trapped all day, every day, with the same group of students. In addition, my appearance had normalized—my teeth were straight and my wardrobe copied everyone else's. Still, there remained something invisible that followed me around—with few exceptions, I was never accepted by my peer group. And so the strongest feeling I get now when looking back at adolescence is one of overwhelming bewilderment at what was happening to me, loneliness, and rejection. As Shir tells Finlay late in the novel, I felt as if something had been taken from me, and I didn't know how to get it back.

Not only does Shir find it impossible to connect with any of her peers in Collier High School, but her family also excludes her. What drew you to write about a character who is so alone in the world?

Because that was the way I felt much of the time as a teenager—completely alone. I was good at covering up my feelings; I never told my family about the peer abuse I experienced in junior high, nor did I tell anyone at school about the sexual and ritual abuse I experienced through my family. Even when my brother Mark committed suicide at fifteen, I went to school a day after finding out, and I certainly never told anyone about my own suicidal thoughts. Instead, I went to Myplace, crawled up onto the bridge's western support arch, and watched the river ripple past, letting it wash away pain and memory, and, ultimately, the truth of my own life so I could go on pretending everything was all right.

We can do so much for each other. It doesn't take much to be a little friendlier, to notice what goes on outside your own circle of friends. If only it was cool to be kind, to be caring, to be generous of spirit. To see past your own reflection in the mirror.

It seems that everything in Shir's world is stacked against her. Where do you think she finds the strength to make her last defiant move against all those who tormented her?

Partly Shir's strength comes from herself. Despite her alcoholism and aimlessness, she is naturally a strong person or she wouldn't have survived this long. Then Finlay comes into her life, and this begins to open up possibilities. I think much of this is due to the fact that with him she experiences creative thought for the first time—thinking just for the sake of itself, as play and exploration. This changes things inside her head, and internal changes tend to lead to external ones.

That being said, her messages on the store wall, Mrs. Duran's sidewalk, and even the school floor, are basically suicide notes—

one moment of truth to throw at the world before everything ends. She survives the crisis primarily due to Finlay's support, as well as her ability to read tiny slipstreams of movement in rivers and crowds. But as she tells Stella at the end of the novel, the fact that she is still alive is largely a fluke; she didn't expect to be.

And so, in a way, the end of the novel is the beginning of another story—what happens next? The truth has been laid bare, both for Shir's schoolmates and family, and the truth is always about change ... and responsibility. The ball is now in their court; how are they going to respond? This is their chance to learn and change, just as it is Shir's. The end of the novel is a question for the reader to answer.

A lot of young adult fiction is written in the first person, probably because that helps the reader identify more strongly with the main character. Yet in Born Ugly, you have written in third person. Why did you choose that approach?

Born Ugly is my sixteenth young adult novel; seven of these were written in first person, nine in third. I find the choice of first or third person narrative depends upon the *voice* through which the story is speaking. Each protagonist is markedly different; each chooses her own unique narrative style. A story won't work if you're writing in first person and it requires third. My job, as novelist, is to listen to the narrator speak, not to tell her how to do that speaking. And while first person may bring the reader emotionally closer to the narrator, I find it gives me less room to maneuver in terms of word play and general description, because it restricts the point of view to only that which the narrator consciously notices. Finally, most of the YA books that I read as a teen were written in third person. Quite probably my "writer's voice" was shaped by this exposure—I read voraciously as a child and teen, still do.

What is there about the creation of young adult fiction that appeals to you?

It's simply the voice that continues to dominate my writing. Probably this is because adolescence was when I felt most vividly alive—my emotions, both positive and negative, were strongest then. I know I write YA novels now for the girl I was then. That part of me still has stories to tell, issues to explore.

What advice do you have for aspiring young writers?

Read *Harriet the Spy* and any poetry by Sharon Olds.

Before you start writing anything, prose or poetry, write the five senses across the top of your page: smell, taste, hear, touch, see. Then incorporate them into your work. If you find it hard to get going, start with a smell or a taste. This will beat most writer's block.

Write bit by bit. No novel was completed in a day, even most poems aren't. If you manage to write one page, even half a page, that's great—you're making contact with your inner voice, keeping the door open to the inner creative current.

Writing is an adventure. You don't have to know it all when you start—you figure it out as you go along. When I begin a novel, I have no idea where it's going. All I knew about *Born Ugly* was that it dealt with the life of a non-photogenic girl who was scapegoated due to her appearance, and that she drank and worked as a delivery girl. The rest revealed itself bit by bit as I worked on the story day after day after day.

Finally, writing is play, but it's also work. No getting around it—if you want to be a writer, you have to write.

About Beth Goobie

Beth Goobie is a multi-award winning author who has published books for both young adult and adult audiences. She has appeared on the American Library Association's Best Books list, been nominated for a Governor General's Award, and won the Canadian Library Association's Young Adult Book Award. Beth studied at the University of Winnipeg and lives in Saskatoon, Saskatchewan.